D1631300

JONCER

Joncer is the nickname of John Mellows, a National Hunt jockey, and we follow him from his apprenticeship and early rides to all the excitement of the Cheltenham Gold Cup. But Joncer is not only a jockey; he is a human being, and the author is as beguiling when he describes Joncer's marriage to the delightful Janet, daughter of a Bohemian professor, as when he depicts the thrills and hazards of horses and betting.

JONCER

A Novel by
NOEL WOODIN

1961
CHATTO & WINDUS
LONDON

Published by
Chatto & Windus Ltd
42 William IV Street
London WC2

*

Clarke, Irwin & Co Ltd
Toronto

For
Naky and Théa Doniach

THREE things make up the Sport, or Business, or Superstition of horse racing—Man, the animal and Money. And the importance of each varies with a particular circumstance. Yet each in turn influences the other two. The jockey's influence ('Man' of the trinity) is generally the most puny.

John Mellows was born forty-five years ago in Poplar, London. He was the fifth, the youngest and the smallest of his family. His father was a docker, his mother a country girl his father had met when on his annual binge-cum-holiday of hop-picking at Paddock Wood, Kent.

Although George Mellows (his father) was a lavish spender and gambler, he was also a hard worker. So the children were well reared. John was tiny and weak at birth; it was touch and go whether he lived. He did. And thrived, although he was always small. And at the age of fourteen he barely weighed five stone but he was sturdily built with a body like a miniature boxer.

His father decided his future. Laboriously he wrote a scruffy letter to Jack Penfield, then one of the leading trainers at Epsom. He recommended his son as a possible jockey, although he didn't mention that the only horses John had then seen, let alone sat, were the Charrington Brewery drays at Stepney. But George Mellows liked nothing more than a day at Hurst, Sandown, Alexandra Park, Epsom, Kempton, and the Cockney's annual idyll (a charabanc with crates of beer, jellied eels, cockles and chips) on Trundle Hill at Goodwood. And with the spectator's almost angelic innocence he blithely imagined that all a jockey had to be was light.

Anyway it was fixed for John to have a three weeks' trial. This news was the first that John had had that his father was planning for his future, although three other equally laboured letters and six weeks of negotiation had preceded the family announcement of it. It was possibly just as well. John was put on the train at Victoria by his placid mother, who gave him 5s. and a bar of chocolate, a placid kiss and a placid hug, and suddenly for the first time in his life he was alone in the world. He was frightened yet curious, determined and in a sort of nebulous way ambitious, although he didn't know then for what; and later, it was to be the events themselves that dictated the way, if not to success, at least to security, to survival. But the confusion of emotions he felt on the train was one he was to know again many times in his life. Just before the start of every race he was to have 'butterflies' in his stomach but with it that quiet determination to control the panic and do his best. Every jockey has to. And strangely, though, even at that early age John's pugnacious jaw, like the strongly composed face of so many jockeys (indeed, it is almost a trade mark of self-made success in men, whatever their calling), was evident.

With it though there was still the child fascinated by the new outside world; for he still had that capacity to postpone his fears for the future until the future came rushing upon him. So it was not until the train stopped at Epsom that he had his first moment of real panic. It was caused as much by the realization that here indeed was the Future as by the fact that he couldn't open the train door. He had nightmare fears of being taken miles and miles further south to what were to him then, a Londoner, the barbaric outposts of rural England. Almost despairing and with two tears just welling up (tears of fear, rage, and of a terrified loneliness), he noticed a short, stocky man in riding breeches, boots and cap, who was watching his ineffectual struggles with interest and amusement from the platform.

"Give us a bleedin' hand, can't yer?" said John,

angry, frightened and defiant. The spectator sauntered slowly over and insolently opened the door. It was then that he saw his saviour was not much older than himself. At the most, he thought, nineteen.

'You for Penfield?' the youth asked.

'Yes,' he replied, jumping out of the carriage with his bag. 'Yes, I am,' and he added as a sort of insurance, and the begrudged expression implying that anyway, 'yes, *sir*.' Even at fourteen John radiated a quality of 'not to be pushed aroundness', a quality of defiant resourcefulness, of intransigence. So the stable-boy, himself at a sensitive age too, took the 'sir' at its face value as a compliment and said, 'Come with me then. The old boy sent me down for you. He's racing today.'

John said nothing. They came into the station yard and the stable-boy indicated the car. 'Put your bag in the back,' he said, 'I'm going for a drink.' John did as he was told and waited meekly. The stable-boy strolled slowly away, but presumably noticing that John was not following him, he turned and shouted, 'Aren't you coming then?'

John was gratified that he was considered able to receive, let alone be offered the adult companionship of bars and smoke-rooms. He knew what the inside of a pub looked like, because on Sunday mornings he had often accompanied his father and eldest brother as far as the door of 'The Cutty Sark'. He would wait there with the other children. And, as subsequent customers arrived and the heavy door opened, he would see them standing at the bar with their enormous pints of brown and mild in front of them, their white silk chokers loosely tied round their necks, laughing and talking with the other customers. They were like kings. And then the brief glimpse would end as the door closed. He had noticed that when the door was open, the heavy plate glass bore, on the inside, the mysterious words, 'RAB CILBUP'. When closed, however, and he was again

shut off with the other children outside, the words
changed to 'PUBLIC BAR'. So 'RAB CILBUP' became a
mystic, secret rubric that stood for the assured, com-
radely world of adults.

And now, for the first time in his life, he was invited
to share in this mystery. His early feelings of defiance
were now overcome by those of gratitude, and then of
inadequacy.

'I'm only fourteen,' he said as he ran to catch the
stable-boy. 'They'll not let me in.'

'Just say you're eighteen, *if* she asks,' replied the
stable-boy confidently, 'but keep your cap on! You
look as tall as Harry Smart, and he's forty!' John had
heard of this flamboyant personality—five times champion jockey, and twice bankrupt, despite five-figure
earnings and (reputed) six-figure betting coups. And a
jockey likely to be champion again that very season
according to his father, to whom Smart seemed surrounded with the dimensions of the heroic and the
attribute of myth. They went in and the stable-boy
ordered John Mellows his first public beer.

It was early but the bar was crowded mainly
with the racing fraternity. The morning work was
finished and, apart from those who had to go racing,
there was nothing to do until the afternoon feeding. So
John sat, happily inconspicuous, with a half-pint of
bitter in front of him, while the stable-boy talked and
laughed with a group standing at the bar. He was nervous; but the fact that no one gave him a second glance
was reassuring. He looked about him at the strangely
elongated horses on the sporting prints, at the glass case
containing—as a card within announced—Fred Archer's
whip and the spurs Steve Donoghue wore when riding
his last Derby winner. And he sipped his beer, hardly
tasting it. He asked himself quietly if it was really John
Mellows who was there. Undeniably, he seemed to be.
He felt his mother's bar of chocolate still in his pocket.

CHAPTER ONE

It had melted. He secreted it behind his chair. It seemed to him then, to represent the guilty evidence of childhood and he felt a mild resentment against his mother for giving it him. His hand in his pocket encountered the two half-crowns.

Even at the age of fourteen a child may have social instincts which are intuitive. After ten minutes or so of sipping beer, of wide-eyed observation of the strange world about him, it struck John that money changed hands with rapidity in a public house. It struck him also that money had been spent on him and that he ought to spend some too. For a while he wondered what to do: whether to continue in the background, implying poverty, ignorance, or at least insignificance, or whether he ought to behave, having been accepted into the adult world—as the adults in front of him did. He soon realized they were spending money on each other. It seemed, therefore, that he ought to spend money on them. He took a plunge. He approached the stable-boy.

'Is five shillings enough,' he asked sturdily, 'to buy a drink?' He held out the two warm coins.

'I should say so,' replied the other, 'you could buy us all one with that.' (You could then, too—it was thirty years ago.)

'That's what I meant,' said John quietly, feeling nervous as the eyes of the group scanned him with interest and perhaps curiosity. 'Will you get them for me, please?' He put the money on the bar and retreated to his seat, not quite sure whether he had done the right thing or not, but fiercely resolved to defend his action should it be questioned. He couldn't see how it could be but then, all this was new to him. He sat there innocently, feeling neither altruistic nor cheated. He knew the Law of the Jungle: he who is new and inexperienced must pay for his novelty and lack of experience. It was the same Law as the one at school: the new-boy had no rights to property nor of alliance; he was alone and all he could expect, provided he accepted his position with, if not dignity, at least an outward calm, was a sort of mercy from the hands of the superior.

His gesture was both generous and clever—there was a degree of calculation in it. The group were impressed and gradually they brought him into the conversation, and without condescension (which he would even then have despised). He pocketed his change casually, restraining what would normally have been his natural impulse to count it carefully, and he tried to appear part of the group yet not obtrusively so.

'You with Penfield, then?' asked one of them.

'Yes,' he replied, adding, 'well, I will be—I only came this morning.'

'He's all right,' the same one continued (he was older than the stable-boy, and quieter, less boisterous), 'I did my time with him. But watch the Head Lad—Stowy Rook—he's a bastard, that one.'

'Yes, I will,' replied John seriously; 'are you a jockey, sir?'

'I ride second for Mr Brazeley,' he answered, not without pride.

'I've never even sat on a horse yet,' said John nervously yet confidentially. The other replied, 'Nor had I when I started.' Although he couldn't have been more than twenty-five the jockey had some of the pompous mannerisms of middle-age. 'Jack Penfield likes to teach a fellow from scratch. He'd sooner have them as know nothing but can learn, to them as know it all and can't.' He seemed pleased with his aphorism. He added, reaching for his drink, 'You'll be all right.' He turned to the group and John watched him with gratitude.

Other advice was given him and more drinks offered. He refused the latter but listened to the former with interest. And so the morning passed.

They left about an hour later and the stable-boy

(who seemed to be called Fred) and he walked to the car. Fred sat in the driver's seat and belched quietly and beerily. 'You'll be all right,' he said. And John Mellows sitting beside him, straining to see over the bottom edge of the windscreen which was level with his eyes, said softly, and more to himself than to his companion, and yet not without some degree of confidence, 'I hope so.'

And he had been. There was little enough time for him to be anything else. After his initiation into the adult world of drink had followed his initiation into the busy, strange and almost monastic life of the Stables. Distraction followed distraction, strangeness followed strangeness: and all his time was taking up with learning and sleeping. There was no time for him to become homesick or to become self-assertive, although it was not his nature to be this anyway and the Head Lad—to all intents his boss—found John a willing pupil, and an easy lodger. (Mrs Rook looked after all the domestic arrangements for the stable-boys. And any complaints she had were soon communicated to her husband, Stowy, whose executive arm among the lower orders was quick, strong and certain as was also his tongue.) And although John was never at ease with Stowy Rook he soon forgot the warnings he had been given about him.

Three months passed before he sat on a horse, but for eight hours every day he was rarely more than a yard away from one. What with constantly grooming, feeding, leading, and saddling them, he began to recognize their various ways. Rook taught him well. 'Some are plain stupid, some 'ave more brains than you and certainly their owners, though that's saying nothing; some are lazy, some are hot pots, and they're all at times contrary buggers. But they've got a right to be.' Rook spat deftly and twirling a whip in his fingers added, 'They're better bred than you and me and most of 'em worth more. You respect them and they'll respect you,' he said.

Both Rook and Penfield soon recognized that John was thorough and conscientious. He regarded his various duties as a job of work for which he received 5s. a week, his clothes and food. He was helped by a calm temperament and this may have been the major part of his natural horsemanship, that affinity, possibly intuitive, that some men have towards horses. Although often tired and occasionally baffled by his various duties he never lost his temper with the animals (nor with his mates) and this quality, probably more than any other, earned him good marks with his masters. He never dreamt of the glories and fame of a successful jockey—indeed it is doubtful if at that age and after a month or so in the Stables he ever imagined himself as one at all. He seemed quite happy as a stable-boy and whatever aspirations he had seemed centred on the forthcoming Stable Boy Boxing Championships where his prospects were promising.

They put him up on a three-year-old handicapper called *Gargoyle*, during the snows.

'Take him round the Walk a hundred times,' said Stowy Rook, who although only fifty years old seemed almost wizened. He stood in front of Mellows, bandy legged yet with an enormous chest and shoulders (it was as if an inverted pyramid rose from his waist) and looked at him with his steady gaze, almost stare, and added, 'If you can count that far.'

'I can count all right,' said John.

Rook hoisted him up and adjusted the girth for him. John took hold of the reins and made a 'bridge' by doubling back the loop end as he had seen the jockeys do. He did that almost unconsciously. His first impressions were of the height he was from the ground—'Hold your back straight,' said Rook grimly as he tested the girth again, 'and pull your elbows in,'—and of the cold. It was February and *Gargoyle* was entered for the Lincoln Handicap then only a month or so away. But the thick snow had brought training almost to a standstill and 'work' entailed little more than walking and trotting round a covered track rather like a circular Dutch barn some hundred yards in diameter. John straightened himself, and feeling strangely awkward the horse and he moved off.

Even a horse gets bored. They walked round the first few circuits quietly enough, but then *Gargoyle* began to fidget, to quicken, to prance.

'Keep him steady,' shouted Rook, 'take a firmer hold.'

John swore to himself but gripped and almost squeezed the horse forward. His boxing had strengthened his arms but even so they soon became leaden from restraining the horse's continual pulling at the bit. Yet although he was exhausted by the thirtieth circuit, he had mastered the animal. Rook watched him in the centre of the Walk like a miniature ringmaster. His silence could only mean some measure of approval.

'You can trot him now,' said Rook quietly, 'but keep your toes in. You're a jockey, not a bloody duck.' There was no anger in his voice though.

John rose slightly in the saddle (perhaps from instinct, or instinct combined with observation and possibly with luck as well) and got *Gargoyle* going immediately into a dignified trot. They completed a few more circuits.

'Half speed now,' shouted Rook. John was not conscious of doing anything. For all he knew *Gargoyle* must have taken the order direct from Rook because they moved into a slow canter and as he dropped his arms and shifted his centre of balance slightly forward, again from instinct, possibly affinity, they cantered. A few circuits later the horse started to quicken, probably from boredom. John sensed the increased pace and gently took a tighter hold of the reins.

'That's it, boy,' shouted Rook, 'that's the way,' but John could only hear the voice, not the words, because of the thudding hooves on the peat and the steady blowing of the animal. The last thing he expected was a compliment so he swore again to himself and decided to ignore Rook from then on. Round and round they went.

'How many you done?' yelled Rook, after a while.

'About eighty,' John yelled back, although he had long forgotten to count or care.

'Slacken off then,' shouted Rook, following him round in a smaller circle of his own in the centre of the Walk, 'slacken off to a trot.'

With his last reserves of strength John took in the reins. *Gargoyle* was unwilling to stop, throwing back his head and snorting. Mellows patted his neck, spoke softly in his ear, and increased pressure on the reins. Gradually they slowed, trotted and ultimately walked. Rook approached them.

'You didn't do too bad, you know,' he said. His manner towards John had changed within the last hour even. Before, John had been an insignificant, though conscientious stable-boy: a promising but very raw recruit before a knowledgeable and rigid sergeant-major. There was not only the difference of rank, there was the void of inexperience facing experience. Now it was as if they had both been under fire together—there was still the difference of rank and immense respect was expected—but Mellows sensed in Rook degrees now of interested tolerance and even a modicum of approval. He felt quite proud of his first attempt at riding.

'We might take you out,' said Rook, feeling the horse's legs for heat—an indication of strain—as he spoke, 'when the snow goes, with the early string.' He stood up now and looked straight at him. 'You've a lot to learn, but you might be able to learn it.' He took the reins and started to lead them both away. He added over his shoulder, 'You'd better do this one yourself from now on, too.' And that was indeed a privilege. Previously John had been moved from horse to horse, from job to job and had been at everyone's beck and call. He'd had to fetch water, feed, tack; had to sweep, muck out, bed down and generally assist whoever asked or, rather, demanded assistance. All for 5s. a week and his keep. He'd done all this efficiently. But this news ended the first stage of his apprenticeship. He was now a fully-fledged stable-boy, entirely responsible for one horse and entitled to certainly more respect and possibly more money if *Gargoyle* did well and the owner proved generous. He rested his aching leg muscles and slipped one foot from the stirrup. They were on the road now, approaching the yard gates. Suddenly a car flew past them at speed and the horse whinnied and reared up. John, day-dreaming happily with self-approval was taken completely by surprise and found himself shaken, bruised and furious, on the ground.

'You daft little twat,' said Rook, not exactly angrily but certainly without sympathy. 'If this had been a race and you'd been first past the post you'd have lost it for us. You mustn't'—John was still on the ground, blinking back tears while *Gargoyle* stood above him supremely unconcerned—'touch the ground until you're in the Winners' Enclosure. You know that, do you?' John picked himself up and took the reins, nodding miserably.

'Well, go and do him thoroughly and next time remember—you never relax with horses until you're sound asleep in bed.'

John miserably led the animal to its box. He sadly reflected (and many men take a lifetime to realize this) that you never take a step forward without some circumstances forcing you to take a similar one backwards. Wearily he reached for the grooming brush as, seemingly, his whole body hummed with bruises. *Gargoyle* munched a carrot.

2

As soon as it thawed John was out riding every day. At first he hated it. The downs on a February dawn are bleak and windswept and much of the work was merely walking the horses (themselves often contrary and restless) for many miles and then waiting, as he shivered in the wind, to be told what to do next. It was as cold as knives.

He was not aware that he showed promise. The memory of the fall was still fresh in his mind and he imagined it must be fresh in those of Rook and Mr Penfield. But whether he considered himself promising or not (and as he was only fourteen such things didn't worry him overmuch) it seemed that Mr Penfield did. The position in the String improved. He was given difficult tasks. Often he would be put on a restless puller and told to track a lead horse at half speed for five furlongs and then to improve gradually and overtake at the seven furlong mark. And not only was it difficult enough to restrain his mount in the early stages, but he had also to keep an eye and an ear open for Mr Penfield who, on an old hunter as broad as an arm-chair and as steady, watched every stride keenly and would shout instructions, insults or reprimands and sometimes all three through a megaphone. He took silence to mean praise. When he was criticized he took it not exactly meekly, but certainly with a willingness. But, unlike many of his mates, he showed no fanatical keenness. He was not sycophantic or flashy; he thought he'd done enough if he obeyed his instructions as well as he could. And then he'd wait for more.

In this he showed unconsciously more of a jockey's mental equipment than did his mates. For a jockey rides for a trainer and a trainer trains for an owner and the owner has the money. He who pays the piper calls the tune. The horse is a sort of medium for money to change hands, and the jockey, however talented, knowledgeable or inspired is merely an instrument in the hands of other powers. He must therefore please the trainer (who is the spokesman, agent and general implementer of the owner's wishes) and respect the trainer without becoming too insignificantly meek or anonymous. It is to be a 'yes-man' but with dignity.

The String—Rook leading the twenty horses—were returning to the Stables one morning towards the end of February. It was a warmer day and John felt that life was not so terribly arduous after all. Nobody had shouted at him, his mount had been well-behaved and after grooming a good breakfast awaited him. The previous night he'd won his bout in the Boxing Championship so that he now qualified for the semi-finals. The owner of *Gargoyle* had backed him. Many wagers were struck at the matches as owners and trainers, jockeys and lads came from the centres of racing—Newmarket, Malton, Newbury and Epsom to fight, or support or bet—and he'd been given a pound. He'd not actually received it. It had been given to Mr Penfield who looked after all the apprentices' extra money. ('You'll need it when you leave me,' Mr Penfield had said, 'I'll bank it for you.' It had been one of the rare conversations the old boy and Mellows had ever had.) And John was quite content as he was naturally thrifty, and apart from that there was nothing he particularly wanted at that moment—nothing, that is, that a pound would buy.

With his increased proficiency he could now sit a horse and walk it home and let his mind drift on to other things. Indeed, the steady rhythm of its movement was conducive to thought, to day-dreaming even. Mr Penfield trotted alongside.

'What do you think of that one, John?' he said suddenly. The horse was called *Postcard*—a lazy, quiet, docile, moderate three-year-old—who was a great favourite with the lads for these very reasons, even though its prowess on the race-course was not remarkable. John looked with something like amazement at the piercing eyes, the bristling eyebrows and military moustache below the sombre hunting bowler that Mr Penfield always wore on the training gallops.

'I . . . I don't know, sir,' he replied lamely—he'd never been asked for his opinion before at the Stable (and never, so far as he remembered, as a child at home). He was somewhat at a loss. *Postcard* chose at that moment to stretch his neck and shake himself. Swaying forward with the horse, he added, 'I don't know enough about horses yet to say, sir.'

Mr Penfield ignored him. 'He seems to go well enough for you,' he said thoughtfully.

'Thank you, sir,' said Mellows, mystified.

'Don't thank me,' said Mr Penfield irritably. 'All I want to know is whether you can manage him in a race or not. Can you?' he added shortly.

'Yes, sir,' replied Mellows, feeling, however, far from confident. He saw that a negative answer would have dismayed the old boy and that a qualified one, in his present brusque mood, would positively have inflamed him. Still, he added with a nervous smile, 'But I don't suppose I'd win, sir.'

'I'm not asking you to win,' replied his master, testily. 'How the hell could you?' Either he or his hunter snorted and he trotted up to Rook at the head of the String.

John's earlier serenity was rudely dispelled. The thought of riding in public made him feel slightly sick and a sudden resentment against his father, against Penfield, even against *Postcard* placidly ambling along, rose up within him. The clear, grey-blue sky looked uncaringly down, and John (who, even at his age then, had a fair-sized vocabulary) swore quietly to himself. *'Why choose me?'* he thought in a mood of terrible lone-liness. *'It's not my job!'* He resolved to see Rook after breakfast—a meal which had suddenly lost its appeal, which, in fact, he now regarded merely as a period of time, of uncertainty—and to try to worm his way out of the threatening responsibilities of the future.

As it happened Rook came to see him.

'Come on,' he said, appearing suddenly in the Yard where John was aimlessly wandering about, 'the guv'nor says you're to have some new clothes.' He jumped into the car and opened the door for Mellows sulkily to get in. 'And after that,' Rook added as they nosed out of the yard and he changed gears, 'I'll give you a few hints about Lincoln. That's where you'll be riding.'

'I don't think I . . .'

'Shut up,' said Rook but not unkindly, 'you're not expected to think. You're not Harry Smart. Not yet, anyway.'

The feeling of helplessness is never so common as it is in adolescence. Perhaps all emotions and feelings are sharper at that delicate age; it certainly seems possible to fall from an unassuming, easy serenity into the black and lonely depths of despair, and all in a matter of minutes. John shrank in his seat, silent and sulky, im-plying at the same time the dramatic agonies of the martyr. Ironically Rook seemed in the best of spirits, whistling and singing as they sped into the town. John gave him gloomy looks out of the corner of his eye but said nothing. He hoped that his silence would convey something of his discontent but, of course, it either didn't or, if anything got across, the older man thought very little of it.

They drew up merrily outside the outfitters, and he was bundled inside. He glared at the staff; an elderly, white-haired, round-shouldered man with a professional smile and a pince-nez, and a young, gawky and drably dressed assistant—with a recalcitrant look of furious resentment. Rook was breezy.

'Measure him up for breeches, riding boots—soft chammy with the firm instep——'

'The racing boots, I take it, Mr Rook . . .' interrupted the pince-nez ingratiatingly.

'—Yes,' replied Rook, 'and a set of silks this pattern.' He threw a tissue packet on the counter and turned to Mellows. 'I'll be in the "Gate" when you're ready,' and he gave them all a gay wave and was quickly out of the shop.

The gawky (and John now saw, spotty, too) youth said with an ironic flourish, 'This way, milord.' He indicated a booth at the back.

'—— off,' said John, remaining sturdily where he was.

The old man looked horrified. The youth, under John's aggressive gaze, looked frightened. John added, having saved a little of his pride '——.' But, still with a heavy heart, he entered the booth. In silence the garb of his destiny was measured.

To be obedient is not always a negative, unambitious quality. It requires constructive if not creative thoughts and implied in the very thing itself is responsibility. John Mellows was not primarily frightened by the idea of riding in public. Admittedly the fact that thousand, of eyes would be upon him (and possibly thousands of pounds would be wagered too, because there were many who backed blindly every horse from the Penfield stable)—this would be like the feeling of 'nerves' he had before a fight. No, it was more that he doubted his ability to do justice to the horse, to his instructions, and he mightily feared the prospect of the purple, bristling face of Mr Penfield, enraged and spluttering after some demonstration of ineptness.

Rook told him (they were driving back now after

Rook had drunk several beers and John one), 'Don't try and win. They won't expect you to. If you're well drawn they might expect you to get placed but no one will jump down your throat if you don't. Just try and get the feel of a race. And above all you want to do just what you're told to do.'

John nodded miserably. '*I know that,*' he thought. '*It's all very well, just saying!*'

With perhaps sympathetic telepathy Rook went on, 'You might think it's hard, silly even. But look at it this way.' He lit one of the cheap cigars with which he always celebrated a winner or a visit to the town. 'Supposing you're boxing then.' Rook exhaled comfortably—he had enjoyed his drink, and braking suddenly three inches from the rear of a lorry his swearing was more from habit than from any vehement disapproval. 'You're in there mixing it up, see?' Leaving the steering wheel to chance he 'mixed' a few imaginary blows. 'Well now,' he said, resuming control again, 'your seconds see more of the game than you do—you're too busy mixing it.' Only the approaching car stopped him demonstrating how to 'mix it' again. John was silent. 'Well,' continued Rook, 'when your seconds say, "play on his body," it's because they can see he's not so strong there, see?' John nodded again, with a little more interest this time.

'A race is the same,' Rook went on. 'We know pretty well what the horse can do and we see more of the race than you do. So we tell you to keep him wrapped up for five or six furlongs and then to wake him gently for the last two—it's a mile, this race at Lincoln. And we tell you that because we know he takes a while to get into top gear and also, if he hits the front too soon, he packs it in—just won't have it—some horses are like that. They stop and look round at you. And we know that because we've seen how he didn't win before and now we reckon we've got the best way of running him.

Tactics, that's what it is.' Rook cornered rather grandly and continued. 'Now, if you do as you're told and you don't win we say, "Tough luck, he's out of his class." If you don't do as you're told and you don't win we say, "That silly little bugger, chucking the race away like that."' (A sort of rhetorical scorn crept into his voice as he said it.) 'And if you disobey orders and by some bloody fluke or other you do manage to win we say, "Ho! A clever sod—you can't trust him," and that'll be the last ride you get from us.'

They turned into the yard and stopped. Rook turned to John and said, taking his cigar from his mouth as if to lend emphasis to the grand finale of his advice, 'Because we might not have backed him heavy that day. You don't suppose'—John was far from supposing anything contrary but Rook, with a mixture of scorn and emphatic ridicule, went on—'you don't suppose that a 20–1 winner is a joy and delight to its owner and trainer. Why, you must be mad if you do!' John nodded. He was quite prepared to own to any vice or defect at that moment. 'I'll tell you what that means.' He thrust a horned finger in the boy's ribs. 'It means that the connections didn't want to win, and that they didn't have a penny piece—not a penny piece—on the animal. And what happens? Next time out he's a short-priced favourite—no price at all. So we lose—and make sure of losing—to get the price right for the next race after. And then as likely as not we get beat. Who got the 20–1? Old women and kids. Who gets blamed for everything? You!' said Rook with contempt and an extra hard thrust at the ribs. 'You for being a silly bugger.'

He sat back in the car seat with the air of a triumphant Q.C. at the successful conclusion of his pleading.

'I see,' said John.

'You'd better,' said Rook.

THREE things happened to John on that windy, sunny March day at Lincoln. The owner of *Postcard*, personally, gave him a pound note, Rook gave him a cigar, and, by the joint action of himself, the crowd and circumstance, he was given a nickname. The name remained with him for ever more. Sometimes it would be shouted deliriously by the happy, generous crowd as he got a hot favourite neatly home, at others it would be bandied about with fury, disdain or contempt by that same fickle crowd when bad luck or a bad horse, or both, caused him to lose. Anyway, it originated like this.

Rook took him into the Weighing Room before the first race. Already some of the other apprentices had changed and were sitting nervously on benches, some looking forlorn, some defiant and none happy. At one end, where the scales were and the officials sat, a few of the older jockeys were laughing amongst themselves, and none laughed more than a bronzed, dark-haired, hatchet-jawed jockey wearing, casually cast over his shoulders, a flamboyant fur-lined overcoat. He, John learned, was the fabulous Harry Smart. The contrast between his group, the assured, experienced, successful and possibly great, and those of the apprentices, the inexperienced, the nervous and unknown, was so pronounced that even John himself noticed it, as he stood there like a stray dog who has wandered on to some playing field. He waited meekly with his saddle and boots under his arm, whilst Rook, who seemed to know everyone and was enjoying this reunion (it was the opening day of the Flat Racing Season), sought out the valet who was to look after Mellows.

An alert, sharp-featured, gipsy-looking man whose

neatly clipped sideboards of blue-black hair extended to just below his ears, said from behind a desk, 'You riding, kid?' He held a narrow board in one hand and a pail of chalky lime in the other—the stuff with which groundsmen mark the lines of a football pitch.

'Yes,' said John helplessly.

'Name?' The manner intimidated John.

'John, sir,' he began, 'John . . .' but Rook reappeared at that moment and led him brusquely away. The ingredients of the nickname were thus presented and an interpretation of phonetics did the rest. Like this. When a jockey is well known, each race-course gets a sign painter to put his name on the boards that are displayed against the number of the horse when it is hoisted for the public. If he isn't well known, and doesn't get many rides his name is merely chalked on a blank board by those in charge—in this case the gipsy. So every jockey starts as a 'chalk jockey'.

The gipsy was in a hurry. He had fifteen names to chalk and the acoustics were only moderate in the bustling Weighing Room. He cannot be blamed for writing 'J. Joncer' and seeing Rook whom he knew to be the Head Lad of the Stable he hoisted the legend 'J. Joncer' against the number of *Postcard*.

Rook noticed it just before the race. He told the trainer and the owner as the three of them were drinking whisky in the bar. He also knew, after a moment's thought, how it had come about and the three of them burst out laughing. This attracted the reporter of one of the sporting papers who felt it was certainly worth a laugh and a whisky and a few lines as well, so by the time Mellows returned from the Weighing Room after the race, the nickname was near enough in print.

The race was not spectacular—not to the spectators, that is. It was an ordeal to some of the riders, a delight to one (the winner), a major disappointment to another (the second), and to John it was scarcely more real than a dream and only barely so.

Postcard's behaviour in the Paddock was exemplary. And after a few words of encouragement and advice from the owner, John was hoisted aboard.

'You know what to do, lad,' said Penfield, with the geniality born of a few drinks inside him, and the certain knowledge of a few more to come, 'take him down to the Start gently, get him well away, keep well wrapped-up until the six-furlong mark and then do your best. Off you go now!' And they left abruptly. The lad led him to the Paddock Gate and Mellows waited his turn to go through on to the Course. A few were watching the horses leave but this being the first race, the animals moderate and the riding unpredictable, the knowledgeable gamblers were leaving it alone.

Postcard broke into a quiet canter and seemed to be enjoying himself. A small bay passed them at speed with the jockey trying to restrain him and Mellows thanked whatever luck he had for *Postcard*'s quiet temperament. At the Start two were playing up, but *Postcard* stood, ears pricked and placid. As they moved round in an elegant circle Mellows answered his name in the roll. It is an occupational disease to feel nervous; some of the jockeys showed it. John did not. He felt to see if his girths were tight enough and, as he was drawn No. 7, he looked for the black and gold colours of the jockey drawn No. 6. He moved alongside. One jockey called out, 'A minute, sir, please,' in a high-pitched treble as his mount refused to come into line. The starter's assistant moved up behind the animal and resentfully it moved in. John watched the Starter, his eyes never leaving the arm that would shortly press the lever to release the tapes.

For an apprentice race it was a remarkably good start. It was as if the imminence, the restrained urgency was guided by one controlling brain. The line of horses

28

(slightly curved) moved slowly forward and the tapes went up. He dug his heels in and *Postcard* sprang away, took hold of the bit immediately and strode out. He tucked him in on the outside of three fighting for the Rails. The noise surprised him—the grunting, the blowing of horse and jockey, the thud of the hooves, the occasional swearing—he had never imagined it to be like this. But he was no longer nervous. They came out of the Dip and he saw ahead of him the slight curve-in of the Rails, that the three ahead of him now would have to negotiate. He pulled over slightly to the left as they passed the three-furlong mark.

At half-way a grey passed him on the outside—strongly ridden. Restraining a sudden impulse to go after him he sat very still. At the five-furlong mark two more passed him on the inside but because of the sudden curve in the Rails they had to check their strides. *Clever bastards*, he thought, and then he heard the first roar of the crowd. For a very short while it unnerved him. He had not only forgotten their existence, but never had he imagined that this noise could be so shattering. He almost missed his mark—an elm tree he'd noticed when walking the Course earlier, as the place to start his finishing run.

As far as he could see he was fifth now. He changed his position in the saddle slightly, gathered his mount up and started to 'scrub' gently at first to quicken *Postcard*, and then, still in the rhythm of the stride, with more force and vigour. He waved his whip forward so that *Postcard* saw it out of the corner of his eye, and pricked his ears. The roar of the crowd was enormous now—it was like rushing into a tunnel. At the seven-furlong mark he thought he was third and ahead and behind he sensed the others riding flat out. He saw on the stands side a bay and a grey about a length in front of him. He sat down and rode for all he was worth. They flashed past the Post.

He hadn't won. He sensed that. He thought he might have come third. *Postcard* slowed to a canter (seeming as fresh as at the start) and John rose in the stirrups, eased his back and drew a few deep breaths. He felt exhausted. Wearily he turned and trotted back to the crowded Paddock Gate where he saw his Lad.

'Where'd I finish?' he panted.

'About fifth,' said the Lad in a blasé voice. He took hold of the reins. At that moment the loudspeaker announced the result. No. 7 was not mentioned, and the Lad said:

'That's it then—go and change.'

John jumped off as they came to the Stall. He wandered through the crowd, a tiny, bizarre figure, until he came to the Weighing Room. He felt tired, and not exactly depressed, but a slight sense of inadequacy. It was, in reality, disappointment, for although he hadn't expected to win, he unconsciously had expected more than the apathetic anonymity and insignificance. Heavily he climbed the steps to the Weighing Room.

Harry Smart, already changed and weighed out for the next race (which most regarded as the beginning of the season anyway, the Apprentice Race being nothing more than a curtain raiser) saw him as he came in.

'How'd it go, Joncer?' he shouted, filled with the hearty assurance of the successful.

John, who at that moment hated him, was also at a loss. 'You mean me?' he asked lamely.

'That's your name, isn't it?' asked another jockey, a cocky, fresh-faced youth, twirling a whip in his delicate hands and feeling confident in sharing a joke with the great H. Smart.

'No,' said John defiantly, 'my name's Mellows.'

'You've been riding under false pretences then,' said Smart with a leer and mock solemnity. 'Show him his board, Ben!' As they all looked at him John felt the same emotions as he had at school when accosted by the bully and his cronies. The gipsy showed him the name-board and its absurd legend 'J. Joncer'. 'That's what you told me, Joncer,' he said, 'and that's what I put down. As far as I'm concerned that's what you are.'

Miserably John said, 'Well, if that's what I am that's what I'll have to be.' A sudden resentment came over him. He added, 'Now, Ben, out of the bloody way and let me get changed.'

The whole room laughed but not unkindly. The valet said to him as he changed from his silks, 'You'll be all right, kid. 'Tisn't a bad name after all.' He lowered his voice and added, 'It's better than Harry's. That's Big Head.'

And John had, of course, to agree.

4

It was as well he hadn't won that day and didn't win for some time to come. If he had, he might have become too unreceptive, too secure: yet still ignorant of the fact that the combination of Man, horse, and luck that produces a winner is indeed a rare one. So, as riding work at home was merely a job of work (and in the spring and summer a far from unpleasant one), he began to regard his career in public in the same light. He learned more and more about horses.

And about owners.

Some flamboyant, vulgar, generous and rich. Not the big gamblers, nor the discreet ones, but those noisy, brash sort of men (and women, too, plump, scented and mink-coated) who become the 'personalities of the Turf', rather than the 'powers': in a word, the sports. Men like Jack Cassell, a magnate of the ice-cream trade, a scrap-iron car dealer, with a chain of butcher's shops, three ladies' hairdressing salons, and many other sidelines; and a man with an unfailing instinct for owning, not exactly hopeless but, at most, moderate horses. A man to whom a win—even a selling plate at a small meeting like Worcester—was an excuse, or perhaps a motivation, a *raison d'être* for a slap-up, nothing-stinted party at some large, ugly commercial hotel in a large, ugly, commercial town. A popular man—how else?—a carelessly generous man, a delight to his trainer, a relief to his jockey, but a joke to the host of acquaintances, the entourage of florid-faced, purple-tinged boozers—who followed in the trail of the five-pound notes, the brandy and the noisy *bonhomie*.

And then the 'County'. Mean, brassy and snobbish. A woman for example like the Hon. Pamela, with her shooting-stick, her metallic voice and ugly hands: who embodied all the rudeness of the clientele of a Cheltenham coffee shop, and all the toughness of a housekeeper at a Borstal Institute. A woman who regarded a win as merely the confirmation of her own supreme judgment, and an unexpected loser as witness of the trainer's or the jockey's ineptness. Until the trainer, with a mixture of charm, sycophancy, humility and gin, would restore the Hon. Pam's belief in her infallibility, she treated them all (the bookmakers especially, although she never left their debt) as if they were wayward servants. Her horses were never at fault. It was as if they were talented gigolos whose frequent failures were due to some cruel, vast and cunning conspiracy of the crowd, trainer and circumstance. She was indeed a difficult woman. But predictable (for there were many like her) and after her complaints and insults had been accepted and dealt with, she was manageable.

And the business men. Sir Henry, a shipowner, company director, underwriter. He owned the finest stud of horses in southern England and bred bloodstock that was exported all over the world. He was a quiet man, not opinionated, or 'sporty' or unduly idiosyncratic: but one of the 'Powers' of the Turf, (and of Finance as well). A man who expected results, invested wisely to achieve them, and paid willingly on receipt: who would sooner lose five times and be certain of winning on the sixth than win, without prescience, three times the same total: whose horses were run to earn prestige—and money, of course—rather than to land some flashy betting coup on the Rails. With in many ways a trainer's mentality and for that reason feared by them. You'd say he was dignified but he was surrounded with that slightly inhuman, chilling mystery of the powerfully rich.

There were others too, but Joncer, as the months passed, began to recognize these three main types. Naturally, at that age (he was fifteen, nearly sixteen now) he didn't identify them as such. But he gradually acquired the correct measure of humility, regard or jolliness that each demanded.

He had ridden a few winners. The first had not been such an event as might be imagined. He was expected to win, he had won, and it all seemed a mere step along some path of inevitability—certainly pleasant but not remarkable: if anything a trifle disappointing. But the crowd began to recognize him: and he, certain members of the crowd.

They would accost him, beerily, with animation or confidentially and demand, importune, hopefully try to wheedle out of him news of some horse that might soon be a winner, as if racing were an empirical process and the jockeys and their trainers, the expert scientists who alone knew the secret and therefore controlled it. All of them had the same look of desperation, in believing that a golden miracle was about to happen. One of them would appear sometimes at dawn from behind a clump of gorse on the Downs. He'd stand like a precocious child in front of Joncer. Quick of speech, wide, yet empty-eyed like an unsuccessful beggar, so very lonely and with the look of one of the very lost, he'd say with specious heartiness:

'Well, Joncer, what d'yer know?' or, implying that he shared the secret too, 'You're trying with *Bagwash* tomorrow then?' Sometimes he'd try a mild sort of bribery—'There's odds to a tenner when you tell us one, Joncer'—nodding his head with the air of a magnanimous conspirator. And John would ride slowly by, at first mystified and later amazed at this tenacious application, and at the *naïveté* of his faith. As he grew wiser he'd reply, 'There's always another trying to win, you know.' Some mornings he'd angrily say, 'How the hell do I know what's going to win?' But most times tolerantly he'd smile and shrug his shoulders and ride slowly on.

CHAPTER FOUR

They were always poor. They'd hang about the entrances to the courses and as he walked towards the Jockeys' Gate one would come up and offer to carry his bag—'Say I'm your valet, Joncer, I'm a bit short today,'—and when he'd got him in—'How's it looking for a once, Joncer—got skint at Hurst.''

Always poor. You could tell a recent win by their shoes—the shiny leather of a new pair accusing by dire contrast the mud-stained, baggy trousers, the greasy trilby hat and the unbelted, swaying overcoat. A win and—shoes. One of their few necessities because they were on their feet all day (and most of the night too, scrounging drinks—not always without grace—in the racing pubs). And yet unchangeable. They never seemed to age or to be ill. A disappearance of some months meant jail, of a day—drunk. They travelled the country from meeting to meeting (Joncer never knew how—they were always there before he was, in the same positions and with the same hard-luck stories) living on a diet of jellied eels, meat pies, ale and trust in a myth, an incredulous myth certainly but seemingly a sustaining one, that one day they would go through the card, or they'd put a crisp five-pound note on a 20 to 1 winner and the winnings on another.

They were the regulars. The rest were like a crowd anywhere. The odd recurring face that you remembered because of its recurrence. And the types—the man who'd taken a day off from work, the one who'd looked in because he was passing, the locals of the vicinity who never missed their home meeting. The old women against the rails of the Cheap Enclosure, with their shrill cries, 'Tell us a winner, Joncer, the old man's on the dole.' The 'wide' boys, identical from town to town, and those few, cold-eyed calculating men who never spoke to strangers, rarely shouted at even the closest of finishing and who did their betting like a dealer buying from an auctioneer (a wink, a nod, a code of gestures each meaning perhaps as little as five or as much as a thousand pounds)—those actuaries of probability who are the professional gamblers.

Like a crowd anywhere. Yes, the ingredients are. But more responsive, fickle, vociferous, indeed colourful, than any other: frightening too, at times.

At Kempton it had been. He was eighteen now and getting many rides. He was returning to the unsaddling enclosure after he'd come second—through no fault of his own—on an 11 to 10 favourite. The Lad was leading him in and the five were waiting against the Rails, four men and a leader spokesman. Anyhow, this one said—his voice was like a cold wind in a fog—'Fall off, Mellows, and we'll get you,' and the ten eyes looked at him from beneath their hats, and the ten eyes were implacable and cruel. Beyond them the crowd wandered nebulously—the five stood like a nucleus of hate—and Joncer felt a tremor of panic. They still watched as he dismounted but when he came out of the Weighing Room they had gone. The memory stayed of the presence of undoubted evil.

On his nineteenth birthday he terminated his apprenticeship with Penfield. It was a Sunday morning. Penfield took him into the office.

'How many more do you need before you lose the three?' asked Penfield. (Until jockeys have ridden a certain number of winners they may claim seven, five, and then three pounds from the weight the horse is given to carry.)

'One,' said Joncer.

'What d'you want to do when you leave me?'

'I don't know,' said Joncer. And he didn't.

'Harry Murphy wants a light-weight. He might give you a retainer—not a bad one either.' Penfield, who was sitting at his desk, leant back and looked calmly at Mellows. 'Then again you could free-lance.' He paused and then said, 'There's your money.'

CHAPTER FOUR

He gave him a cheque for £800. Mellows was amazed, at the amount first, and then at the numbing idea of possessing it.

'What's . . ?'

'It's what you've earned. Presents included and interest and I've made it up to a round figure. You'll need a car if you free-lance and for Christ's sake get some new clothes. That's all the advice I'd give you—you've had all the rest from me during the last five years. Except for one thing more'—Penfield came forward in his chair and looked keenly at Mellows—'and that's Money in general.'

He lit a cigar. 'You should be making five thousand a year soon. And you'll make it for about fifteen years or so, unless you break your neck, gamble it, or put people's backs up. It's good money. Save it.'

'Yes, Mr Pen . . .'

'Save it. Nobody will remember you when you're forty-five and riding losers. Nobody wants you—because you won't be any bloody good then—unless you're a freak like Harry Smart—and he has more off days now than on. So that's when you'll need money. To buy yourself a pub somewhere. You might make a good trainer but I doubt it. That's what you ought to do—buy yourself a nice pub—with photos on the walls of yourself being bloody brilliant at Ascot, of the King giving you a cigar, a finish of necks somewhere and you just there by a whisker—that's what I'd do any-way!' Almost nostalgically, almost enviously, Penfield sat back in his chair and dreamily continued: 'A good bar trade and grub for the snobs—Virginia Water, Cobham, some place like that and you mine host.'

It was as if he was painting an idyllic picture for himself more than Mellows. But he suddenly became brusque again.

'Get what you can out of racing, and don't let any

bugger get it back. And hold on to it. I know when you'll need it most.

'Now business. You can ride *Whisper* next week and stay on with me for a month or so. While you look around. I'll give you a ride now and then until you're on your feet. You'll be all right. Until you're forty anyway. I'm nearly twice that so I ought to know.'

And suddenly he did look an old man. Not that John realized any more than this mere fact. It's doubtful if he felt sympathy or admiration for this rough practitioner of a rough trade, because Joncer was young and rich, unexpectedly, romantically, fantastically rich. He thanked Penfield and walked out into the light-hearted spring sunshine. The tremendous possibilities of the very present and the immediate future reached out and dazzled him. John Mellows had grown up.

The following week was the Derby. Joncer won the Caterham Stakes, the sprint that precedes the big race. He weighed in, was congratulated by the owner, and sat down in the Weighing Room. A feeling of tension was pronounced amongst the waiting jockeys—the next race was the Derby, the richest race in the Calendar, a race in which a horse could start worth 3,000 guineas and finish worth 100,000. A race in which a jockey could make a thousand pounds for himself, and a reputation for ever. Or conversely lose it. Joncer himself was not riding—only the most experienced jockeys, Irish, English, Australian and French rode in this race. So he sat there—he had a ride in the last race—waiting, feeling the tension, and in many ways thankful to be out of it. With surprise he noticed Harry Smart on the scales. Lately he'd had either bad luck or else age was indeed beginning to tell, because he hadn't been in the Winners' Enclosure for the last thirty rides. Whispered gossip said Smart had lost his nerve, or that debauchery had taken its toll, or age was creeping upon

gesticulating, animated lad
Blower money.'

'And then, they book you ag
It went steady a moment or s
they didn't—small amounts
wanted to get on—they stepp
again all the way down to eig
eight and a half monkeys laid i

The lad stood there like a p
fore a general, breathless, ama
thing like it, not since *Tuppence* w

'I'll win it,' said Smart quietl

'Old women, kids, all of then
bard himself—they're all on.
Books'll be smashed empty. I te
walk home.'

He moved over to another g
never seen anything like it ever

'I'll win it,' said Smart. 'I've g
Stakes for me.'

A bell rang to tell the jockeys t
Smart got up and made for the c

'You'll win it,' said Joncer.

'Yes,' said Smart, and out he v
clamour, the sunshine. The ot
Joncer waited where he was, in
empty now except for the Clerk
up and moved to the door.

'He'll win it,' he said.

'Yes,' said the Clerk, 'I expect

If it was simply a matter of
petence, at work upon things whi
would be no horse-racing. Or, if tl
would be trained mathematicians
and the bookmakers charitable in
thing more than that. Only a litt

him and even a few, the superstitious, white heather
types, said Harry had a jinx on him. Despite all this,
one owner preferred Harry to all the others. Joncer
heard Harry say to the Clerk of the Scales:

'Number 15. H. Smart. Nine stones, blinkers,' and
then step off with the saddle, weight cloth and blinkers
over his arm. He came and sat next to Mellows.

'Well, Joncer?'

'Well, Harry. How do you feel?'

Smart twirled a cigarette in his fingers and quickly
drew a long pull at it. Exhaling he said, 'All right,
Joncer.' And then he repeated it, distantly. 'All right.'

They sat for a minute in silence. Mellows said, perhaps embarrassed by the silence, 'Sooner you than me,
Harry.'

Smart spat between his knees. 'Why's that, kid?'

'The Derby, Harry! . . .'

'It's just like any weight-for-age mile and a half race,
Joncer. If you know your horse and do as you're told,
you can't do wrong. I know. I've won four.'

'Thought it was three, Harry.'

'Four. I'll win this one.'

'The Ring don't think so, Harry.'

'That's what you know. I'm quitting after this.'

'What'll you do then?'

'That's the trouble, I don't know. I could ride for
another twenty years and still get 'em home. But no
bugger'll believe me. The twats say there's a jinx on me
now.'

He paused and then said quite calmly, 'I'll just have
to show them, that's all.'

'Hope you do, Harry.'

Perhaps a slight element of disbelief crept into
Mellows's voice. Smart said, almost laughingly, 'You
think I'm finished too, don't you, Joncer? They all do,
so why shouldn't you?' He dropped his voice even
lower.

'So I'm going to win t[...]
come clamouring for me t[...]
wards I'll say, "No, you [...]
That's what I'm going to [...]
them they can stuff them a[...]

'How you going to win, [...]
sideways towards Smart an[...]
than faith in his question.

Smart said, quickly and [...]
wait in front, Joncer. I'm g[...]
wait behind me because the[...]
than any. So they'll all try[...]
tucked in. So, round the Co[...]
They'll wait. At three from [...]
two from home the same a[...]
I'll just sit there still. And [...]
they've left it too late becau[...]
death. They'll all panic an[...]
show the whip and have ha[...]
Post. That's how I'll win it.'

Joncer nodded. Smart h[...]
assurance of the great. And [...]
believed him, while in his bel[...]
hope, of sympathy. Even th[...]
they have to kid themselves[...]
gesture against the suffocati[...]
stance; against age, gossip, lu[...]

'Good luck, Harry, anywa[...]

'Luck,' said Smart, 'I spit [...]
as if a spark crackled along t[...]
nerves. 'No such thing, luck. [...]
that's generally something el[...]
to be clever enough to avoid.'[...]

A stable-lad came hurrying[...]
gone mad for yours, Harry—[...]
that——'

'—the Blower'—said Smar[...]

but this addition is to know the colour of destiny, the vague tenuosity of the future. Not only to know it (and knowing is really a feeling, an intuitive surge) but more, to assimilate the mysterious knowledge and act upon it with the inward conviction of the mystic.

So it is indeed strange that the foul-mouthed, arrogant Harold Smart, a practitioner of a highly skilled physical trade, should have some of the qualities of a Buddhist sage. And yet, of course, he'd have to, since the very ingredients of his trade implied some attempt to predict the future. It is implicit in the act of any jockey getting up on any horse, that he can narrow the field of probability. And the degree of his conviction in doing so is some measure of his prowess. Either that, or his brashness.

There's a bit of bluff in it too.

They got away to a good start. Joncer couldn't see much of the early stages—he pieced it together from the chatter of the jockeys in the Weighing Room afterwards but they seemed to settle down to a steady gallop. Smart was close up fourth. After three furlongs he shouted to the leaders, 'Hold it, boys—you're flogging it,' and because he was such a good judge of pace they all took a stronger hold. He moved up—'let me through for Christ's sake'—and took up the rails position at the top of the hill. The others settled down behind him. The stamina of Smart's mount was suspect —most judges seemed to think he'd get a mile with the best, but the Derby's half-mile extra (and up hill at that) would find him out. They thought this because the animal was French bred, by an unfashionable sire, and had never yet raced over an undulating course such as Epsom. The weight of money (from 33 to 1 to 8 to 1 at starting) was something to off-set this, but most—all the other jockeys—expected him to drop back in the straight. They knew that Smart was nursing him and so rather than get 'lost out in front' in the early stages, they let him stride ahead, while they tailed him, biding their time.

They came down Tattenham Hill, Smart two lengths in the lead. He took the Corner, tightly against the rails, and shook his mount up slightly to counter the sudden blare of the fair-ground, the roar of the crowd and the peat track that some horses tried to jump, to give him something else to think about. The jockeys behind him forced their horses forward, but Smart settled his down again and they thought they could overtake whenever they wanted. At three from home a length separated them (two behind Smart and another close up fourth), Smart sat very still and his mount pricked his ears at the first roar of the crowd in the stands. The others moved alongside. Smart, still riding with his hands, kept him going. They reached for their whips (they were two from home now) but Smart still 'waited in front', composed, rhythmic as they passed the last furlong post. At 100 yards there were three in a line. Smart, almost insolently, hardly moving, as all one with the horse, pushed him forward. He won by a neck, and half a length, amid a deafening Derby roar from the crowd, whose lives seemed suspended in an eternal moment, not of Truth for that is pretentious—but a moment of stilled excitement, that hung instance of decision.

'Yes,' said Mellows but no one heard him.

'A great, a grand race,' shouted a reporter from the *Sporting Life* as the cameras flashed, to photograph the American owner (he was a large Texan with a florid Texan smile) leading in his French horse and his English jockey. The crowd surged round them.

'Yes,' said Smart, looking grey, relaxed yet implicitly triumphant. And they didn't hear him either. The owner took the clamorous congratulations with the same unchanging, almost inane smile. He led into the

Winners' Enclosure followed by a more assertive congratulatory section of the crowd.

'Tell us, Harry,' said the *Sporting Life*, 'when you knew you'd win.'

'Before,' said Smart. He'd dismounted now and was removing his saddle and blinkers from the steaming horse. 'Before I'd started I knew. I had to.'

'Yes,' said Joncer eagerly, coming forward from the Weighing Room. 'Yes, that's right. That's what he said.'

But he was still ignored. Smart, his saddle and tack under his arm—a tiny, laden figure, monkey-like amongst the crowd—said, 'I've not won till I weigh in —will you——?'

And they all stood back to let him pass. He entered the Weighing Room, and the crowd—the French trainer, dapper, voluble with the polyglot French of Maisons Laffitte, the owner, the Press, and other owners and jockeys, followed him in. He sat on the Scales: they registered nine stone one pound.

'You've put on a pound, Harry, then,' said the Clerk. (It was within the margin; he had weighed out with nine stone but the sweat from the animal soaked up by the saddle cloth added the further pound. It often happens.)

'I've put on £50,000,' said Smart bluntly. He meant sterling.

'Yes, it's right,' said Mellows, 'and he said he'd win.'

'What made you so sure you'd win, Harry?' asked the reporter.

'Me,' said Smart, 'who else?' He stepped down from the scales and pushed his cap back with his whip. Almost angrily he said, 'You don't suppose the horse knows, do you? Once in a while a jockey wins a race.' He paused. 'Not the horse. Not luck but the jockey.'

'What I like about this guy,' said the American owner, with his hearty smile, 'is his modesty.'

CHAPTER FOUR

Smart gave him a quick look but said nothing.

'What are your plans now?' the reporter asked. Smart had moved to a corner of the Weighing Room. He sat down and his valet tugged at his boots.

'I quit,' he said, looking up at the circle of faces, 'I quit. It's a mug's game.'

'Come on, Harry, quit now! At the top of your luck?'

'There's no such thing, I tell you,' he replied, perhaps wearily. The other boot was off now so he stood up to remove his silks.

'That's right,' said Joncer again eagerly, but quietly too, to himself more than anyone, 'he said he spit on it.'

'I've got enough money,' said Smart, 'I'm going to sit back'—fastidiously he tied a neat bow-tie—'and I'm going to eat cream, roast potatoes, drink beer—the lot. That's what I'm going to do—enjoy myself. They can get some other sucker to ride the pigs from now on.'

'*Cochon?*' asked the French trainer, mystified.

'*Oui*,' said Smart, neither his voice nor his accent changing, '*donnez moi* my saddle.' The trainer gave it to him. Holding it, balancing it in one hand for a moment, Smart then lobbed it towards Mellows.

'There you are, Joncer,' he said, 'use that on your forty-fifth birthday if you believe in luck. It's the lightest ever made and every pound (money as well) when you get to that age counts. I know.'

Joncer caught it. 'I don't believe in Luck neither,' he said, 'but I'll keep it all the same. Thanks.'

He was photographed as he said it, for in a sentimental way it was news.

'You'll be all right,' said Smart as he made for the door, 'you're mug enough for a mug's game.'

And then he was gone.

'Like I was saying,' began the Texan, 'what I like about that guy is his . . .'

'You don't know,' said Joncer quietly, quickly, 'he

won the race. Was him, not your horse. And he said he would. Not boasting nor showing off. He just said he'd win and he did because he had to. He won plenty of money too. But what else do you want? Him to blush? Say it was luck when it wasn't? Pretend that anyone could have done it when we all known damn' well that they couldn't? He's not a disc jockey you know. He's,' he paused and then added, with an awkward youthful exuberance, 'he's great.'

'Yeah,' said the Texan, 'so he told us.'

'Yes,' said Mellows, 'he told us. But that don't matter.' But he said it to an uninterested, dispersing crowd now. He added to himself more than to anyone as he stood, clasping the saucer-sized saddle in his arms, a small, lonely figure suddenly amongst disbelievers—'It don't matter.'

The jockeys for the next race lined up in front of the scales. Joncer returned to his bench and waited.

5

HE kept the saddle. He had no need of it then because he rode comfortably at seven stone. And even, just after the war, when he was thirty-five he did seven stone ten at a pinch, and seven twelve. But the lightweight saddle stayed with him.

I know this. Some of what I've just told I've had to make up and some of what I'm going to say. And I've left a lot out, like girls: like seeing Singapore, Calcutta, Nairobi, because he'd ride there in the winter months, and I never went that far. And though he told me a lot, now he's quit racing I've forgotten some of the jokes. And I've forgotten a lot of the hardship, the unfairness, at times the feelings of hopelessness that no one can avoid. When you feel like chucking the whole thing up and taking a seven-pound-a-week job. I'm a racing man myself and I say that. That sort of thing is always happening.

But if you're in racing and you stay in racing you don't change. Joncer Mellows hasn't. I knew him when he was a kid at Penfield's. (I knew Stowy Rook who married my cousin and I can tell you he was a bastard—you wouldn't believe it but I've known him keep some kids' winning money as if it was his right: he'd not pass it on to them, the presents, when the owners handed it over. No, he'd keep it: he never did with Joncer, mind you, because you wouldn't do that to someone like Joncer; you couldn't push him around. No one could.) Anyway he hasn't changed. And Harry Smart, when he was a kid, was always cocky, bigheaded, generous mind, but he knew it all—you couldn't tell him anything. He's probably the same now on his South African farm. He'd tell the oranges how to grow.

Of course, Harry was one of the great. He was an

Artist of the Saddle if you like. Often when he got beat (and they'd all moan, I can tell you) he'd no right to be even second. Even donkeys went well for Harry.

Joncer was different. He was good—he'd never have got where he was if he hadn't been—but he was just short of being a genius like Harry. He had style, mind you. He was strong—he could drive them. And he could save a horse up and pounce at the Post. You cheered Joncer home like he'd done you a good turn. But Harry—you were speechless for a while by his sheer mastery—you knew you'd seen something that no one else could do—even when he'd come second. Like I said, I'm a racing man myself and I have to say it.

I liked Harry, even if he was a bit of a handful.

We were doing the Southern Circuit one year, Folkestone, Brighton, Lewes, Goodwood and home. I was travelling Head Lad then and Harry and me would go out nights together. He was a restless bugger. If we were in a pub he'd have to play darts. And he'd have to stay till he'd won—that generally meant till he'd got his opponents drunk and probably himself too. And girls—any bits of local talent there were—Harry had to make his play. Generous certainly. You didn't need any money when you were out with Harry—a fiver on the bar and he'd tell the landlord to treat 'em all and tell him when it had gone. Some would cheat him—you couldn't spend ten quid in half an hour on eight people —not in 1938 anyway—not spend it and leave them sober, without even a wobble amongst the lot. It would break my heart, I can tell you. And as likely as not we'd end up in some hotel two or three in the morning, with some tart or other, and Harry would be riding the next day and I'd have my work to do from seven o'clock in the morning. It was killing.

But he'd be there next morning, bad tempered, irritable to dukes and less, and yet ride like an angel. You had to like him.

With Joncer it was better. He liked his fun as well but it was quieter. He was fond of a bit of fishing, so after racing we'd go down to somewhere like Fordingbridge for the evening rise and then a few pints. And he liked listening to folks talking, to play dominoes, to sit back and take it easy, to forget racing. I never had to worry with Joncer.

I never knew about his girls. He had one or two I suppose, and I think he was sweet on some widow in Ayr. He'd grin a bit when he'd tell me he was 'riding' up North on such and such a day especially when they sent him up from Newmarket to ride a filly called *Bedtime* at Hamilton Park.

'She's in the Handicap nicely at seven stone ten,' said Joncer.

'Some widow,' I said.

Harry quit before the war and went to South Africa and we never saw him again. Someone received a post-card signed 'His Reverence H. Smart, S.J.' and we forwarded it to the Jockey Club. It was cheery and saucy, so we reckoned it would do more good there than round the Stables. And one of the boys who'd been riding in Jo'burg said he saw Harry patting the President, or at least the Admiral of their Fleet, on the back in the Members' Enclosure so we knew old Harry hadn't changed. And as far as you forget anyone we forgot him. The war came then anyway.

I missed it. I was fifty-two in 1939.

Joncer was twenty-five. He'd ride a bit on his leaves and once or twice we'd have a drink together. He was a corporal in the cavalry (or whatever they call their ranks) and doing all right. Enjoying it almost.

He missed his chance on a Derby winner; we had a good 'un and we booked him to ride it (the war permitting). So he turned down another ride. Ours breaks down before the race and Joncer (who'd got leave) watched from the Stands the other one win. It was at Newmarket that year.

'Tough luck,' I said as we came away.

'Yes,' he said, 'I could have done with the money.' And that's all he said. No cussing ranting like some of them would. He just forgot it and went back to his tanks—or they may have had horses still at that time—it was a pretty crummy war to begin with.

Then it was over and Joncer came back. He rode for the Lambourn Stables. He'd put on weight. He seemed to have grown even. He did eight stone. For a while we had to watch it and it was Turkish Baths for him once a week during the season. But for a couple of seasons he did well enough—anything around eight stone in the Long Distance Handicaps—you couldn't ignore Joncer. And somewhere in '49 or '50 he rode his hundred winners in the season, rounding it off with the nicest Cesarewitch I've ever seen—although I may be biased myself because I backed him—at 33 to 1, six times. He told me he made a bit for himself too. Mind you, Joncer was never poor. I'd have put him at £20,000 in 1950, though I never knew what it was in, or how much he made. But he could have retired. And not gone short of a drink.

But he didn't. It wouldn't have been like him anyway. You might think it strange to retire at thirty-five, but when you're a jockey at this age you're on your last stretch. Unless you're Harry Smart. But at thirty-five normally you want to think about life ten years hence, unless you want to end up cadging drinks in the bar or telling stories in the Cheap Ring. And with Joncer there was this thing of weight. In 1951 he could just do eight stone four and with top weights at nine stone (a few over up to nine seven, but not many) there weren't a lot of rides available. Not on the Flat anyway.

He realized it. Because this had happened.

6

THIS man Singer had come around the tracks. No one knew him well; you knew him in the same way as you'd know another, but at the same time mysterious, regular at your local. He was like the man you say 'good evening' to, and he nods back. And each of you continue in your respective isolations. He was six years younger than Joncer, but he looked more like an untidy undergrad. You'd see him standing in the Members' Bar, on the outskirts of some group or other, speaking when spoken to, occasionally buying drinks, but for the most part nothing more than an accepted eavesdropper. He'd become such a familiar sight, that I suppose everyone thought he must be a friend of somebody else. He wasn't shy: just remote. Not unfriendly, but certainly never convivial.

He hasn't changed much in these last ten years. He's still got that dank, straight fair hair, and he's still six feet tall and thin. An intelligent face apart from the eyes (blue, large and in a faraway, mystical way they seem somehow fanatical) and if the weather's good tomorrow at Cheltenham Races, he'll still be wearing the same baggy, worsted trousers, the same leather-patched sports coat and his suède chukka boots. I'll bet on that.

He's got an Aston Martin now. The floor littered with old race-cards, cigarette packets, pie crust and the dried mud of some twenty different race tracks. There'll be a couple of old cheque books in the cubby hole and the counterfoils will all read in at least three figures and all the names will be bookmakers. He wins more than he loses though. Because Singer is a gambler. Not lucky, not superstitious—you can't be—but quick, clear-cut and tenacious. Shrewd too.

Why he bothered I don't know. He's rich to begin

with (from what or why I don't know). And he doesn't seem to enjoy gambling either. I've stood next to him during a race. He looked gaunt, as if the uncertainty of it was concerned with more than so many hundreds changing hands—as if it were a terrible sort of test, a proving ground, some sort of compulsion from which he couldn't escape. Yes, Singer was neurotic, if you like.

I didn't dislike, or like him. People I don't understand I can't feel anything about. But with Joncer it was different. Maybe he understood Singer. Whatever it was, they became, as far as such a thing was possible, something like friends.

Joncer came second in the last race at Warwick a few years back. He should have won. He'd starved (even then he rode a pound overweight) and he must have been as weak as a kitten. He just couldn't drive the animal home.

He fainted in the Weighing Room. I was there. I was collecting the tack together and then I was setting off for Newmarket. Joncer still lived at Lambourn those days.

We got him on his feet.

'You'd better have a drink,' I said, 'before you go.' He nodded. He was still a bit weak and I saw he wouldn't be able to drive his own car. He changed out of his silks and we went to the bar. There weren't many there. Singer was on his own—one end. Joncer and he must have got talking whilst I bought the drinks. I think it was the first jockey he'd ever spoken to.

'I thought you'd win, Mr Mellows,' said Singer, eagerly, 'I had five score to one, yours, but I'd a small saver, the winner. I thought you'd win though.' He sipped his whisky, carelessly—as if it wasn't there, as if the glass was something you had to hold, to gesture with, when you spoke. 'I thought you'd win.'

'So did I,' said Joncer. He still looked white, and I knew the signs—he looked middle-aged (he was forty then). He said it wryly. Singer didn't know about the weight trouble.

I had an idea. I ignored Singer—not rudely, there wasn't any need for rudeness—you could ignore him like you would a child.

'What you want to do,' I said, 'is to get yourself a Head Lad's job somewhere.' (I'm one myself, I knew what I was talking about.) 'I don't suppose you'd want to be a trainer yourself.'

Joncer grinned. We both knew we hadn't the front, the way to cope with, not only jockeys, lads, feed bills, money generally, but owners as well. And owners can be as tricky as the nappiest 'dog' in any stable. I went on:

'In some National Hunt Stable. A few rides for yourself when you fancy them—no weight problem there—ten per cent of the presents, a thousand a year anyway—why—you'd be laughing.'

In a way I was right—it would be a comfortable life. His earnings would drop certainly. There just isn't the same sort of money in the jumping game. But he wasn't short and a thousand a year plus extras is enough for any single man who's got a bit tucked away as well.

I could see how he felt though. It might mean saying good-bye to fasting, Turkish Baths and continual travelling, but it meant saying hello to middle-age as well. He wouldn't exactly be 'hanging up his boots' but he was certainly entering the last stretch.

'I never did use that saddle,' Joncer said.

'What saddle?' I asked, but I knew the answer as soon as I said it.

'Harry Smart's,' he said. I knew then that he agreed with me.

We drank our drinks quietly. 'We may as well have another,' said Joncer, gathering the glasses. 'I can put a stone on now if I want.' He went to the bar.

'Drive him home,' I said to Singer, 'and give him

some food half-way.' It was cheeky of me to ask it, but I thought Singer wouldn't mind. Fact was, I suppose he thought he'd get a few tips from Joncer, so he jumped at the chance. Maybe he was just lonely. I don't know.

When Joncer returned Singer said, 'Can I give you a lift, Mr Mellows—I'm staying at Newbury.'

And Joncer said, 'Thanks.'

7

I SUPPOSE that was the beginning.

I was up North for the rest of the season and so I didn't see much of Joncer. I read in the *Life* that he'd taken the Head Lad's, stable-jockey position with Cedric Verepont in Gloucestershire. And if my daughter hadn't married a few months after (she married young Billy Locker who rides the light-weights for the Malton Stables—a good boy, you want to watch him) and if my wife hadn't said it was time for me to quit, I doubt if I'd have seen Joncer for a year or so. Only she was from Gloucestershire herself and so we sold up and I try and grow roses (on limestone soil) while she's a big noise in the W.I. You wouldn't know us now! Anyway we ended up in the next village to Joncer. I tell you, he thought he'd seen a ghost that evening I walked into his local.

Joncer told me. 'And this Singer—he talks horses all the way back, even when I'd got to my digs. I have him in for a drink and suddenly it's two in the morning and he's telling me how he backed some two-year-old I'd ridden way back, and how he won a monkey. But I saw he knew nothing about horses, as horses that is. To him they're all prices on a bookie's board, nothing more—might just as well be the Stock Exchange and him buying on the margin.'

I nodded. I said, ' 'Tisn't a bad way of weighing them up after all—the way they bet is a fair indication of how good an animal is, or should be.'

'I know,' said Joncer, 'if you're one of the mugs who has a day's racing once in a while, it's about all you've got to go on. But Singer—he was at it every day, and he hadn't learned what "weight for age" meant—he couldn't tell a well-bred animal from a £20 hack—he just had no interest that way.'

We both drank a little.

'I was getting fed up with all this talk about betting,' Joncer went on, 'it was three in the morning and I was tired. I said, "You want to buy a horse yourself, Mr Singer, and have yourself some real fun."

'I don't know what he does for sleep. He said, "Yes" and then he said "Yes" again like he'd made a discovery or something. "Will you buy one for me?" Well, I'd been thinking about what you'd said—going over to the Jumps—and I thought that if I turned up at some Stable after a Head Lad's job with a patron as well—they ought to fall over me.'

I nodded. Even at three in the morning Joncer could be smart. 'So?' I said.

'We went to Ireland,' said Joncer, 'Singer and me, and we bought one. A six-year-old by *Fortina*—a nice, strong-looking chestnut called *Pentameter*.'

That was the first time I heard the name. '*Pentameter?* What does that mean?'

'Means five feet,' said Joncer.

'Five feet what?' I said.

'Just five feet,' said Joncer. 'Singer said he remembered it from school."

'Has the animal got five feet or something?' I asked.

'Funny thing is,' said Joncer (he was enthusiastic about the animal—he was interested in all sides of racing—a lot of jockeys will give you a moronic stare when you ask them about a simple thing like breeding even), 'funny thing is that he stands over a lot of ground (he's near seventeen hands) and he's got a slow, strong action. So if you've had a pint too many you might think he's running on five legs.'

'Some horse,' I said.

'You wait till you see him then,' said Joncer.

'Who'd you see in Ireland?' I asked. I bought some more drink before he went on.

'The lot,' said Joncer. 'It took us three days to get

the owner of *Pentameter* sober enough to name a price, and I had my hands full with Singer. No one liked him. He's too restless, he never relaxes—and you can't hurry an Irishman over his drink. Singer should never be the one to do a deal. He isn't——' Joncer paused for a while—I knew what he was going to say—

'Happy enough?' I said.

'That's it,' said Joncer. 'You see, we were at a small meeting down south—Tramere—and there's this Novice Chase: 5 to 2 on one, 6 to 1 *Pentameter* and any price the rest. Of course Singer wants to back the lot but I take him down to the Paddock—Paddock?—it was a bit of string pegged out in a field really—and as soon as I saw this *Pentameter* I knew that here was our horse. I said so. Singer thinks I mean it's the one to back, so he runs off and has six ton to one. I meant it was the one to buy, but if he must back something I can't stop him. I meant that *Pentameter* looked every inch a Gold Cup horse—say in a couple of years' time.

'Anyway Singer goes off to clout the Books and I watch the parade. You remember Maxie Mahon who got warned off over here?' I nodded.

'Well, he gets up on this 5 to 2 on shot and he looks as if he means business. I can see that Singer can say good-bye to his £100. And when I see that *Pentameter*'s jockey is his owner and that his owner is three parts cut —it took three men to get him up and even mounted, his breath was scorching the grass—I knew the race would be painful.

'Singer just doesn't know how lucky he is. He stands next to me during the running. He looks grey and if I ever saw a nerve case it was him. Maxie settles down on his and off they go, *Pentameter* about third. They all get over the first jumps and then they come past us. The owner of *Pentameter*—O'Rourke his name— this O'Rourke rides like a bloody cowboy—he gives a "yippee" at every jump—they'd hear it at Limerick, and he waves his arm like he's got a lasso ready. Maxie rides, Oh so quiet! and off they go into the country. I try not to look at the jockey but at the horse. Even with this sack of potatoes on his back I can see the horse can jump—measuring his stride nicely and coming to them with his ears pricked. At the turn for home Maxie wakes his up and the 5 to 2 boys begin to shout.

'But you wouldn't believe it!

'Maxie wasn't cheating—I could see he wasn't—he was all out on his. But this *Pentameter* takes it into his head to go—O'Rourke is played out now—not enough energy left for a tiny yippee. He hangs on to the neck and two from home Maxie and he are together. *Pentameter* flies it (they tell me this—I couldn't look—it hurt so!) and at the last is two lengths clear. O'Rourke wakes up, rides like a windmill, drops his whip, loses his cap and wins by six lengths with Maxie looking as black as coal.

'You know what Singer said?'

'No,' I said, though I could guess.

'He said, "That O'Rourke can ride!" and off he went to draw his six hundred quid.'

We both drank deeply. 'Then you bought this five-footer?' I asked.

'No,' said Joncer, 'we opened negotiations. O'Rourke's in the bar treating the world. I lose Singer for a while and introduce myself. Turns out all the newspaper boys are there and they remember me. O'Rourke is impressed. So we all start drinking and talking, like the Irish do. Along comes Singer, his pockets full of money, walks up to O'Rourke and says, brusquely, and without offering him a drink, "How much do you want for *Pentameter*?" '

' "Have a drink," says O'Rourke.

' "No," said Singer. "No, I want to buy your horse."

' "Englishman here," says O'Rourke to the whole bar, "wants to buy my horse."

' "Yes," says Singer, standing there like a priest in a brothel. "Yes, how much?"

'It's not the way to do it. O'Rourke says, "Englishman here, won't have a drink."

' "I'm not thirsty," said Singer. I ask you—what a thing to say in an Irish bar!

' "Now who had it in their mind to ask if you were thirsty?" asks O'Rourke. He turns to the barman and says, "Give the Englishman who isn't thirsty and wants to buy my horse, a drink."

'I stepped in then. "As one jockey to another, Mr O'Rourke, will you allow me the privilege of buying this round?" That pleased O'Rourke. We all became pally and they forgot Singer. I told him that some bloody thing or other—I forget the name now—was a certainty for the next race and off he goes to back it.

'We all drink for a bit and then we get in a car and go to Limerick. We have some more there. Then we somehow (the next day it must have been) find ourselves in Cork. O'Rourke and me are pals for life now. "Dublin next stop," he says, "for a real drink," and Dublin it is.

'I bought *Pentameter* there.'

'How much?' I asked.

'Four fifty,' said Joncer (he meant guineas—it was cheap, very cheap), 'though I'd spent £50 extra on drink—you know how it is.'

I do.

'Singer was at the hotel in Dublin. I don't know where he'd been the last few days—he talked a bit about some greyhounds he'd backed—but that's all I gathered. "I've got you *Pentameter*," I said.

' "How much?" says Singer.

' "Six hundred," says I.

' "Fine," says he and pays me out in cash. And everybody's happy. A hundred for me and a horse for Singer.'

We both laughed, and sat back for a while smoking.

There was a girl in the bar, a young girl about twenty-one or two I should say.

She had fair hair which was tied in one of those pony tails and a fine-featured face. I mean eyes, nose, mouth were delicately set. And her whole face sort of moved well with a wide range of expression. I'd noticed her as well while Joncer was talking—I wouldn't say she was pretty—more that she was interesting. But Joncer obviously thought she was all this and more.

I'd have said then she was arty—she wore a long skirt—I wouldn't know what material except it looked silky—and a man's shirt—a dark green one—with a chocolate silk scarf tied cowboy fashion round a slender neck. Chocolate and green are famous racing colours— *Bahram*, *Mahmoud*, *Palestine*, *Tulyar*—ask any racing man whose these are. I pointed them out to Joncer.

And I knew she was arty when she went up to the bar and ordered a whisky—not just that I mean—it was when she said, in a clear, lady-like but pleasant voice, as she opened her purse, 'Oh what a bloody nuisance, I'll have to change a fiver.' The whole bar heard. Joncer was up like a greyhound. 'You have that with me, miss,' he said, the money out and on the bar before she had time to say yes or no, or 'thank you, but' or whatever she had in her mind to say. Joncer was always quick that way. He led her back, gallantly, to our table. I stood up.

'Please,' she said, 'don't bother—I'm not used to such good manners.' Nor am I usually so I sat down and grinned, and Joncer brought out his cigarettes.

'Thanks,' she said, taking one. 'Daddy's such a mean bastard, he won't let me buy any.'

I couldn't make her out—all this swearing and yet she was the very reverse of a tart.

'Who's Daddy?' asked Joncer.

'Oh, I'm sorry,' she said, 'you don't know me. I've seen you, though. You're the jockey at Mr Verepont's, aren't you?'

Joncer nodded. ·Well, I live two houses away—when we're not in London, that is. My name's Janet, Janet Miller, and Daddy is Professor Miller—he knows Mr Verepont.'

'I'm John Mellows,' said Joncer. He introduced me as well and we all shook hands and drank. Without asking, Joncer bought some more.

When he returned she said, 'Daddy thinks Mr Verepont is a fool.' She was outspoken all right. Of course we all thought that in the trade too—he could cope with owners, could Verepont, but if he knew a good horse from a donkey, I'm a Jesuit. Joncer said, 'Daddy's right,' and he drank deep. I hadn't had time to ask him about his boss, but he said this with such conviction that I knew now how he felt.

I know a bit of a funny story about Verepont so I told it. 'He used to have a reputation,' I began, 'around the Stables—a few years back.' The girl leans forward, her chin between her tiny hands, slanting her eyes a bit like a cat and says, 'Tell me all. I love a bit of gossip.'

'Well, miss,' I said.

'Call me Janet,' she says quickly, 'not Jane or Miss Jane. Janet.'

'Well, Janet,' I said, a bit shaken, although I didn't know why, 'it's not really gossip. It was all because of a mistake. You see, a lot of us in racing aren't what you'd call educated. We're not daft or stupid, but we don't get much time for the finer points.'

'Thank God for that,' says Janet, 'you should see some of Daddy's students if you want to see those who have.'

I wouldn't know about that, so I said so and she told me to go on with the story.

'It seems,' I said, 'that one of his stable-boys was showing Lord Longdon and some other gent round the stables. Verepont used to train for his Lordship, and the boy hears the gent say about Verepont, "Oh yes, I knew him at school. He is a bigamist." When they've gone the boy comes rushing back and tells his mates (Mrs Verepont not being very popular).'

'Which one?' asked Janet with a laugh.

'Well that's it,' I said. 'Of course the boy hadn't heard right. But he swore that's what the gent said. "A bigamist." And so they all got to thinking. And Cedric Verepont was always taking trips abroad—France and Ireland looking for horses, so they put two and two together——'

'Making five of it,' said Joncer, grinning. 'Making five certainly,' I said, 'they reckoned there was another Mrs Verepont somewhere.' I drank a bit and then I went on.

'The rumour spread round all the stables—as far as Malton because that's where I heard it—and for months it persisted—there's still a few today who if they don't exactly believe it as it stands, reckon there's something strange about Cedric—all from this same story.

'It was Jack Cassell's son Billy—you remember Billy?' I asked Joncer and he nodded, 'he got to the bottom of it. Turns out that old Jack thought his son ought to be educated properly. So he sends him to some posh school or other, and when he was on holiday and round the stables he hears the story—the same stable-boy was here telling it.

'Well, you can guess, can't you?'

'No,' says Janet, 'I can't.'

'I'll have to tell you then. There's a public school—Wickham, I suppose—anyway wherever it is, the old boys from it are called Wykehamists or something like that, and, of course, Cedric is one as well.'

'Oh, how lovely,' says Janet, clapping her hands, and downing her drink, 'Daddy will love that. He went to Winchester.'

'That's the place,' I said, laughing too, 'Winchester. And that's where Jack Cassell sent his son Billy, and of course he knew.'

So we all sat there grinning and drinking, as if we were old pals. That's the funny thing—I'm the oldest—seventy, and Joncer he's over forty, and Janet, though she wasn't then more than twenty-two—we could all talk like we were the same age. You had to like her, she was a good listener, and although you never knew what she was going to say next, nor how she was going to say it, it was good to be with her. And she had such pretty ways, Joncer fell for her then and there, even though he had one or two rough passages.

'So you're living in the village now?' he asked.

'Yes,' she replied, 'I'm looking after Daddy while he writes a book. Mummy's gone off with Geoff, to America.'

'Who's Geoff?'

'Well, it's a bit complicated. Daddy didn't want to go to America on this lecture tour because he had this book to do. But Mummy likes America, so Geoff—he's a historian like Daddy—got Daddy's lecturing job and because he's fond of Mummy, he's got her as well for a year. I'm jolly pleased. She's such a bitch and so very good-looking. I don't get a chance when she's around.'

'What happens after a year?' asked Joncer, mystified.

'Why, she comes back to Daddy and I can go on the razzle.'

'Oh!' said Joncer. I was a bit slow too.

'You mean that she's living with this Geoff and your dad——'

'Yes,' she said gaily, 'Geoff is Mummy's lover now but in a year's time she'll come back to Daddy. Oh—he's very pleased. It gets her out of the way while he does his book—she can't stand living in the wilds—so everybody's happy.' She finished her drink. She was getting really talkative now.

'Geoff is quite nice really—he's a bit younger than Daddy and much better looking. He's not so clever though. Daddy says he's really a Marxist but I think all history is balls anyway.'

I said, 'Is it?' Well, how would I know?

'And Geoff is not so popular with the rest of the Faculty. But he's not mean like Daddy. Nor does he booze so much.'

'So your father likes a drop,' said Joncer. He was feeling a bit lost too.

'I'll say he does,' said Janet. 'Haven't you seen him down here the minute it opens? Tall, thin bloke?'

Recognition seemed to strike Joncer—it was no good asking me—this was the first time I'd been in the pub. Joncer said, 'I know him. Drink sherry?'

She said, 'Tell me a university teacher who doesn't.'

Joncer went on, 'He tries to get off with Mrs Whitman, that's the publican'—he said to me—'a well-spoken, good-looking fellow, not much older than me. Hair's going a bit grey, and he wears fancy waistcoats —that your father?'

She nodded. 'It must be—especially if he's nice to the lady of the house—he's terrible with women.'

I think she was quite proud of her father over this. She took a cigarette and Joncer lit it for her.

'What nice hands you have,' she said to Joncer, 'do all jockeys have hands like yours?' Joncer said he didn't know and they looked at each other. I began to feel I was in the way. It was all very tender. And this was strange for Joncer. When he had been after a girl in the past he was the life and soul of the party, making jokes, lavish in his spending, noisy really—a lot of jockeys are like this—I suppose it's to cover up a feeling of inferiority from being small (although Janet and Joncer were about the same height). I'm sure this was true with old Harry, for instance. And with Joncer it had been the same. He seemed a bit cocky, a bit flashy, though he wasn't like this at all when with me or his mates. If anything you'd have said he was quiet. But he was being very quiet with Janet. They were holding hands now and she was laughing at something he was saying. It struck me that Joncer was still a good-looking fellow—strangely enough in a kind of Irish way—dark hair, blue eyes and an open, quiet sort of smiling face. She was right about his hands too—they were good, small, strong yet delicate (there were few who could ride a horse with a bad mouth better than Joncer—he didn't need a whip, he could drive them with a feather). And he was fit, strong, compact: there wasn't much of him but what there was, was good. I don't know whether he looked his forty-odd years—I'd have said not but I'm no authority—but I know for certain he didn't feel them.

And here he was near enough in love.

And that's where a three-score-years-and-ten bloke says good-bye. It was pretty late anyway.

'I'll come round and see this five-footed horse then,' I said as I got up to go. Joncer looked blank and Janet looked polite.

'This *Pent*——'

'Yes,' said Joncer, suddenly coming up for air as it were, 'we're taking him to Stratford Thursday. Why not come along?'

'To the races?' asks Janet.

'Yes,' says Joncer, I thought a bit hopefully.

'Can I come too?' she asks.

'My goodness, yes!' said Joncer. 'You'll bring us luck.'

'We'll all go,' I said, feeling pleased myself. 'I'll see you all on Thursday then.'

They said good night. 'Give my regards to the missus,' said Joncer just as I was leaving.

'Christ,' I said, 'I forgot. The Peace Offering,' and I
went up to the bar for her bottle of Guinness, while
they laughed. Since we'd moved down here my wife
would watch the clock like an office worker when I
went to the pub. I don't know why. Probably because
she had never known when to expect me when I was
Travelling Head Lad. Now that I was at home all the
time though, she'd know damn' well what I was up to.
And when I should be back. So I always take her something just to show I thought of her. Women lead
strangely lonely lives in some respects.

8

THE trouble with Singer was that he lacked that spark, warmth anyway, which makes a personality. He seemed personality-less—a cold piece of flesh if there ever was one.

We knew he was an orphan and maybe that explained it. Women—mothers, wives, girl-friends, daughters—they all work on a man somehow, they put the warmth in him. Seemingly Singer had never had these influences. I can imagine the lonely holidays from school, spent locked up in his own solitude, without even a sister to warm his poor, frigid and, in my opinion, rather nasty soul. I don't understand him so I only guess.

Yet when his uncle died (there was an uncle and it was from him that he inherited the money—it couldn't have come from anyone else) he had a choice; if not a choice, an opportunity. He could have (and should have, I would say) laid his lusting hands on as many women as he wanted—starting probably as an act of defiance against the gender and possibly ending the debauch no less defiant: but in the process absorbing something of that softness, and tenderness, which walks hand-in-hand with the procreative sensibilities. Even if the debauch had never ended, even if he were now a cruel, insatiable philanderer—this would have been better than a cold, colourless neurotic.

But he didn't. Maybe he couldn't. Perhaps this world of scented, twittering women, so terrible and so lovely, so fecund and so deadly, had such a huge dimension of strangeness, that Singer, hopelessly shy of course, found himself terrified and weaponless on the verge of its joys. If he ever came so near as to be at the verge.

Certainly women disliked him. Janet for one said he gave her the shivers, just sitting in the same car, just an ordinary proximity like that. It might have been simply because Singer showed no interest in her, in any women come to that. I don't mean a carnal interest—a look, a certain preening grace—of course there was none of that in Singer and women don't always want that; no—he just showed no reaction at all. Not even standing up when introduced, not even acknowledging their presence in any different way from the way he'd acknowledge the milkman, the postman, or someone else in a train. He'd show no live response at all. No wonder they disliked him. Even my wife for instance. Even she, at sixty-five, expects that slight concession from the male, that certain effort which makes the presence of a man and a woman a composite thing different from the presence of just a man and man, or woman and woman. Every woman does and I wonder if they go so far as even to demand it. Surely it's something that the mere juxta-position of the sexes creates; the dynamics follow from the ingredients of a man (whatever age) and a woman (whatever her age too) being present together.

But with Singer, no. He was like a lump of rock.

All that inborn energy—sex, lust, love, fear—it's got to go somewhere. With Singer it went on gambling. They tell me it's sex-substitute. I wouldn't know. But if it is it's a very poor one.

I was looking forward to the racing at Stratford. For one thing I hadn't been to a race meeting for a few months (for some years to one exclusively devoted to Steeplechasing—under National Hunt Rules as it's called) and I'd never seen Joncer ride over the sticks. So I took £20 out of the bank, told my wife I wouldn't be late, and drove over to the Stables.

The first person I saw was Verepont. Naturally he's

a fool. A man who can go around with the reputation of being a bigamist—who lets such a daft story like that have the smallest modicum of credence—is a number one clot. Anyway he says to me as I got out of the car (he was standing in the middle of the yard dressed in a grey tweed suit and brown brothel creepers), 'Hallo, old man, long time no see.' He was like a parson who doesn't quite remember the name of one of his old parishioners—behind the greeting a far-away feeling of worry, insecurity, loss. At the same time—let's face it—if I'd been Lord Longdon he'd have known my name.

'Morning, Mr Verepont. Last time I saw you I was with Stanley Yarrow at Malton.' (We turned out two Derby winners, a Grand Prix, and about two hundred others, so even Cedric should remember that.) 'I was his Head Lad.'

'Of course,' Verepont said and I saw he did remember me then. He was a bit disappointed. I think he hoped I was a rich farmer—the sort who made up the bulk of his patrons—and that I might be a prospective owner. Being also in the game of course spoiled it for him. Still, even I could own a horse if I wanted. I could afford it and I pay my bills a lot quicker than farmers. In fact I might get myself a quiet chaser yet—do a bit of hunting early on and race him in the early spring. But old clot Cedric—he wasn't clever enough to see that.

'Thought I might go with Joncer today,' I said. The two of us were face-to-face in the yard now, Verepont with his hands thrust in his jacket pockets, gunman style, and me facing him.

'Yes,' said Cedric, 'we're taking two.'

'Which two?' I asked.

'*The Bishop* and *Pentameter*,' he said. '*The Bishop* has a chance, but *Pentameter*—we'll have to see.'

If *Pentameter* was as good as Joncer said, he could win

every race at Stratford. *The Bishop* was a selling plater
—he'd win enough to pay his feed bill and that's about
all. I said, 'Mr Singer will be coming then?'

'Yes,' said Verepont. 'Yes, he's somewhere about.'
He was looking over my shoulder towards the boxes—
Cedric Verepont would never look any man in the eye
—he wasn't exactly shifty—just uncertain. 'I'll have to
go now. Please excuse me. John Mellows will be back
shortly.' And he went towards his house.

I'd heard horses in the lane while we'd been talking
and as he went Joncer came through the yard gates
leading the string. And a minute afterwards, in a black,
close-fitting dress and a large grey hat, like a damn'
great carving-dish, came Janet. She looked lovely. I
saw why, too; I'd not noticed it in the pub. She had a
figure all right—a French figure like a *belle pouliche*.

'Well, cowboy,' she said to Joncer. Neither of them
had seen me.

He said, 'Well, Princess. You got up in time then,'
and they turned and saw me.

Somehow I felt a bit depressed. I felt a bit un-
wanted. Mind you, that's only age talking and I know
how to ignore it. But you can't avoid the feeling.

'There's himself,' said Joncer dismounting.

'Dressed like a prince,' said Janet. (I was too—when
I go racing now, I don't stint myself, and I was wearing
my thirty-guinea Lovat tweed.)

'Hallo you two!' I said and grinned a bit. Almost
sheepishly, I suppose, although I don't really know why.

I helped Joncer unsaddle. The other lads were leading the horses away and I heard the clattering of
buckets, someone singing, a tap running—I smelt
horses and it was suddenly good to be around again.
Only when you're a racing man do you get that feeling:
it's worth thousands.

'Where's the five-footer?' I asked. 'This other *Golden
Miller*?'

'All right,' said Joncer, resting the loosened saddle for a moment on the horse and looking straight at me—he thought I was ribbing him—'All right,' he said as he heaved the saddle off—'you wait and see.' We moved to the Tack Room. Janet was stroking one of the animals in the loose box.

'It's the chestnut, four down,' said Joncer, nodding the direction. 'I'll be with you in a moment.'

So I went and had a look.

At first I thought I'd gone to the wrong box—it seemed empty. All the others had the horses' heads poking out because this was feed time and they were ready for it. Then I looked closer. *Pentameter* was sound asleep in the shadowed corners. Well, I've heard of lazy horses—but never at feed time. For a moment I thought he was off-colour.

Joncer came and we went in. *Pentameter* graced us by opening an eye. Then with an almost studied carelessness he stood up, yawned and shook himself. Joncer slipped on the bridle and we led him out into the light.

He looked magnificent.

When you look at a horse for the first time you try to fault him. Since there is no perfection—except in the mind's eye—it is by the least number of faults that you assess a horse's worth.

I was silent.

Joncer looked at me with a quiet air of, if not triumph, at least vindication.

'Yes,' I said.

That's all I could say. I walked round the animal, looking very carefully. He looked in wonderful condition too—not fully wound up, of course, since Joncer wanted to win the Gold Cup in March and this was only September.

'Yes,' I said again, and because you have to say something—it's almost expected—I said, 'Feet seem a bit on the small side.' But I didn't really mean it. And Joncer knew I didn't.

'So are yours,' he said.

The first thing that struck you about *Pentameter* was power. A huge chest and lovely legs—straight and strong. He was a big horse and he stood over a lot of ground. And like a lot of lazy horses he had an intelligent head, a kind eye, and a thing I'm fond of—he was lop-eared. (I've never come across a lop-eared horse yet who wasn't a hundred per cent honest.) Of course, size means nothing—and when you've been used to flat racing all 'chasers seem enormous—but I still say that a good big 'un will beat a good small 'un. They know how to keep themselves in trim. They never do more than they're asked to, they're always reliable, and when you're riding them you always feel you've got a bit more tucked away when you want it. Like an overdrive on a car. And as I said a lazy horse is an intelligent horse. Some hot pots we've had (and won races with too) are a handful I must say. Put down a bucket of best oats and one of cyanide—they'll go straight for the poison.

A lazy horse can hardly be bothered to go to either.

Joncer said, 'There's not much the matter with him, is there?' And I said, grinning, 'No. You might win a few point-to-points with him in a year or so.'

Of course, as far as I could see, they could win whatever they wanted.

We put him and *The Bishop* in the horse-box and saw them off. Then we tossed up to see whose car we'd go in and Joncer lost so we set off in his. Coming out of Evesham a red Aston Martin passed us doing about ninety.

'That's Singer,' said Joncer.

Janet shuddered. 'That man!' she said. I didn't know she'd met him till then but we all three agreed.

9

I ALWAYS used to enjoy the couple of hours before the first race, and now that I was only a spectator I enjoyed them even more. Especially as I had Janet with me—Joncer being busy with one thing and another. It was a perfect late summer's day as well.

Stratford-on-Avon Races is a small meeting, devoted entirely to Steeplechases and Hurdle Races. The prizes, compared with Cheltenham, Newbury, Aintree, that is, are small, and in general the class of horses moderate. But it's a pleasant place, not far from the river, about a couple of miles out of town. I've never ridden there myself (nor had Joncer—that's why he was walking the course beforehand) but they tell me it's quite a sharp little track—not an easy one like Worcester or Ludlow. Still, all the big trainers (and hundreds of smaller ones) send horses there, so you get large fields and plenty of sport.

By about noon most of the professionals have arrived. The bars are not full, but certainly active. Trainers and owners and the Press buy each other drinks, a few punters study form, outside the eel man is putting up his stand and the first florid faces of the bookmakers appear.

I met a lot of folk I hadn't seen for years and I got a few playful, old-fashioned looks when I introduced Janet. And after an hour or so I was feeling pretty merry all round as I'd had a fair amount to drink.

Janet was fascinated by it all. And I suppose if you've never seen it before—the horses being led from box to stable to Paddock, the mounting crescendo of activity among bookies, paper sellers, tipsters, trainers, jockeys and lads, the clean look of the track, the feeling, a mixture of urgency and expectancy—all this must

add up to a bit of an eyeful. Even I still find it exciting.
I left her for a few minutes while I looked in the Weighing Room but when I returned she was in the thick
of it.

'And what is a "monkey to a half"?' I heard her ask
someone in a group of the 'fraternity'.

'It's five hundred pounds of theirs to fifty of yours—
that is to say, ten to one, miss,' said a familiar-looking,
sporty type—I couldn't place him then and there.

'I see,' she said, rather primly. 'And a "pony"?'

'That's twenty-five pounds,' said a bookie.

'Well,' she said, finishing her drink, 'I've got ten
pounds I want to put on two horses that Mr Mellows
is going to ride—how do I do that?'

It was time for me to step in—we didn't want these
sharks to know what we were going to back. And then
I recognized the sporty type—it was Jack Cassell.

'Hallo, Jack,' I said. I said it very quietly—this was
about the only way to make a noisy type like Cassell
hear you: perhaps, surrounded as he often was by the
raucous voices, noises, activity of the racing world, the
soft, clear voice, whisper almost, was the most compel-
ling address. Anyway I said, 'You don't look any older.'
He didn't either—it's a strange thing but, like old
soldiers, racing folk don't seem to age. When they die,
they merely disappear. They aren't there any more.
Not missed either, until someone says, 'Where's old
so-and-so?' and someone else remembers that he read,
heard, knew, or hoped, he'd died some while back.

'Nor do you, you old villain,' said Jack and I
winked at Janet. 'This young lady was saying she was
waiting for you,' he went on, 'and I didn't believe her.
Never thought you were still alive. Surprises me
though, that you never told her a few of the things you
know.'

'He's told me a few things all right,' said Janet
brightly, and they all laughed.

And we set to for a while. Then Jack moved away, and we all seemed to disperse, and Janet and I moved out to the Paddock.

'You like Joncer then?' I asked suddenly. I don't know why I asked it then but I did.

'Yes,' she said, 'but it's nothing to do with you.'

It wasn't. I knew that. And she wasn't really angry.

'No,' I said. We were watching the horses parading now and *The Bishop* was amongst them. I pointed him out. I resumed. 'No, it's nothing to do with me. Except this though. I'd like to see you and him hit it off. Don't ask me why, but I think you'd get on fine. I shouldn't say you'd get on. I mean, you obviously do. And I'm nosy only on account of the fact that I've seen this. I'd like it to work—the thing between you whatever it is.'

'You're still nosy. There's nothing between us.'

There was though. I said so. 'There is, you know. You're both—well, I don't know you so well, but as far as I do—and I've known Joncer for most of his life— you're both different when together. Happier, I'd say, certainly jollier, younger if you like. You laugh a lot. And when you laugh you get—everyone does—you get a lot more tender.'

I don't know why I talked like this. Maybe I fancied Janet myself. 'Don't think I'm wise or anything. And I'm not all that old,' I said (I lied there, because I was very old compared to them, compared to nothing—I was seventy). 'But he's a nice bloke and you, well——' I paused because although I believed it and could say it outright, I thought it best to be a bit bashful. It worked.

'What about me?' said Janet, like any woman very, very curious because she knew that only flattery could follow. And perhaps knowing that what I was going to say was true as well.

'Well,' I said, 'when someone—like you—has a happiness in their heart and this someone—you, I mean—

meets someone like Joncer—and he's a happy person—
it's right that they should be together.'

It didn't really mean anything. We were both leaning on the Paddock Rail watching the horses go by.

'For a hard-bitten racing man you're terribly sentimental all of a sudden,' she said. I might be. I said,
'Well, it's a good thing to be, isn't it?'

'Of course,' she said warmly and squeezed my hand.
And suddenly I felt twenty years old again. Then I saw
Joncer entering the Paddock with the other jockeys.
There was only ten minutes until the first race. I had a
lot of explaining to do.

At this meeting the races are named after Shakespeare plays or characters. I don't think Shakespeare
would have minded. Anyway the first was the Falstaff
Handicap Selling Hurdle Race of 200 sovereigns. A
Selling Race (I was telling Janet this) is a race where
the winner is put up for auction after the race. The
winning owner collects the stake money, but whatever
is bid for the winner is divided between the owner of
the second and the Race Course Company. Naturally,
the winner's owner can bid for his own horse, or again
if no one bids for it, the horse remains with him. The
class of horse in any Selling Race is moderate, but often
some tremendous gambles go on.

Look at it this way. Suppose we have a fairly com-
petent animal and we want to make sure of landing our
bets. We put him in a Seller. Maybe we only get 6 to 4
or 2 to 1 for our money in the betting, but we know it's a
certainty. We win. The owner gets the £200 stake
money plus whatever he's won on the betting. The
animal we'll say, for sake of argument, is worth £400—
that's the price for a moderate horse. Then comes the
snag. The owner of the second knows that if he bids in
the subsequent auction for our animal he has only to
pay half. So he can bid £400 for the animal and get
him for £200. He's only got to win one more race with

him afterwards and the stake money alone will cover what he's spent. The owner of the winner may be loath to let the horse go; so he's got to buy him back—and whatever he bids (for his own horse) half will go to the second. A smart man will see that if the second can edge the bidding up he could make himself more than the stake money itself.

There were eight runners, and in the paper they read like this:

010 *Matchbox* carrying 12 st.

> ridden by C. Jenks

004 *Cypriot* carrying 11st. 11 lb.

> ridden by R. Smith

003 *The Brush* carrying 11 st. 6 lb.

> ridden by P. Donnelly
> (allowance 7 lb.)

201 *Manuscript II* carrying 11 st.

> ridden by T. Maxy

000 *The Bishop* carrying 10 st. 9 lb.

> ridden by J. Mellows

002 *Birdland* carrying 10 st. 8 lb.

> ridden by F. Beer
> (allowance 5 lb.)

000 *Hopeless* carrying 10 st. 8 lb.

> ridden by The Owner

002 *French Mustard* carrying 10 st. 2 lb.

> ridden by J. Stephens

The figures before the horses' names showed where they finished in their previous races, and the difference in weights was the assessment of their relative chances by the Handicapper. (In a handicap, if it worked out all the horses should finish in a straight line.) Even if a horse (like here, *Manuscript II*) had won his previous race the Handicapper will take into account the class of horse he'd beaten before and not necessarily give him

top weight. Every punter weighing up the handicap-
ping will have his own ideas—will try to detect a flaw
in the figures—and when he's done it that will be the
horse he'll back.

I always have an immediate preference towards
the top weight because the Handicapper in this case
has said to himself—'this is the best horse—this is one
we've got to stop'—and you can't stop a good horse
completely. At the other extreme he'll say—'this one
has never come anywhere near winning—we'll make
all the others give him weight'. That will be the bottom
weight. And I say to that, if an animal has never looked
like winning before, I can't see why he should suddenly
turn into a flying machine.

Anyway, that's briefly what I told Janet. We moved
over to look at the betting. It was just beginning to get
interesting. Singer was in the thick of it.

'They've gone 7 to 2 *Manuscript* and *The Brush*,' he
said, eagerly, and at the same time craning his neck to
watch the next move. 'There's some 4 to 1 over there,'
he said quickly and made as if to move off.

'Hang on!' I said. 'The market hasn't settled down
yet—this is only the suckers betting. You ought to
know that, Mr Singer.'

It did sober him down a little.

Not that he was drunk—just a bundle of nervous
worries, seemingly shut off from the rest of the world.
And why he should want to back a horse just because
someone else had I'll never know. Another thing too—
he must have talked the race over with Joncer (I had
for certain) and Joncer must have told him that *The
Bishop* had as fair a chance as any and that *Birdland*,
ridden by the young boy who claimed five pounds and
therefore reduced the weight to near enough bottom,
was the only danger, the only other horse that was
going to be backed.

'There's 4 to 1 *Birdland*, Mr Singer,' I said. 'That's

the one to have on your side.' I said it as if the whole thing was a war, battle, fight, because that's how I thought Singer imagined betting. A fencing match with money as the weapons and the horses, something like the scenery, place, battle-ground.

'Yes, Mellows said that one too.'

'Get it then,' I said. 'You won't be the only one so get it quick. Ask for four and a half.'

We heard him talking to his 'Rails' bookie. A book-maker who bets on the 'Rails'—the fence that separates the Members' Enclosure from where we were, in Tatter-salls—is a big operator. And since he will wager in certainly hundreds and sometimes thousands, all bet-ting is done on credit and only with approved clients. He does little shouting and has no blackboard with the prices thereon. The proceedings are conducted quietly and discreetly—even when someone like Jack Cassell walks up with a couple of tons to lose.

'Ah, Mr Singer,' said the bookie.

'*Birdland*,' said Singer brusquely. That was his manner.

'4 to 1,' said the book, 'he's popular.'

Singer turned as if to walk away.

'A 9 to 2 once, Mr Singer, and only to you.'

'It's a loser now,' said his clerk after quickly running his eye and pencil up the column.

'We don't mind losing to Mr Singer,' said the bookie with blatant hypocrisy.

'All right. A nine hundred to two,' said Singer, coming back to us, and scribbling in his notebook. He had to do that as a reminder; he backed so many.

He'd done quite well. The smaller men for the most part were only prepared to trade at 4 to 1 and I could see 7 to 2 on a lot of boards. *The Bishop* hadn't moved from 5 to 1.

'Shall I?' asked Janet, feeling in her hand-bag.

'No,' I said. 'We should get 6 to 1 if we wait.'

'Why,' she said, 'that would be £60 I'd win if Joncer does it.' She seemed amazed.

'That's right,' I said.

'Is it really that easy?' she asked.

'No,' I said, 'but when it is, it's wonderful.'

Birdland suddenly went to 3 to 1—for a minute or so and then 11 to 4, 5 to 2 and in no time at all everyone wanted him. I saw 7 to 4 being taken in places.

'How's that then, Mr Singer?' I said. 'You could trade a bit of your 9 to 2 now if you want.' I meant that he could offer some of the smaller bookies a price over the one they were laying, so as to cover himself. If he turned bookie for one bet—say £600 to £200—and if *Birdland* did win, he'd still make £300 profit. If it lost he would have had a free run for his money.

'No,' said Singer, 'I back 'em. I don't lay 'em.'

He sounded rude, but as I say that was his manner.

I looked again at the betting. The horses had left the Paddock and were cantering slowly down to the Start. The final exchanges in the betting were hectic, so I moved into the fray. Janet followed me.

The betting was 7 to 4 *Birdland*, 9 to 2 *Manuscript* and 6 to 1 *The Bishop*.

'That's us,' I said, 'get your money ready, girl. This is where we step in.'

We both had £60 to £10 each with the same bookie so that finished his 6 to 1. As we left he'd only show him at 4 to 1. Singer had stepped in £2,500 to £400 on the Rails.

'There's a hundred for Mellows if he wins,' said Singer. He was sweating already and looked grey. I must say I'd be jittery with all that at stake. Joncer rarely had a bet—for one thing it wasn't allowed, although plenty of jockeys did, Harry Smart for example—but if he was going to receive £100 anyway for winning, there wasn't much need for him to risk his own money as well. That would be plain stupid: greedy certainly.

They were walking around at the Start.

I think I know what makes a Racing Man—a jockey, gambler, bookmaker even for all the raucous vulgarity of these tribes. It is a quaint kind of faith. I don't mean religion, that mystery, incense, and the clatter of holy relics, nor the smug, tin chapel carry-on, but faith in the ever-slipping, somehow eternal, and certainly continual moment (I say that as an old man for I know only too well how moments do indeed slip by). Because faith means something like a conviction to act. To act and possibly benefit from all the tense demonstration of a man on a horse. Even it means to participate in that event, present, there, in your eyes, and mind, where the future is a result (not a dream, a hope or something that will or might happen some day), but a concrete decision which resolves all the preceding probability (until the next race anyway). There is neither time nor place for what's vague, however superstitious you may be over incidentals. You think of nothing but the event, the result. You will be richer and poorer. You, for a shilling or £1,000, take some part. Then there is a lull. And then a new set of probabilities as the runners for the next race appear, and you have the choice before you and certainly the vision of personal riches. I mean, it's strictly a matter of you, the race and the bookmaker. Not like voting in an election (when you're anonymous) nor like praying in a church (when in terms of the Almighty you are certainly insignificant if not entirely unheard). It's a personal thing. It's an actual thing. You win. Or you lose.

To say this is about as close as I can get to explaining Singer (never understanding though), who saw the whole thing in terms of himself versus the bookmaker.

Anyway the race. As I saw it, that is. And from what I heard from Joncer afterwards. You'd not be able to

read much about it in the papers because it was—as far
as the racing world in general goes—considered a small
affair. As far as those present, and as far, perhaps, as
those all over the country, who had bet their shillings
at street corners or pounds over the telephone, it was
an exciting one. We saw it, of course. For those who
opened their evening papers in somewhere like Glas-
gow, Bootle or Brighton it was exciting, too. For a
briefer moment, and in a more vicarious way, but still
exciting.

Joncer adjusted his goggles. We could see him
plainly although he was a good half-mile away. He was
the only rider wearing goggles—he found that even in
good going the mud flew up in your face if you rode a
waiting race and they were some protection.

The eight horses formed a ragged line. For some
reason or other *Manuscript* decided at the crucial
moment to whip round.

The Starter's Assistant ran behind the horses carrying a long, ringmaster's whip. The Starter climbed the
steps of the Starting Gate and the White Flag was
raised and that meant that the horses had officially
come under his command: all bets that had been made
now stood irrevocably, win or lose.

Back in the Grandstand the loud-speaker announced,
'They're under Starter's Orders.' A hush settled.
Singer, hemmed in by the crowd, stood quivering and
sweating. We stood behind him. A few bookmakers
were still shouting the odds and when one said, 'Seven
to four *Birdland*,' some of the crowd rushed up with fists
filled with fivers. Singer seemed to consider it and then
decided no. He trained his binoculars on the distant
smudges of colour at the Start. They seemed to be in
line now.

The horses moved slowly up to the tapes. We saw
Joncer with his eyes fixed on the Starter's hand. His

ankles were slightly out-turned and his elbows half-raised like a drummer about to give a quiet tattoo. And suddenly it happened.

Back in the Grandstand the loud-speaker said quickly, 'They're off,' and everybody seemed to sigh, not with relief so much as with decision.

There were twelve flights of hurdles in front and two circuits of the course to complete. Even with a lazy horse—one which takes a furlong or so to get into his stride—Joncer believed in trying to be first at the first hurdle. Then you could let the field settle down around yourself. You didn't have to fight for a position.

Only instinct rules the immediate start. The first twenty seconds are impossible to reason or predict. He dug his spurs into *The Bishop* and gave him full rein and waited for what would happen. *The Bishop* seemed to enjoy it. Somehow they got away and he strode out and seemed quite happy to keep the leaders—they were *Manuscript* and *Cypriot*—just in front of him. The run towards the first hurdle narrowed, and Joncer gently urged his horse on. He wanted a clear run at the jump. *The Bishop* responded and *Manuscript, Cypriot* and he met the jump together, Joncer on the outside. *Manuscript* landed first and turned towards the Rails. The jockey on *Cypriot* swore but took up second position and Joncer brought *The Bishop* in behind him as they approached the second. He told me then he thought, 'Where's *Birdland*?' but he didn't dare look round. He didn't want to be pace maker and he saw little future in tracking *Manuscript* who was reputed to lack stamina. One thing comforted him: *The Bishop* could always be relied upon for a bit more speed if you got to work early enough on him. You had to find it, as it were, but he was a lazy horse, too, and so it was there. *Manuscript* was three lengths clear at the second hurdle—the one before the long bend by the railway—and strode away, going easily. He's trying to steal the race, thought

Joncer. And the boy on *Birdland* obviously thought so too, because he suddenly drew alongside *The Bishop*, riding the horse with his hands, urging him gently forward. Joncer let him go and tracked him in fourth place. The race as he saw it was taking shape.

They approached the third. *Manuscript* flew over it, with his ears pricked, keen and fast. *Cypriot* followed him, now some eight lengths second, but not going half so well. The jockey was forcing him, even in this early stage. *Birdland* took the jump half a length clear of *The Bishop* and Joncer settled him down behind the favourite as they turned into the straight for the first time round. There was a long run before the fourth hurdle and *The Bishop* started to stride out. Mellows held him back. He sensed there was a horse close behind him but he didn't look round. *Matchbox*, he thought, grinning a little, Charlie Jenks never did trust me. And he saw the gold sleeves of the jockey out of the corner of his eye a second later as *Matchbox* drew alongside.

'What you got there, Charlie?' he shouted as they matched paces for a few yards.

'You'll see,' said Charlie Jenks, half turning his head towards Joncer (they were opposite the Stands now and we could see they were having a bit of a barney) 'when we get back.' He forced his horse forward, sort of pumping it with his elbows and drew ahead.

When they came to the next hurdle the order was *Manuscript* ten lengths clear of *Birdland* who had moved up into second place, *Cypriot* and *Matchbox* were some three lengths behind the second horse, and a length behind them in fifth place came *The Bishop*. There were a few mild shouts from the Stands as they passed it the first time and one bookmaker shouted, 'Evens *Manuscript*.' Singer looked back at me with a wild, yet secretive, look in his eyes. I shook my head. He won't last out, I thought. Joncer hasn't asked *The Bishop* for anything yet. I felt confident even with ours lying fifth.

They passed the Stands in the same order and set off into the country again. Joncer was some twenty-five lengths now behind the leader. He told me then he thought, *now we wake him up, now we start racing*. The sixth hurdle was a narrow one and just after a bend. It was not the usual place to consider overtaking. But Joncer began to close. *Matchbox* ran a bit wide at the bend and Joncer quickly pushed *The Bishop* through the gap and at the hurdle he rose and landed ahead of him. This manœuvre unnerved *Cypriot* who, trying to match paces, took off too soon and landed on top of the hurdle and blundered through. This cost him whatever chance he may have had; from then on he tailed off and ultimately finished last. *Matchbox* was straightened up and began to track *The Bishop* who was now third and close behind *Birdland*. *Manuscript* was still six lengths out in front and as yet didn't seem to be tiring. But this change in the order caused excitement in the Stands. 'What price *The Bishop*?' shouted a gambler more rhetorically than curious. We saw the shape of things to come. We were happily expectant.

They turned the bottom end where the Start had been. *Manuscript* was being caught, steadily overhauled by the favourite with Joncer tracking him, taking the shortest way round rather than pushing his horse too much. The next hurdle loomed up. *Manuscript* first, two lengths clear of *Birdland* and *The Bishop* close by at the favourite's quarters. *Manuscript* we could see was tiring and both the second and the third knew they could take him when they wanted. But *Birdland* seemed unwilling. And Joncer waited. *Matchbox* drew alongside again, but was being really pushed to maintain even this waiting pace. *Birdland*, just before the seventh, swerved and Mellows seized this opening and moved into the Rails position. They took the hurdle together and drew alongside *Manuscript*. All three galloped in a straight line towards the eighth and Joncer landed first with *Birdland* close up with him. The boy touched *Birdland* with the whip and the two of them galloped round the Far End absolutely together, matching paces, stride for stride as they went. The excitement in the Stands mounted. 'Two to one, *The Bishop*,' became a general cry among the bookies who were still relying on *Birdland* to win and who wanted some covering money. Janet was delirious. There was a little man in front of her and she was pummelling his shoulders with her fists and shouting. He was shouting too and didn't seem to notice.

They were three hurdles from home. They came to the first, rose and landed together. And on the Flat they continued. Joncer said that he thought *Birdland* was going better than *The Bishop*, that, in fact, *Birdland* had that extra touch of class, of speed that was just enough to beat *The Bishop*. The excitement in the Stands now was intense as Joncer and the boy got down to serious riding. At the second from home they rose and landed again together and set off on the Flat neck and neck.

It was experience that won the race. As they approached the last hurdle before the short run in to the Post, Joncer steeled himself. The hurdle came nearer and nearer. The two horses were still inseparable and both were under the whip. But, at the jump, Mellows forced *The Bishop*, even though he was not perfectly balanced, to take off a fraction before *Birdland*. It was a poor jump. But it caught the other horse, it caught *Birdland* unexpectedly, this 'putting in a quick one' as it is called. *Birdland* leapt and knocked the top of the hurdle with his front legs. He somehow blundered through and lost a lot of ground on landing. Mellows sat down and rode for all he was worth and although *Birdland* recovered quickly and was soon in his stride again, at the Post, in a frenzy of shouting, cheering and swearing, *The Bishop* won by a neck.

The Official Return was:

1st   *The Bishop* ridden by J. Mellows at 5 to 1
2nd   *Birdland*   ridden by F. Beer 7 to 4 (Favourite)
3rd   *Matchbox*   ridden by C. Jenks 10 to 1
Distances : a neck and ten lengths. *Hopeless* was fourth.

When they pulled up *Birdland* and *The Bishop* were the furthest from the Paddock. They turned and trotted back together.

'That was dirty riding, Mellows,' said the boy on *Birdland*, angry and disappointed, and feeling disappointment as only a youth can; 'real dirty I call it.'

'If you think so, son,' said Joncer kindly with both his hands on the saddle and arching his back to to take off the strain of so much crouching, 'you object to the Stewards. But in my opinion it'd do you more harm than good. You want to remember never to match strides for too long. You give the game away. The other fellow can anticipate your every move. Stay in front, or wait behind ; don't race alongsides.'

The boy didn't reply. Sulkily he quickened and entered the Paddock gate ahead of Mellows. His stable lad took the bridle and led him in. Someone in the crowd shouted, 'Hard luck, son,' but the boy looked straight ahead. He dismounted in the enclosure reserved for the second horse.

There was a cheer for Joncer as he came in. The tweedy lady who owned *The Bishop* came forward and took the bridle rein, delighted with everything. She patted *The Bishop* and looked up to Joncer, smiling and vastly happy. 'Well ridden, Mellows,' she said, 'a lovely race.'

'Thank you, ma'am,' said Mellows, smiling also, 'I enjoyed every minute of it.'

He dismounted in the Winners' Enclosure, and I winked. A small crowd had gathered round him. *The Bishop* was now to be offered for sale. The tweedy lady asked him, 'Shall I buy him in? What do you think, is he worth keeping?'

Joncer unstrapped his saddle from the sweating horse. 'He'll always win a few races like this one, ma'am, and he might do well in the Handicap over three miles' heavy going. But ask Mr Verepont. See what he's got mapped out. I'll always be very pleased to ride him for you.' He hoisted the saddle over his shoulder and entered the Weighing Room. It was a trainer's job to advise; the jockey merely gave opinions. I followed. He went straight to the Scales and said, 'Mellows. The winner, ten stone nine pounds.'

The scale flickered and then settled on this weight.

'Correct,' said the Clerk. 'Will you check the winner, sir?' He called to the Steward, a dapper, bowler-hatted gentleman chatting in the corner. He came over, looked at the scales on which Mellows was still sitting, and said, 'Ten stone nine. Correct?'

'Yes, sir, and thank you,' replied the Clerk and Mellows got up and left. The verdict was irrevocable. We had won £60 each, Singer a couple of thousand, and seemingly the rest of the world a bit. We were very happy.

Inside the dressing-room Joncer took off his racing silks but decided against changing his breeches. The champion jockey and Joncer were talking so I joined them both.

'So they've let you win again, Joncer,' said the champion.

Joncer grinned, 'They have to call on the old 'uns now and then, Champ,' he replied. 'What have you got today, yourself?'

'Two pigs and a hot-pot. I wouldn't back any of them with bad money.'

'Make sure you don't bounce then.'

'Not me. Not at £7 a time. Doesn't even pay my insurance.' He adjusted his silk cap over his crash helmet.

'I heard you were quitting this season, John. I can't see why. You can still put in the quickest one in the trade.'

'You hear so many things around race-tracks. I once heard of a bookie who paid out a shilling bet in pounds.'

'I know. I once heard of a good thing. At twenty-five to one on. And you know where that finished.'

We all knew. A punter had once laid a thousand pounds of his own money to win forty of the bookie's. The horse had finished third out of four.

'Well, that's the game. Don't eat grass.'

'I'll try not, John. Be seeing you.'

And Mellows and I wandered off outside, met up with Janet and then saw Singer.

'You did it then,' he said quickly. 'I knew you would, I knew it. They all thought *Birdland* but I knew. A twenty-five hundred to four I took. I'm laughing. And it's all going on *Pentameter*. What a day it'll be! We'll get 'em on the run today, by golly. Here's a present like I promised.'

Impulsively he handed Mellows a roll of notes, his eyes shining and feverish.

'Thank you, Mr Singer,' said Joncer. Like Joncer I thought that he was only half sane. He shouldn't be allowed out without a keeper. 'But I shouldn't step in too deep on *Pentameter*, if I were you, Mr Singer,' Joncer added. 'After all it's the first time he's run here.'

'What do you mean?' said Singer, clutching his arm nervously, 'he's a good thing, I thought you said.' He was transformed suddenly into something like a harassed harridan.

'Sure,' said Joncer wearily, 'he's a good thing. But even good things can come unstuck. I shouldn't put more than a hundred on if I were you. We think he'll win but we don't know. No one knows.' We turned away as he said, 'Good luck anyway.'

I left Joncer and Janet together. He'd brought her

along, I suppose, so he could show off. And I had enjoyed escorting her while he'd been busy. But she was
his girl and full of fun now that she won, and I was in
the way. And on top of this I felt like sitting down for a
while and having a quiet drink; to gaze into space,
away from fanatics like Singer, away even from youth,
from Janet and Joncer, although I suppose strictly you
wouldn't call him young. Anyway to be on my own for
a few minutes. I ordered a large whisky (I shouldn't
really drink it as it plays me up the next day but I
couldn't resist it). And I sat down with my thoughts in
the corner. I was happy enough.

I won't tell you much about the other races. *Pentameter* won his race by roughly a quarter of a mile, and
the last race was won by the boy whom Joncer had
beaten. Funny thing Joncer and I were in the Weighing
Room afterwards to say good-bye to the Champ and a
few others we knew. We heard the boy telling his mates
how he'd won.

'You never want to match strides for long,' he was
saying. 'You give the game away, because the other
fellow can anticipate your every move. Stay in front or
wait behind. Don't race alongside. I came from behind
and they never knew what hit them.'

He turned and saw us.

'That's right, isn't it, Mr Mellows?' he said sheepishly.

'Yes,' said Joncer, 'that's right.'

We laughed about it later.

10

I WOULD say that Joncer was an intelligent man, but I wouldn't say he was knowledgeable or particularly a thinker. He'd read the back page of the newspaper and he liked American thrillers. I've seen him curled up on a bench in the Weighing Room deep in one. Then the bell would go for the jockeys to enter the paddock. He'd go out, win a race, weigh in and take up the book again, with its lurid cover and possibly lurid contents, and become deeply engrossed in it until his next ride. If you spoke to him all you got in reply was a grunt.

He likes a song and he can sing well enough. In a bar somewhere, that is. He'd never get the words right but that didn't matter—he'd make them up himself. And they were a bit saucy at times too. As we used to say, when he quit being a jockey he could always be a disc jockey.

He was always a keen if impatient fisherman and a deadly shot (we'd go out Sunday mornings after pigeon—he'd get three times my score—and I reckon to be useful).

But that's all there was to Joncer—apart from the fact that he's the best friend I've had, and he's tough, generous and kind to one. You wouldn't call him an intellectual, I mean. But I suppose you wouldn't call the Professor one either—you'd never think to look at him that he was anything academic even.

I suppose at first Joncer made a point of being respectful, because he was knocking around with Janet. But after a month or so I think they genuinely enjoyed each other's company. The Professor would do most of the talking, of course. And even when I was there, too, he'd have an interested audience. He certainly knew a thing or two. He liked his drink and he was what I'd call an energetic man. Respectful to us as well in a kind of way—he knew how to draw a fellow out. After talking to the Professor you felt you were a lot wiser. Mind you, I think Joncer went a bit too far; the *Manchester Guardian* may be a good newspaper, but it's no use to a racing man because it doesn't have a racing column—not even a list of runners. So I used to smile to myself when I'd see Joncer reading all that close print—before he'd met Janet I expect he thought that Suez was the name of a horse.

One night the three of us were talking.

The Professor was wearing a dark grey suit that night, with a maroon waistcoat with a faint blue stripe and a polka-dot bow tie. With his grey hair, his height, his presence generally, he looked like a distinguished actor. (Janet used to say, 'Like any St Martin's Lane ham.')

'There is in all of us an incipient snobbery,' he said.

'What's "incipient" mean?' asked Joncer. I was pleased he asked because I didn't know either.

'Beginning,' said the Professor. 'But I suppose you could stretch the point here to cover unconscious. Let's say unconscious snobbery anyway.'

I nodded. There are plenty of people I don't like. And some I dislike without knowing why or bothering to know why I do.

'So the people I feel vastly superior to are the comfortable, self-contained millions dedicated to the myth of security, prudence, thrift.' He paused to sip his sherry. Mrs Whitman, the publican who was a full picture of all the Professor's dislikes, although neither she nor the Professor realized this, listened enthralled. 'Surely thrift is the deadliest virtue?' he resumed. 'And extravagance the grandest, most dignified sin.'

We nodded again. Even Mrs Whitman. I don't know whether we agreed but we nodded.

'When I was a child I used to see an advertisement for a building society,' he said. 'It consisted of the symbol of a £ slightly humanized, sitting in a chair. The caption read, "Thrift is the Armchair of Old Age". It terrified me then. I was always broke as a child. But I soon realized thrift was pernicious. For thrift is also the death of youth, of exuberance, of talent, chilling the blood-stream of culture, anti-social—a thrifty person sets himself away from society, entrenched behind the barricades of his pound notes, squinting at the world through the grime of lace curtains and the deceptions of his security.'

'You're mixing up mean people with thrifty people,' said Joncer.

'No, I'm not.' He turned to me. 'You're the oldest. When you were young did you worry about what would happen to you when you were seventy?'

'No,' I said. It was true. I didn't. 'No. We never had enough money in those days even to be thrifty. When you got your 5s. you blewed most of it straightaway, because to spread it out so much a day made it disappear without effect. Better one good night out than several miserable half-pints. Mind you there's this about it. I was good with horses—had an instinct for them if you like—and so I could always get a job. I knew I'd never starve. But I never had more than the change from a pound until I was thirty—till I got married and I became Travelling Head Lad. I needed more then. I got paid more of course, I made more. But the only security was in the job, in me, myself. In me, the wife, us.'

And that was true. 'Naturally,' I went on, 'as we started to turn out winners and I backed them I began to have more than we needed then and there. So we saved it—there were kids then—and later I invested some of it too. But if we wanted anything we didn't stint ourselves—we got it and to hell with the cost.'

'The correct attitude,' said the Professor. He was on his fifth sherry now—I wondered what he'd change to.

'The future will look after anyone if they have enough faith in it and enough assurance, belief in themselves to exist through the present. And I wonder if it's even faith in the future—it may merely be that the quality of whatever one does during the immediate moments, dictates, or anyway takes care of, the vast unknown of a few years hence. It might be the satisfaction of doing whatever one does, the mere joy, delight of being, say, a jockey——'

'What do you mean?' said Joncer, not perplexed so much as realistic. 'I'm a jockey because I can't do anything else. There is no choice for anyone, not after the age of twenty-five anyway, not unless you are a freak. And I didn't have a choice—I was put to it at the age of fourteen—was lucky. Lucky because I was good at it, had the instinct for it if you like. Delight? Joy? I don't know about them. I do know that I've not got a lot of years left, so I clean up while I can.'

It was a long speech for Joncer. Shows you what love can do. He went on: 'But what about those without any skill—what's the word——?'

'Aptitude? Instinct? Affinity? They're all there.'

'Affinity then. What about those without that, bar turning a handle on a lathe, running around for a quid a day for some small bookie, those——' He paused. 'Well, those who aren't lucky—they've got to be thrifty and watch the pennies.'

'That's where you're wrong,' said the Professor, 'the unskilled are not thrifty. They can't afford to be.' He turned to me. 'Like you in your early days, they haven't enough money to save. So they spend, colourfully, exuberantly, gaily, recklessly, they spend and make the brewers rich. But how much wiser they are—happier too—than your careful, respectable, thrifty, middle-class man. How much better informed, livelier, humane and nice your unskilled, boozy worker is than the parasitic suburbanite.

'Dignity is the only thing. And the dignity worth having comes from what a man does, his trade, job, art, profession, calling. Not from his possessions, his television set, his premium bonds, his careful hoarding of a pound or two. Thirft is always undignified.'

Well, that shut both Joncer and me up for a while. It sounded right even if it was a bit beyond us. To bring it down to earth I said, indicating my empty glass, 'Well, you must be hoarding a few pounds, you haven't bought a round since we came in.' He hadn't either.

'My apologies, gentlemen. What will it be?' he said. We ordered. Janet used to say he was mean, of course: but it wasn't quite like that. With us he seemed forgetful more than anything, perhaps because he was so wrapped up in what he was saying. Anyway he didn't seem to worry about being reminded. It was as well that I did. 'Twouldn't do to hold forth against thrift, meanness, respectability, when you're drinking on somebody else.

I knew one thing. Joncer was dying to get the Professor talking about his wife and the mysterious Geoff. So was I to a certain extent, although I wasn't so interested as Joncer because I wasn't aiming to marry into the family.

"Your wife will be back soon, I suppose?' I asked the Professor, mainly from devilment.

'Yes,' he said, not the least put out. 'She is with a colleague of mine at the moment and unless he extends his tour I expect them back by Christmas.'

'That would be Geoff—the colleague—would it?' asked Joncer keenly.

'Yes,' said the Professor, a little surprised. He finished his drink and said, 'Of course. Janet must have told you about the arrangement.'

'Arrangement' was good, I thought to myself. I've heard it called many things but never that.

'She mentioned it,' said Joncer, still retaining his level stare. 'Sounds all right to me.'

'Ah well,' said the Professor, somewhat nostalgically, 'Marjory is a difficult woman. And a fascinating woman. It seems neither fair to me nor to her admirers that I should keep her all to myself. Absence doesn't make the heart grow fonder—it merely gives it a space, a calmness, to breathe in. I shall be pleased to see her again but within a month we will be rowing, I know we will.'

'And Geoff?' I asked.

'Well, I think that she merely tires of him. He's a very restful person and I suppose after a year of cosy, restful protectiveness she gets a yearning for the dynamics and fireworks of the marriage hearth. In her letters she speaks already of how she looks forward to Christmas.'

'We'll see her then?' asked Joncer.

'Oh yes,' said the Professor. 'Christmas will be spent at home in the bosom of the family.'

He glanced at his watch.

'But I must back to my book now. Good night to you both.' And with that he went. His departures were always that sudden.

'I can't make him out,' said Joncer after he'd gone.

'No more can I,' said I, although this wasn't quite true. It's not for me to disapprove and I certainly didn't envy him—no 'arrangements' for me but as I say, I wasn't aiming to become intimately connected with the family.

'Janet and me,' began Joncer, 'we're——'

'Congratulations,' I said. 'It's about time too.'

'It's not definite yet,' said Joncer, a little taken aback. 'I thought we ought to wait for her mother to come back—do it right, you know—and you're the only one I've told, but we seem to get on all right, so I popped the question.'

'What did she say?' I asked.

'She said, "Of course. When? Where? And how?" ' said Joncer a bit blankly.

'Well, there you are, boy,' I said. 'You couldn't have it plainer than that.'

'No,' said Joncer. 'What surprised me was that she seemed to expect me to have asked her. No surprise nor anything. I might have been a grocer asking her to buy some biscuits.'

'What did you expect her to do,' I said, 'blush, look at the stars and go all coy?'

He thought for a bit. Then said, 'Well, do you know, that's probably what I did expect.' He grinned.

'Joncer!' I said, and we had another drink.

11

THEY arranged to get married on the day after Mrs Miller returned. The Professor seemed to think that this was enough of a concession to her; whether or not she approved or disapproved of the son she was gaining was neither here nor there—at least she would be present at the ceremony.

It was mid-October now—the National Hunt Season was well under way, so Joncer was busy. So was Janet. The two of them had bought a cottage about a couple of miles from mine, and she was redecorating and furnishing it.

Why does a young girl of twenty-four (she was this, it turned out—she looked even younger), well educated and I suppose well connected, marry a middle-aged jockey of forty-five, certainly not well educated, and certainly not well connected. It is to beg the question to say because she loves him.

I think it's something like this. There is in some men a quiet confidence. They are restful to be with, placid almost, but after a while you find that their company makes you feel good. Joncer was like that. His company didn't make you want to go and do something big or extraordinary (no one can do that, no one can make you want to do things beyond your powers), but you do come to feel that your own little world is a strangely exciting place. And it wasn't so much due to anything Joncer said, but more it was this calmness, strength, humour—as I say—confidence that Joncer seemed to be never without.

And that's part of being a good jockey. And another thing—although he objected to the Professor talking about the 'joy, delight' of being a jockey—it was the choice of word, or even the mere expression of something he considered should remain unsaid, that made Joncer speak up. Because he did enjoy riding horses. He'd made himself good at it—therefore he enjoyed it. He was a master and his sureness in himself and in his competence got over to you and made you feel good and strong and at peace with the world.

Yes, says the jockey, I'll ride your horse. For £7—that's all they get per ride—£10 if a winner, and he has to pay valet, travelling, saddle, etc. out of that. I'll not only ride it, he says, I'll ride it the way you want me to ride it. I'll square my own feelings and opinions and I'll do just what you tell me to. I'll do that.

So a jockey risks breaking anything from his neck downwards for £7. Naturally he has to enjoy it. And any man who makes a living (even any man who tries to make a living) doing something he enjoys, is worth a girl marrying. Even if he's only barely five feet five inches tall.

All I can say is that Janet, after listening to the talk of her father's professor friends and finding it on the empty side, and after meeting all sorts at her many society engagements, had to wait until she met Joncer to recognize a real man. Because when you got to know him you couldn't help feeling that here was a man with more guts than most, honest as the day, who could be a hero one minute and forget it within the next and who'd never be so presumptuous as to talk about himself until you forced him.

Maybe she saw it that way. Or possibly it was just the usual thing of two pairs of eyes meeting and saying more than words were meant to say. After all you couldn't strike a spark like theirs by clever talk. No one could. And a look carries all sorts of meanings, private and intentional, that no one else can see. It can break down the bars we erect to defend our privacy—not that privacy isn't at times a wonderful thing when you want it. But it might have been the oldest story of boy meets girl.

Well, of course, it was that anyway. But possibly Janet saw in Joncer these other things.

Jockeys who are in love are not known to ride better than those who aren't. There's no form to go on anyway. However, the fact that in the next two months Joncer rode thirty winners—if it has nothing to do with love—may be due to this thing like luck, the cycle of good fortune coming round, or perhaps good fortune being concentrated for no apparent reason in one specific space. But then again love may have been the spur, if not to getting the winners home, at least to bringing about the wave of self-confidence that, if it isn't Luck itself, is how you know it's there.

It might have been with Joncer a sort of unconscious peacock act, the young blade showing off his prowess to his 'intended', one of those bits of daredevilry you might see any teenager do up in the park on a May evening when the swarms of giggling girls go by. That might have been what started him off.

Janet went with him once or twice more but after that she stayed working on their future home. She seemed to lose interest in racing. Or perhaps I should say there were greater interests. She would back Joncer —she'd often ask me to put the ten bobs on with the local bookie—but beyond that her interest faded. More in her line then, was what colour to paint the living-room, how much to pay for carpets and so on. For the first time in her life she had a lot of money to spend. I suppose that the Professor never gave her much because there wasn't much left to give—unquestionably they spent all his income on good living now and had spent a lot on educating Janet previously. And with her languages—she spoke French and Italian—and her attainments generally (piano playing, her wit, her frankness, her liveliness) these were dowry ample enough for Joncer, who after all could still make £2,000 a year. And spend it, too.

So she prepared the nest while Joncer won the bread.

And what bread it was too! The sort of stuff that your two bob each-way-treble punter dreams of. At Cheltenham he rode three winners all from Verepont's Stable, at 10 to 1, 100 to 8, 4 to 1. Well, you multiply those odds together and then by whatever you might have been prepared to stake and you'll see what I mean. And success breeds success. Other owners watching these doubles and trebles come up decided that Joncer was the jockey for them and quite often he'd have six rides in six races. Naturally, the more rides you're given the more winners you'll get.

Pentameter won again—at Birmingham in November. He was odds on, of course, and the papers were already describing him as 'one of our best novice chasers'. Joncer and Verepont didn't over-exert him. One race every six weeks or so, and easy races at that—to give him confidence, get him used to the different jumps, different courses, and the different sorts of going. Even Singer became more interested. So he ought—he was the owner after all. He was calmer, keener on the finer points, so that racing, instead of being a process of hectic wagering merely, became more of a sport, a relaxation—in his case, like a cure for nerves.

Then they entered *Pentameter* at Newbury and he won there too. I'd gone that day and, after racing, Joncer, Verepont, Singer and I were driving home in Joncer's car. Singer had smashed his, trying to straighten a corner on the A40. And whatever muse, power, god or fury it is that looks after gamblers, looked after Singer: he was thrown clear as the car turned over after crashing a wall and he landed in a muck heap. Smelly yes, and shaken a bit, but quite unhurt apart from that, he walked to the nearest hotel, had a bath and a double whisky and went to sleep. And I bet he slept imme-diately too.

We were all, in our various ways, happy.

'Well, Mr Singer,' said Verepont, 'you've certainly got yourself a good horse.'

'Yes,' said Singer, still a bit vague, still a bit else-where. 'Yes, I'm very pleased with him.'

'What would you like us to do?' resumed Verepont. 'We can pick up a few more easy races this season and wait until next year before we go for the big prizes. Or else we can enter him for this year's Gold Cup and take on the "cracks". It's up to you.'

'Is he good enough,' asked Singer, 'good enough now I mean?'

'There's only one way to find out,' said Joncer, turn-ing slightly from the steering wheel. 'And that's to try it and see.'

I put in a word. 'Not often a novice wins the Gold Cup, Mr Singer, but *Pentameter* is an exceptional horse. And again, you think of the odds you'd get against him. They must give you at least twenties. Unless you race him against the best you'll never get a good price.'

'That's true,' said Verepont. He knew as well as I did, how to dress up a proposition for Singer.

His eyes lit up. 'Right,' he said. 'We'll win the Gold Cup with him this March. And no messing.'

We stopped shortly after this for a drink to celebrate the decision, and we all enjoyed it. I even liked Singer for an hour or so. It was a nice evening.

12

Marjory Miller, Janet's mother, returned on 13th December. On 14th December Joncer and Janet were married. I met Mrs Miller the day she arrived. I had been helping Janet with the house. So had my wife. She made all their curtains and would have done a lot more if they had let her. She had always had a soft spot for Joncer, and although at first she was a little suspicious of Janet—'she's a bit of a miss' was what she'd said at first—she soon came around to liking her. Anyway that was our wedding present—I paid for the curtain material that Janet had chosen and my wife knocked it up. Janet and I were hanging them when we heard the garden gate close. Janet looked out.

'There she is,' she cried and rushed to meet her. I looked out and saw a very smart woman of about forty dressed in a close-fitting black and white check costume. They kissed and chatted excitedly for a while. Then I appeared and was introduced.

She was a very attractive woman. Slim, graceful, perhaps tall. A clear, well-preserved skin with only the tiniest wrinkles round the eyes: they were kind, humorous and, I was surprised to see, dark brown. I noticed her legs first—I do with every woman—who doesn't? and they were long, slender and beautifully shaped. Although no filly she was one of those attractive types that you'd see at Ascot and Longchamps—dressed to kill. She was a real charmer and clever with it too. And she knew it, but you'd never hold that against her. You knew she expected to be admired—like I was saying earlier, every woman expects some response and this was what she demanded—and you did that with appreciation. I could see why Janet said she never had a chance when her mother was around. Yes, I could see what men saw in her and I even came around to seeing that her annual change of men, husband to boy friend, the mysterious Geoff, was not so strange after all. When you were with her it seemed perfectly natural and right. You might go so far as to say it was only fair to the men.

'Pleasant trip, Mrs Miller?' I asked.

'Yes, thank you,' she replied, and her voice was soft, low pitched and vibrant. Somehow it filled the room with comfort and some strange promise.

'Geoff, of course, poor dear, was miserable,' she went on. 'But I told him he mustn't be greedy. So he's gone back to Cambridge both disgruntled and purified.' She laughed and lowering her head slightly, entered the cottage through the low front door and its canopied porch.

'I must have a tiny peep at your love nest, Janet,' she called from inside and for the first time I saw how Janet not only felt, but suffered from feeling, over-powered and outshone by her mother. Since she felt drab, she suddenly looked drab; there was no sparkle, only a listlessness. Mind you it was not so obvious as all that. It was more that I knew Janet as a lively, cheerful girl and now I suddenly found that though outwardly she seemed the same, her mother seemed to bring out a hundred blemishes to dampen her natural sparkle. If you'd met them then you'd have thought her the mere dutiful daughter. I knew her, of course, to be far more than this.

'Yes, surely, mother,' she called out and we followed her into the cottage.

'I'll finish off those curtains,' I said, 'while you show your mother around.' And Janet said all right.

Now, why is it that mothers, whoever and wherever they are, because my wife is the same, the whole blessed tribe of them—why must they interfere? The cottage is called Pipers' End because it is on land once belonging to a family called Piper and it is the last cottage on this land if you're going westwards.

'What a quaint name!' said Marjory with what I was to know as her brilliant but bitchy smile. 'Do the Pipers of Pan come here to die?' Now I would not say that the inhabitants of Tite Street, S.W.3, are all drunks; but I kept quiet. I admired her; yet I could see how she'd get on your nerves.

'No,' said Janet with a weak smile and she went on to explain.

It was a good house. It was built of Cotswold stone, but it wasn't heavy looking; it was light and sunny because the windows were large, especially the bow windows downstairs, both sides of the porch. I suppose it was about two hundred and fifty years old. As you went in there was a fair-sized hall, even if by modern standards the ceiling was low. Still, neither Joncer nor Janet were giants. They had painted the walls white and the woodwork grey. Marjory stood in the centre, turning like a model and said, 'Darling, you must get some pictures: this is like a Trappist cell.'

Give 'em a chance, I thought; they've not moved in yet, but we both, Janet dutifully, if a bit wan, and me, smiled and said nothing. Leading from the hall was a large sitting-room running the whole length of the house. That's a thing I like; better one big room than two small. Marjory went in.

'What a size,' she said, 'how on earth will you keep warm?'

Now, there was a bloody great inglenook fireplace in the centre big enough to burn a railway carriage, plus enough power points to run the Blackpool lights—but still I said nothing.

Janet said rather helplessly, 'Oh, I think we'll manage.'

'But how grand you are—the piano, my dear!'

I was with Joncer when he'd bought it for cash at a

sale. Joncer knows very little about music—Beethoven to him is a four-year-old trained at Malton—but he was lucky. Janet said it was a good piano and when you heard her play it you knew damn' well it was too. So we were proud of our efforts.

Janet said defensively, 'Yes. It's John's wedding present to me. It has a lovely tone.'

Marjory, I later learned, was not musical and maybe that explained her lack of appreciation. A piano to her was a piece of furniture that you put flowers on.

'How sweet of him!' she said. They went into the dining-room then and Marjory went through wearing a distant smile. I was listening so hard that I hit my hand with the hammer.

'Oh, dash it,' I said, quaintly.

A bit of a polite barney went on in the kitchen. That's a natural place for it too, but I couldn't hear exactly what went on. But as they came back Janet said, 'But, Mummy, I'm sure it will work and John likes it.' And Marjory said, 'Yes, dear. We'll see.' She sounded a bit threatening and I guessed they were talking about the central heating.

'I've finished,' I said. 'I'm away now.' I reckoned I was best out of it.

'I hope we meet again,' said Marjory and a long, elegant arm came at me like a snake in a glove and I took it, shook it and said, 'Yes.'

'I'll come to the gate,' said Janet and she left Marjory for a moment. I suddenly felt a bit shy—what do you say to a bride on the eve of her wedding?—but she didn't notice it. 'Thanks for the curtains,' she said, 'and don't forget to thank your wife as well.' I nodded and then I had an inspiration. I said, 'I think your mother's jealous of you—being young, your looks and of you getting married.' (It was unreasonable of me to think this as I'd only met Marjory twenty minutes back, but the way she'd said 'love nest'—indeed, why use the expression at all—'home' is what it was going to be and that's what she should have said—made me think this.)

'Don't let her get you down,' I said as I turned to go.

'No,' said Janet. She suddenly smiled. 'No, I'm damned if I will,' she said, and she ran into the house.

I know I'm a gossip and, worse than that, I tend to see myself sharing in the lives of those I gossip about. That's probably old age. But this was one time when it paid off. I cheered Janet up. By playing a hunch I'd managed to pierce a sudden barrier of loneliness. I went away feeling I'd done a good job, and it's not often you feel this at any age, let alone seventy plus.

'QUITE happy, thank you. I am populating a vision of my own private splendour,' the lank-haired, dapper undergraduate said as he spilt champagne over my shoes. He was a friend of Verepont's son, Vivian. As you may have guessed from that, the wedding reception was just about in top gear now.

'I'm pleased to hear that,' I said as I moved on with the tray of drinks. There were about thirty of us there and the cake had just been cut and the photographs taken. A lot of the older folk (myself excepted) were university colleagues of the Professor, but he himself was listening enthralled to Joncer's father—George Mellows, who was dressed in his racing suit—the blue-striped and double-breasted and round his neck the white silk choker.

'I ain't never worn no tie,' said George Mellows, 'and even if my boy is got married—and it's a big event for us as well, Professor——'

'Quite.'

'—I ain't going ter dandify myself today for no bugger. You takes me as I am.' He stood there both appealingly and defiant, with his arms slightly extended (one hand holding his glass of whisky) until—it was as if defiance got the upper hand—he finished the whisky with a gulp. A short, stocky man, about my age, still with a good head of hair, originally black but now grey and close cropped, and dark blue, piercing eyes that glared at the Professor.

'Why, of course,' said the Professor, 'you don't realize how pleased we are to do that very thing.' He moved to the table and secured a bottle of whisky and winked at me and George Mellows. We all three moved over to a quiet corner.

'I'll be frank with yer,' said George. 'Joncer's a good boy, he always was to us, he's thoughtful like and he's tough, takes a lot to get him down. Not like my other boy—the one with the pub in Leeds. Anyway, Joncer.' He poured himself a drink. 'I won't deny he's done very well for himself marrying into a well-connected family like yer own. I'm pleased fer him. I am truly.' He drank some more and wiped his rather ferocious moustache with a scarlet handkerchief that appeared from his sleeve. The Professor listened intently. He had deliberately shut himself off from the other two noisy, chattering groups—one surrounding the happy couple, and another centred on Marjory Miller—the academic, older group this, although I saw many a wistful glance cast across to her from the friends surrounding Joncer and Janet.

'I'm pleased for him,' resumed George, 'and at the same time I'm worried for him. Not because he's older —we're game to the end in my family—it's more that we're different, used to different ways of carrying on, and your girl's been used to one and my boy to another and I worry so as he won't let her down like, lower her, you might say.'

He said it with quiet dignity and I liked him for it. What he said outright and at the right level—one family man to another—was, even I could see, what all the others were saying too. Because to a university man a jockey must be one of the lowest of the lower orders. A social gulf, if you like, that love would find itself powerless to close because love is more like a condition, and not what you'd call a weapon, a social asset. The Professor's wife for one, I felt, hoped even then that the Gulf would become the Void, and the tenderness that joined Janet and Joncer now, would become the strangling cord. I felt that about her anyway. 'How quaint!' some of her friends were saying, with an undertone of smallness which did them no credit. I expect they were afraid. Afraid that it would encourage their own children to bring a bunch of misfits into their precious, silly society doings. Thinking, 'If this should happen to us, if my son marries a Woolworth girl and I have to entertain his common, saucer-drinking, fish-and-chip in-laws?'

But when I say 'thinking' the thought hadn't really gone that far then (it had with Marjory Miller, but she was that much closer, and involved, more than that—she was almost partisan). With the others, as they politely avoided the Mellows family or were extravagantly polite when face-to-face, the thought was not yet a threat; it soon would be. But at the moment it was only a hint in an atmosphere—there all right but not yet vicious. It soon would become this too. I sensed that, anyway.

How quaint, they were saying—except for Marjory Miller. She must have thought all this the height of vulgarity—she must have felt lost amongst it too, because never in her wildest dreams had she expected Janet to marry a jockey. All that I can say about that is: never imagine anything with daughters. Let them go their own sweet, mysterious way. They are generally a lot smarter than their parents. But don't for heaven's sake think, as she was thinking, *how ghastly* and *how can I rescue my little girl from this?*

Yes. She was thinking this, I reckon. More than thinking: a sort of emotional commando strategy was already in action in her conversation and gesture.

Joncer's mother didn't notice it. The reception was being held upstairs in Mrs Whitman's and she and Mrs Mellows (senior) were both in the throes of maternal, tearful, gin-coloured happiness. And the other sons—the publican, the butcher, the car dealer—their own heartiness like a tidal wave carried all before them. It would be later when the hang-over gripped them, when the flood had abated and the mind surveyed the wreckage and the flotsam—it would be then that the subtle weapons of Marjory Miller and the others would begin to score. They would all have dispersed, of course. But they would carry away the scars of a delayed-action attack.

'He won't,' said the Professor. 'He won't let her down because there is nothing to let down. It's a question of joining, of becoming. And it's the same with Janet, she'll have to connect and become, as well.'

'Yer don't see——'

'I do see. But the brittle society of the teacup and sherry glass—that will—has already, perhaps—evaporated. Indeed, in Janet's case it never existed—it bored her. My friends bore her because they lack the robustness, the vigour, the good-heartedness——'

Marjory interrupted then. You've got to hand it to her. She did it like a queen. I don't know why she did it, but she did. Perhaps this was a declaration of war—the first skirmish.

'Now, William,' she said to the Professor, 'you mustn't monopolize Mr Mellows. We won't be seeing much of him in the future what with his work and yours'—this was so much an afterthought that it was insulting—'we must make the most of him now.' She gave George Mellows such a radiant smile that he hiccupped.

'Yerss,' he said, standing up. He was clearly at a loss so the Professor rescued him.

'George,' he said, 'that's an order. Let us join the ladies.' He turned to me. 'And you,' he said. 'It's not safe leaving you alongside a whisky bottle!' It isn't either so I grinned and we moved over to a group who were all holding champagne glasses and pretending that this was the most natural thing in the world. Which is silly because you normally hold a teacup at that hour, so I for one would have expected a bit more joy and excitement. But, of course, I was pretty drunk then.

'This is Mr Mellows,' said Marjory. 'You have been dying to meet him, I know.' And indicating me—'And Mr Sherrif, an old friend of John's.'

I grinned and George Mellows said grandly, 'I'm very pleased ter meet yer all, I'm sure.' He stood there with a mixture of defiance and humility. And I just stood.

'Sir Theodore,' resumed Marjory, indicating a tall, elderly, but very erect man, dressed in a morning suit and soft grey waistcoat, 'is most interested in dockland conditions. He is Chairman of the Commission.'

'Ho yes,' said George Mellows with evident fright.

'A fascinating subject, Mr Mellows,' said Sir Theodore from his great height, and from behind his large, cold, grey eyes. 'I envy you working right in the hub of things.'

'I do night work mostly,' said George Mellows.

'How interesting!' said Lady Theodore. Whoever you think Sir Theodore looks like, imagine that dressed in purple and pearls round the neck and you have his wife. I've never seen a couple looking more alike.

'Yerss,' said George Mellows.

Two lesser men were introduced. One, who was a most unhealthy-looking thirty-five I would have said—round, fat, almost bald, like a monk on the razzle—gave him a beady look and said, 'No doubt the Factories Act, 1948 created quite a stir in your circles, Mr Mellows?' Without waiting for an answer he turned to Sir Theodore and said, 'When I was asked to sit on the Brocklebank Committee, Sir Theodore, we were overwhelmed by misinterpretations of the Act. I must say——'

'Is that the one what gave us the time and a half?' asked Mellows.

The other answered. He was medium height, wore glasses, dressed well but without character, and spoke with a slight Yorkshire accent.

'No. It was more to do with safety measures.'

'It weren't no bloody good, then,' said George. Marjory said, 'Really!' and I said to the Yorkshireman, 'Where you from, lad?' to save us from a dangerous moment.

'I live in Chelsea,' he said.

'No, I mean, where were you born?'

'Oh, Leeds.' He didn't like saying that.

'Leeds?' said George. 'You'd know me boy's pub then. "The Goat and Compasses." Best pub in Leeds—music every night and variety Saturdays. Turns over £2,000 a week, so he should worry.'

'I'm afraid I——'

' 'Corse you'd know it—your old man would then. Back of university.' George Mellows was on safer ground.

'I hardly ever go into pubs,' said the Yorkshireman with embarrassment. 'I'm not against them—they serve a very useful purpose—but I have no cause to use them.' He smiled bleakly.

'Well,' said George, 'the next time you're home you go to my son's place. Say I sent you—he'll give you the best in the house.' A thought struck him. 'That goes for all of you,' he added. 'You needn't spend a farthing, and you'll have the time of your life.'

Lady Theodore said, 'Thank you.' And the others put on their smiles. I laughed like a madman to myself.

'A royal invitation,' said the Professor, but this was lost on the others. They were talking a bit hysterically amongst themselves now.

'I expect George could do with a drink,' I said—always the soul of diplomacy.

'I know I could,' said the Professor and so we led George back to the whisky. Marjory gave us a rather cold look as we went.

Well, Marjory had tried to make a go of it. She was silly even trying, I thought, but still she did. You can't blame her nor George. If anything, you've got to blame her friends, although it's probably going a bit too far saying that. You just can't mix people together like that and expect something to come out of it. Not unless they're in love.

We were sitting quietly in our window seat, the bottle between us.

'You can't blame anyone,' I said, I suppose to the Professor but as much as anything I was thinking aloud.

'No, Harry, you can't,' said the Professor. He was at his best now.

He'd drunk enough to be imaginative and at the same time carefree. George Mellows seemed mystified.

'That's a sensible lad,' he said. 'That one from Leeds. Doesn't waste his money on booze and all that. 'Spect he's worth a bit even now.' He drank some whisky and after a moment of reflection said, 'And that's the first "Sir" I've ever met. I bet he knows a thing or two.'

'He knows how to kiss the right arse,' said the Professor, 'and the bald-headed one is trying hard to be runner-up.'

George Mellows was hurt. ' 'Corse,' he said, 'it's all new to me.' He seemed to shrink even.

'On the contrary, George,' said the Professor. 'You'd know their type after ten minutes of working alongside them. They are the plague that England suffers from. They are the inept whose only talent is to hide their ineptness, to dissemble and appear—a crowd of bloody actors. They wouldn't last ten minutes, I tell you, anywhere bar amongst themselves. In numbers lies their only strength.'

It was then we heard them chanting. We were nearest the window. Looking out I saw the crowd.

'WE WANT JONCER AND JANET,' they were saying. I was aware of it first—perhaps when the Professor was saying, '. . . they are the inept whose only talent . . .' and I knew who they were. Before I stood up to look out of the window I could have guessed five or six of those below. Because in a kind of way I'd been expecting them.

The others hadn't heard, or if they'd heard it hadn't registered any more than it strikes you when you first hear the sea that the tide is coming in, or going out—you'd merely hear the soft roar, a quiet growl in the sea's throat, and that is all. That's how the Professor heard it until I said, 'It's some of the racing boys, come to wish them all the best.'

The chant was clearer now, both as a chant and in what it said, 'WE WANT JONCER AND JANET. WE WANT THE HAPPY COUPLE.'

I recognized from the window some of the faces of those below. A couple of tipsters, a small bookie, a jockey or two, and some of the hangers-on. And they were jovial. The Professor stood up. The rest of the party, aware now of the disturbance, stopped chattering and looked towards him with surmise and amusement, and some with something that looked like sympathy, but wasn't.

'Marjory,' he said, 'some extra guests have arrived. Mrs Whitman, would you be so good as to admit them?' And everybody started talking again, although all were more subdued and some looked at this latest development with an 'I told you so' air of vicarious satisfaction. Marjory Miller put a brave face on it even though, behind, one of her friends was saying, 'and this is the sort of thing poor Janet will have to deal with,' and this friend knew Marjory heard her say it, and no doubt knew that she expressed Marjory's own thoughts too.

In one way it was very funny—luckily neither Joncer nor Janet knew or sensed the undercurrents of disapproval, or if they did they were so self-contained in their happiness that it mattered little. Might have amused them even, I don't know exactly. But you can imagine that among the invited guests (numbering thirty) with an overweight of the academic, since Joncer's family present numbered five, Verepont and his son would fit in anyway, there came now this invasion of the hearty, and slightly criminal representatives of Joncer's own world. My world too. All you could say about them—although the Professor, who had strange ideas on everything—said far more than this—was that they meant well.

First through the door was Gus. Gus was a large man and large in everything he did, especially large (or tall) were his stories. He was a good tipster. By that I don't mean that the horses he tipped were certainties or that if you backed them you'd get rich. If that had been the case Gus himself would have backed them. No, he was a good tipster in that his 'front', the personality he radiated to the gullible was impressive. 'I was having lunch on the train today,' he would begin in a voice of brass and the accent of what he considered the 'county', 'when I met Lord Rosebery. "Hallo, Gus, old man," he said——' and then would follow an involved story, intricate, robust and extreme that gathered the crowd around him like so many mesmerized sheep. 'That's the sort of man I am. No bluff with Gus,' he would finish up, 'only half a crown for a week's wages without work.' On a good day the half-crowns would rain on him—as much as £7 or £8 in a day.

And with Gus came Bert Brooks (he bets under the name of Les Acton now because he'd gone broke under his own many times before—a small bookie need never go broke any more than a big one—but Bert's trouble was, he would lay them and back them). A good sport though, and if I'm ever on the cheap side I bet with him. Both he and Gus wore Homburg hats. What was funny was that neither ever took them off and that Bert was half the size of Gus—a small, sun-tanned man of about fifty, with sharp, brown eyes, lively hands and a mixed accent behind the bookie's whisky, rasping voice.

CHAPTER THIRTEEN

From a distance they looked like an absurd caricature of father and son in a comic strip.

Behind them came members of the fraternity who were a little more respectable. Harry Blackwell, for instance, a jockey not much younger than Joncer, who'd come to pay his respects to bride and groom. Then Wally Parks, who rode a Grand National winner before the war and trains one or two horses now, as well as running 'The Starting Gate', a nice little pub outside Prestbury. And many others. They had three things in common: they were all connected with racing, they all liked Joncer, and they were all uninvited.

Because in our world you can't do things formally. All the news gets around without the help of announcements in the paper anyway, and if Joncer were to invite one he'd have to invite the lot. And more than this. Everyone knows that the groom is little more than a figure-head at his own wedding. He's expected to get happily drunk, make a speech that finishes with a grin and a hiccup, and then quickly escape with his bride to a secret destination that everyone knows. The bride's mother is the queen. The bride is the princess, and the bride's father the Chancellor of the Exchequer. There is your trinity of power. Marjory had only one day in which to assume command but she managed it as only a prospective mother-in-law can. Her command was now not exactly threatened; it was simply not given a thought by the invaders who, in a matter of seconds, had found themselves drinks, and had taken over the proceedings.

'We've all come 'ere,' said Gus suddenly in the loudest version of his professional voice he could muster. He rapped the table with a bottle and succeeded in stunning the others to silence. Marjory and her group tense and quietly furious in one corner, and Joncer's brothers near the happy couple in another listened to the booming voice, the one with a sullen, furious resentment and the other with a good-hearted willingness. Yet I heard George Mellows say to the Professor, 'What bloody cheek; who the hell——' but he was overpowered by the broadside *timbre* of Gus.

'We're all 'ere,' he said, 'to wish our old pal Joncer and his lovely bride all the very best.' A chorus of 'hear, hears' and other remarks arose. Gus commandingly lifted his hand. 'We all know that Joncer's one of the cleanest, straightest, cleverest and most decent blokes on the Turf.'

Again the chorus. A thought struck Gus, 'One of the decentest blokes anywhere,' he glared and thundered. The academic group tittered, 'quite, quite'. 'And now I say, he's one of the luckiest. I'm not selling tips today, I'm *giving* you one. I'm telling you that Joncer and Janey Mellows are a cert for the Happiness Stakes.' A merry uproar of approval greeted this. 'A cast-iron-past-the-post certainty. We'll drink to it!' He lifted his glass and the others followed suit, Marjory with reluctance and irritation. Gus turned to the newly-weds. 'Here's Long Life and Happiness,' he said, 'and if you ever want a week's wages Gus will get them for you.' We drank and Bert Brooks said, 'No adverts, Gus,' and we laughed. Seemingly out of nowhere a large silver tray appeared, the edges rimmed with horses, each one engraved with its name. Just the sort of useless, expensive thing, I thought, that they would decide on. 'We'd like you to have this,' said Gus shyly. It wasn't often he gave anything away. He added to Janet, 'If Joncer gets obstreperous dot him over the head with it.' And again a noisy roar of laughter filled the room.

Janet was touched. 'Thank you all very much,' she said, and Joncer said, 'Yes, fellows, thanks a lot. I've just made one speech.' He had, earlier—it was terrible. 'And you won't want to listen to me when you came to enjoy yourselves. But thanks. And don't forget any time you're passing don't be frightened to look us up.'

'Yes,' said Janet, I think, quite serenely happy, 'any of you, any time.'

And then it all became general. Well, that's not quite correct. It became a matter of splinter groups—the Mellows boys mixing in with the newcomers, creating that public bar friendliness that was, with them, always near the surface. And Marjory, putting on the tragedy queen act, moved amongst her friends. And George Mellows, the Professor and me. We suddenly heard the car start outside and rushing to the window we realized that Joncer and Janet were off. We all shouted after them as they drove happily away.

Their departure did a lot to ease up the tension. Until George Mellows said, 'Yer shouldn't have let that rough lot in, Professor. A bunch of common tipsters—no good to anyone.' At first I thought he was joking but when I saw the look of self-righteous disapproval on his face I realized he still believed in the stern morality of the old-time working class. The Professor saw it too.

'You're a snob, Mr Mellows,' he said quietly, perhaps angrily.

'Whad yer mean—snob?' demanded Mellows. He was certainly angry. He was standing up now, a squat bundle of defiance against the Professor. It struck me that 'snobs' meant a completely different thing to Mellows. He probably confused it with 'rich' or at least 'moneyed' and so felt that he was being included among the ranks of his own natural enemies.

'I can see nothing untoward in these gentlemen,' said the Professor. 'In fact, I find their gesture in coming here both generous and loyal.' He said this frigidly and quietly.

'Yer don't know them like I do,' said Mellows almost patronizingly. 'I tell yer, they're a bunch of scrounging, lazy, noisy layabouts. There's not one of them has done an honest day's work in his natural——'

'What does that matter? What possible virtues

accrue to a man because he clocks in at eight and clocks out at five-thirty for five days of a dreary week. That's merely an economic time-table. I say a man can still be human despite it. You're saying he is, because of it.'

'They wasn't invited. They barged in here to my son's wedding like they owned the bloody place and you——'

'It's as much my daughter's wedding.' He was quietly furious now. 'And I am delighted to see them. You must take my friends as you find them, Mr Mellows. I don't have such high and astringently puritanical standards as you do.'

George Mellows looked squarely at the Professor. People, I thought, are never so absurd as when they try to be dignified. He said, 'So I'm not welcome?'

'On the contrary, everyone's welcome. But I don't think either of us have the right to disapprove, neither do I find the slightest necessity to do so. They seem quite charming to me.'

'Well they don't to me. They lower the tone and I'm not staying alongside of 'em.' He turned away quickly, strode over to his wife and said something to her. She looked surprised, got up on her feet and shortly they were through the door and away.

I looked at the Professor and I grinned. What else could you do?

He said, with a mock, tragic sigh, 'Well, that's one up to Marjory, I suppose.' I laughed then.

'I suppose it is,' I said.

'And having declared my feelings of charity I'd better circulate amongst this class-ridden gathering.'

I laughed again. 'We must be charitable,' I said.

'Yes,' he said, 'we must. But do you know what I find so irritating?' He didn't wait for me to reply. 'It's this. The desire to be fair, tolerant, equable—as you say, charitable, gives one, as its corollary, the appearance of a ditherer, the appearance of some half-baked ineptness, even, in the eyes of some beholders, the tincture and smack of cowardice. I have precipitated the in-law rift—the very thing that Majory must have wanted from the immediate moment after she heard of the marriage—and I shall be blamed for it, even though it was her first objective. I am Nature's fall guy,' he said grandly. 'How awful it is being me.'

I laughed a lot then. And I liked him a lot then too.

'Come on,' I said, 'let's go and meet Gus. A few more drinks in everyone—nobody will give a damn.'

'If alcohol can fuse this gathering into the momentary appearance of a jolly oneness, I will offer a prayer to Bacchus every day of my life.'

'Come on,' I said, 'you talk too much!'

We joined the mob and within an hour or so something near conviviality was going on. At least the barriers were down. At seven-fifteen I saw Gus try to kiss Marjory. And as far as I could see, he succeeded. After that, I thought anything could happen. So quite happily I went home to bed—well, my wife put me to bed—all I remember is getting home.

Now I'd better tell you what the story turns on. It is something that brings the duke and the working man together and breaks down the barriers for a brief moment. And all it is, is a horse. And in this case the horse is called *Pentameter*.

I'll have to tell you a bit about horses and about owners. Great horses; *not* great owners. Not yet, anyway.

On the Flat we've seen since the war some, well, anyway three, of the great. An Italian animal called *Ribot*, an Irish-trained animal called *Ballymoss*, and I'd put *Tulyar* in this class too, to make up the three.

All right. Tell me about *Pinza, Crepello, Airborne, Alcide*. My short list of three stands unshaken at *Ribot, Ballymoss* and *Tulyar* although *Tulyar* has not been brilliant at stud. But I'm not talking about the subsequent covering careers of the animals; I'm talking about how they ran and how they were; how they fulfilled their own, rather absurd, destinies—to run over set distances faster than their competitors. That's what horses have to do. All else is irrelevant to what I'm talking about.

So these three, *Ribot, Ballymoss, Tulyar*, are my three great ones. On the Flat that is.

Over the sticks it's different. No question of subsequent stud value here—performance is the only test, and not only test but occupation too. And in my opinion breeding counts here for very little. It's more how a horse looks, behaves, has matured, that matters. There's this though—the difference between the Flat and the Jumps: a lot of failures from the Flat are found hurdling or chasing at five years and upwards. And some of them make good. Well, at least they win a couple of times. But whatever their breeding, the quality of their previous failures—this is nothing if you're trying to predict the equivalent greatness in a steeplechaser. My three for the Jumps since the war are *Cottage Rake*, *Kerstin* and *Sir Ken* (a hurdler, I admit, but by God, a good one). None of them fashionably bred, and only *Sir Ken* what I would call a good-looking horse. But all three were stamped with a degree of greatness from six years onwards. It is either luck, or a hunch or this plus potted experience which costs money, that makes a man buy such animals. But when he does, how lucky, pleased and inspired he is. Like Joncer was with *Pentameter*.

Because *Pentameter* is one of the great steeplechasers. To think about alongside *Cottage Rake*. And he's only seven years old now.

Over the past fifteen years any racing man can make a short list of what he considers the great. All of these lists should contain one of the three in mine. I should think that a good proportion would include *Pentameter*.

Now the owner of a great horse on the Flat stands to make a packet of money, not only in stakes but from the subsequent stud fees. The owner of a great steeplechaser can only make money from the value of the races and by betting. He doesn't make as much because the prize money is less, but he can get as much as ten years' sport out of the same animal.

Well, why don't we all own great race-horses and live on champagne and run Bentleys?

Here's the answer.

There are some four thousand horses each year in training. About one-fifth of these will win races, some of them more than once. And yet some of these are very lucky when they win because 60 per cent of the winning animals are moderate, who manage to beat the even less moderate. There are owners of 3,000 horses who never see their colours first past the Post. The academic student will say—why keep a moderate horse? It costs as much to feed and train him as it does a good one. Why not, therefore, get rid of the less talented and concentrate on those who will at least help to pay for their keep?

Well, it's like this. A few owners do precisely what your academic student suggests. They probably have a family fortune behind them, so that a slow and expensive policy of 'weeding' can be carried out. And at the Ascot, Doncaster, Newmarket and Leicester Sales you will find plenty of rejects up for sale which have come from the Big Stables. Sometimes they make a mistake. I saw a horse sold as a four-year-old—a big, rangy, bent-looking thing, well bred but ugly—for eighty guineas. As a seven-year-old—after a season's hunting —he won the Grand National, worth that year £8,500. That sort of bargain can happen once in a lifetime. But you'll find hundreds of tweedy county characters bidding at all the Sales, firm in the belief that the bargain will happen to them.

This is the essence of the majority of race-horse owners. They prefer to buy dubious bargains, to hope that the animal will show unnatural improvement. It's more than hoping really—it's more a wild faith that they can see more than the experts can against all the rules of the game. Because the owner is little more than a figurehead with a cheque-book. The roar of the crowd is not for him and rarely does a punter bother to see who owns the horse he's going to back. The jockey and trainer have all the visible glory. The owner finds himself cast into a background of tolerated, although possibly flattered insignificance. The sensible owner knows this, accepts his position, pays his bills, takes the trainer's advice and generally wins money. The stupid owner doesn't, but changes from one trainer to another, from jockey to jockey, sure that it is they who are responsible for the generally poor performance and also for failure as well. This sort of owner believes that his animal is blameless, and that it is the deep plotting of the sharp-featured, shifty-eyed trainer which stops the horse from fulfilling its promise.

So—in an eight-horse race, seven have got to lose. And some of the losers would lose in a two-horse race. A winner is therefore a rare event. And many owners become superstitious. They think in terms of luck (Harry Smart spat on it, only the great can afford to), and how to pursue it, how to trick luck over to their side of the fence. The first superstition is to believe that luck really even exists. The second is that it's catching, that it follows a select few, and therefore if these ride or train your horse, luck will follow. Owners will confuse luck with skill.

Joncer had ridden thirty winners by Christmas, by the time they got married that is, because they quit then for three weeks and went to France for their honeymoon. All were good wins—there were no flukes—but, as I said before, success breeds success, and the super-stitious owners thought, 'Ah, here's a man to drive my so-and-so home!' So Joncer got offered all sorts of horses to ride.

Some jockeys are more wary than others about accepting a chance ride. Even Harry Smart in his heyday would think twice before getting up on a horse he knew very little about. And he wouldn't worry so much about whether the owner had a reputation for meanness—he worried more about the character and potential of the horse itself—was it a pest, a rogue, one with a contrary streak and had it any chance at all of winning? Those were the things Harry would weigh up before he'd put a foot in the stirrup. And Harry only rode on the Flat where the risks to a jockey's life and limb are far less than at the jumping game.

Joncer, however, would ride anything for anyone. I think he was damned silly. Twice he'd had six rides in six races. In other words, he'd ridden on each day a total of some fifteen miles, jumped about fifty jumps or hurdles, and even when you're at the peak of condition, that's some ordeal, I can tell you. The equivalent (in energy required) would be to ride a bicycle up a one in 5 hill for fifteen miles at an average speed of twelve miles per hour. Try doing that five days a week, in winter weather, when you're forty-five and you'll see what I mean. But more important than that was this. When you know a horse—what it can do and what its favourite conditions are—you can ride it with confidence. But when you have to feel your way at every jump, to guess at temperament and ability, you can't be expected to do so well. And you have to take a lot on trust.

Joncer and Janet had been back about a week, and he started riding again at Cheltenham—the January meeting. There was nothing running from Verepont's stable but Joncer had a ride for one of the Yorkshire Stables in the third race. The horse was fancied too, so I think he was just stupid to accept this ride in the First.

A young farmer came up to him while we were chatting in the Weighing Room.

'Ah, Mellows,' he said, 'would you be interested in riding my horse in the First?'

He looked like a schoolboy, although he must have been easily thirty. A round, open face, ruddy complexion and straight, floppy hair. He was well over six foot tall.

'Who trains him, sir?' asked Joncer politely.

'I do myself. There's some gallops on my land and I've put up one or two jumps. And of course I hunt him. But he's too good for Point-to-Points.' He spoke confidently, perhaps a bit fresh, but he didn't fool me. I know these home-trained animals. They are generally gift horses (*always* look a gift horse in the mouth)—castoffs from some small stable or other and they're more trouble than they're worth. And then, on top of this, they are badly trained. Rarely is the animal given enough walking, and never with regularity. The usual thing is that someone takes him round the lanes for half an hour or so, after milking, and when they return he rarely 'does' him properly. Hardly any grooming, which is as important as exercise. Twice a week the farmer (twelve stone) gets up and gallops him full speed for two miles till the poor animal is just about clapped out. Just before racing they make him jump a bale of straw—that's what they call training. So I was surprised when Joncer said, 'Well, I'll have a look at him.' They wandered off towards the Paddock, and presumably Joncer agreed then to ride the thing.

When I saw *Fountain Pen*—that was its name—I knew Joncer had made a mistake. It was a horse with a mean eye—real mean—tiny ears, narrow shoulders, and he was jittery as electric sparks. I wouldn't have got up on him for a thousand. He quietened down a little when Joncer mounted but before that he'd been sweating and bellowing like a gorilla. I suppose Joncer must have been feeling carefree that day, over-confident, a bit bumptious. Jockeys are sometimes like airmen—they both have 'accident prone' periods due to this unconscious relaxation. A slight letting up as it were.

Out of curiosity I had a look at the betting. *Fountain Pen* was 4 to 1—a ridiculously short price and due no doubt to the blind, trusting followers that Joncer had—those who back the jockey not the horse, old women and kids, and even a few big punters.

It was not a premonition. I just knew that *Fountain Pen* was no good, and shouldn't have been allowed on any race-course anywhere.

They got away to a moderate start and Joncer, who'd been told to 'get out in front and stay there', led at the first jump. *Fountain Pen* laid his ears back and crashed through. Somehow, or by something a million times stronger than strong glue, Joncer managed to stay in the saddle. But I knew then he was for it. He did himself, too, I think. He should have pulled the damn' thing up then and there.

But he didn't. Wouldn't have been like Joncer to do that anyway.

They went at the second in a bunch. And then it happened. I couldn't see exactly what went on but I felt it. There was a crack as *Fountain Pen*, hardly rising at the jump, blundered through the closely packed birch and then I saw the damn' fool animal riderless out in front. He ran at the rails, jumped them and scattered the crowd. Whatever else he did there I didn't see. I knew Joncer had fallen under the hooves of the rest of the horses and I also saw that he hadn't got up. The Flag was raised for the ambulance and I left the Stand.

There are times when you feel like committing murder. As I pushed through the crowd I saw a thug of a fellow tearing up his bookie's tickets. He said, 'That nit, Mellows. He couldn't ride a rocking horse.'

Well, I didn't stay, because I'd have lost my temper and at my age that's unwise. But it shows you how fickle the crowd can be.

When I got down to the jump the St John's men had Joncer on a stretcher. I said, 'How is he?'

'Out cold. He must have got kicked as well. We think the collar bone's broken and maybe an arm.' The silly bugger seemed quite cheerful about it.

I nodded and felt a bit useless. Anyway I waited till the ambulance came and he was loaded aboard.

'Can I come?' I asked the driver.

'Not allowed, old timer,' he replied, again cheerfully. I must have looked glum. I certainly felt it.

'Telephone the hospital tonight,' he said. 'There's nothing you can do now.'

The crowd started roaring then. The horses were

approaching this same jump—it was both the second and the last because they had to go round twice in this race. They passed us and one of them won. I don't know which horse and I still don't care.

I wandered out on to the road and wondered whether I ought to telephone Janet. I found an empty telephone box but there was no reply. Perhaps they'd already let her know.

So I walked rather aimlessly down into the town and on to the hospital.

That evening we heard how he was—he was still unconscious—his crash helmet was dented so he must have been concussed pretty bad—very badly bruised too and the collar bone broken. Which, taking all in all, wasn't too bad. Well, we thought so then. But after two days and he still hadn't come to, we started to worry. And Janet especially was frantic when after four days Joncer had shown no response. But the fifth he stirred and on the sixth day after he opened his eyes and smiled. They tell me that on the seventh he tried to get up but they soon put paid to that.

He was in hospital for the rest of January. It had been a mild winter up to then and except for a bit of flooding at Worcester no racing fixtures had been lost through fog or snow. They say that you've only got to empty a bucket of water in the River Severn where it rises in the Welsh hills, and Worcester Race-course floods: that's because it's right next to the river. Anyway, you can discount Worcester—Joncer, lying in bed, was missing plenty of rides.

I said to him, one day in hospital, 'You were daft to get up on that *Fountain Pen*—that thing should have been turned into meat pies long ago.'

'We're daft getting up on any horse. Look,' he moved suddenly in his bed and winced, he'd forgotten his collar bone, 'I make a living by letting it be known I'll

ride horses, and then by actually riding them. If I'm
sitting around the Weighing Room and a bloke comes
up asking me to ride one, I've got to say yes. If I just
took one ride a day I'd never pay the valet, car expenses, things like that. I can't afford to be choosy. I
know before I get up that some are hopeless animals,
but the owner's paying me to ride, so that for a brief
minute or so he can feel that the unexpected might
happen, and happen to him. And sometimes, once in a
blue moon, it does happen.'

'Because you're a jockey, doesn't mean that you've
got to ride everything on four legs that comes along.'

'If I'm asked to and paid to, I've got to.'

'I don't see it.'

' 'Course you don't. You didn't have to make your
money that way.'

'You're not making much lying in bed, are you?' I
said. 'And another thing, what about *Pentameter*?
You've only got to win the big race on him and you've
made yourself a year's money—you know as well as I
do that Singer will see you all right—specially if he gets
33 to 1.'

'If I win. There's horses like *Fountain Pen* in every
race——'

'Not in the Gold Cup, Joncer,' I interrupted.

'—comparatively speaking. I mean, a horse can fall
and bring down a good 'un. And if that happens to
Pentameter, where am I? I tell you, if a bloke says "ride
this"—you've got to ride it.'

His hand was feeling on the bedside table for his
cigarettes. I got them for him and we lit up.

There were other beds in the ward. The fellow in the
next bed had been listening to us. He now plucked up
courage to speak.

'Joncer,' he said. He had a voice like a cement mixer.
'What about *The Bishop* tomorrow? Think he'll win?'

'How the hell do I know, Charlie?' Joncer replied. 'I

haven't seen a horse for three weeks and even if I had I wouldn't know. I only just won on him last time, if that's any use.'

'So I shouldn't back it then?' said the cement mixer. Joncer looked at me helplessly. I said:

'If you fancy it, mate, you back it. You never know—it might win.'

'All I was asking,' he said reproachfully, 'was whether they were going to try with him.'

Amongst the punters you often get this fairy tale—that all the trainers, jockeys and owners get together the night before, over a bottle of whisky, and allocate each other their respective winners. 'You have the two o'clock, George, we'll have the three-thirty'—that sort of thing.

It was Joncer who put him wise. 'When a horse is as moderate as *The Bishop*, Charlie, you've got to try with him all the time.'

Charlie was one of these big, bulbous-faced characters, with small eyes and close-cropped hair. The sort of fellow you're always seeing—with much bellowing and grunting as he just catches a bus, where he'll stand on the platform smelling of a public bar, sweating slightly, and you'll see the three protuberances that are part of his eighteen–twenty stone—the Guinness-coloured nose, the selection of chins and the vast balloon of a belly.

'So you are, then?' he asked, looking at us dumbly.

'Yes,' I said, 'we're trying.' Lowering my voice I said, mainly for devilment, 'Only don't tell the whole world—we want a good price.'

'Ta,' said Charlie. 'Ta. I'll see you all right, don't you worry.' He sat back in his bed supremely happy. Joncer winked at me.

Then he said, 'How is *Pentameter*?'

I told him that he was well and that Verepont's son was to ride him in his next race—the last one before the

Big Race. This presumed that Joncer would not be fit. I asked him, 'How long will you be in?'

'Another week,' he replied, a bit defiantly I would have said. 'You can tell them I'll be riding again the second week in February.'

I nodded. 'Gives you three weeks before the Big Race then.'

Joncer said, 'Yes.' He paused a bit and then said quite softly, 'I'm going to win, you know. It's strange, but I know I'm going to win it.'

I said, 'I expect you will Joncer,' although, to tell the truth, I didn't expect him to be out of hospital in time. But Joncer was so serious when he said it, defiant almost, and as that wasn't usually like him, I didn't say any more. Janet came into the ward then, anyway, and it was time for me to go. Especially as she'd brought her mother as well.

As I left, Charlie growled, 'Thanks, mate.'

I winked back.

Incidentally, you might think it was a bit mean of me to tell Charlie to back *The Bishop* when, as both Joncer and I knew, his chance was moderate. But the Charlies of the Racing World are legion. What they really want is for someone else to make their minds up for them. In this case, Charlie wanted to back *The Bishop* anyway—he fancied it. The fact that some of the connections were present too, that made him even keener. And when I said we were 'trying' he reached a peak of happiness. He was in the know. So whatever happened in the race was incidental. Charlie thought himself smarter than the ordinary punter. We'd given him a direction in life and he took it.

And as it happened we also gave him a winner because *The Bishop* duly obliged the next day at 15 to 2. I hadn't a penny on myself.

SOME say that all husbands are compelled in the end to woo their mothers-in-law harder than they wooed their now-carefree wives.

I know I had to.

Anyway, I'm not unduly inspired when I say that I reckon that Joncer had to woo Marjory, and that it didn't take him long to realize the necessity for the wooing.

I know I soon realized it, when I got married.

But it's only conjecture on my part when I say he won her round in record time. Again, there are no statistics. Who holds the record, anyway, for making mothers-in-law house-trained? Can you tell me?

You can't. But I think that Joncer comes pretty near it. Because of three things. The first is to me the strangest —and probably only a guess too—but it turns on the fact that some women are drawn, not necessarily irresistibly, but certainly with a fascination and, from that, with a mothering instinct, to a maimed man. And Joncer was that—for a month anyway. It obviously went against the grain for Marjory to be distant and therefore aggressive, whilst he lay, cheerful enough, but unquestionably an injured man in his hospital bed.

This happened one day. I drove Janet and Marjory to the hospital. Marjory was incapable of driving a car —she simply couldn't understand gears and what they were for. And Janet wasn't much better—I mean when, after three hours' tuition, someone says, 'And what is the clutch for?'—you feel like saying—'Not for you, my darling'—and leaving it at that. I'd tried to teach her, but we hadn't made much progress even though she had learned that when you turned the steering-wheel the front wheels turned accordingly. Anyway I drove them to see Joncer. Well, when I say that it's not quite true; Janet naturally wanted to see him, but Marjory, I suspect, was more concerned with getting to her hairdresser's in time for her appointment. I managed that, and Janet and I had a drink while she was inside.

'How goes it?' I asked Janet when we were seated.

'Well,' she said, 'not too badly. I've at least got Mummy to come and see John. She has been so absent-minded on purpose whenever I've mentioned him lately. Distant—you know?'

I did know. 'But she's had to be fairly pleasant now that Daddy's gone back and Geoff—well Geoff, I think, has found himself a bit of local talent.' She grinned. Janet's slang was always unpredictable.

'Oh?' I said. 'Who?'

'She's the daughter of the Lord Lieutenant of the County. Up North somewhere. You couldn't get anything more local than that, could you?'

'No, I suppose you can't. And is she "talented"?'

'Very much. A smasher in fact and with a new M.G. in her own right.'

'How do you know all this?'

'Because,' said Janet with delight, 'I used to be at school with her and she wrote me recently telling me all about Geoff. She doesn't know *our family connection* with her intended. It's a scream, isn't it?'

I thought so. I said so. 'What about your mother? How much does she know?'

'Only what I tell her and that's not much. But after the way she's treated Geoff she doesn't deserve any mercy. I think she guesses I know more than I say. It subdues her somewhat.' She drank a little and added, 'It's all very Modern, isn't it?'

This was Janet at her best. Slightly wicked, relaxed, chatty and daring—like the Janet we knew when we first met her.

CHAPTER FIFTEEN

I laughed. 'So your poor mother is on the shelf?'
'And about time too!'

She came in shortly afterwards and we bought her a
drink. It's a strange thing but women never look at their
best when they have come straight from the hairdresser's. Probably they know this. They go to great lengths
saying how awful they look, possibly hoping that someone will say, 'not at all. You look wonderful.' Marjory's
hair had been waved but to me it looked as if a ton of
glue had been plastered over it. I'm sorry, but there it is :
that's how it appeared to me. Of course, I might have
felt sympathy for her on account of her lost Geoff as
well, but her hair-do didn't help any. For a moment she
really looked her age.

I obviously wasn't as clever as Joncer.

We left when the drinks were finished and walked
round to the hospital. I was silent while the women
chattered amongst themselves. We went in and found
Joncer.

Mind you, he was an interesting, lively (even saucy)
invalid. And when Marjory came to see him he may
have known deep down that this was the time to woo
her. He might also have known that since she was on the
shelf, if only for a while, she was vulnerable to whatever
charms he had for her.

He looked up and grinned as we came in. He kissed
Janet, nodded to me and smiled nicely at Marjory. He
winced slightly as he moved in the bed—it was a lovely
wince with just the right amount of the casually tragic
in it. I nearly burst out laughing.

'Ah, Mrs Miller,' he said, 'how nice you look.'

She smiled and an eyebrow curved. 'Thank you,
John. But I'm afraid I must appear a trifle drab.
I've just come from my hairdresser. I feel he's ruined
me.'

'Not at all,' says Don Juan Joncer, the heart-throb of

Tattersalls. 'Not at all. You're a delight for sore eyes, I can assure you.' He smiled winningly.

'Anyway,' said Marjory with a gesture that waved away, but only just, all these compliments, 'anyway, how are you, John?' Her voice was low with sympathy and I felt that now we'd all sit down and discuss our wombs. You know the way women have of talking about illness?

Joncer winced again, ever so slightly and said, bravely, 'Oh, I think I'm getting better, you know.' I loved that 'I think'—there'd be a big cheer go up if this were the Weighing Room.

'Not too tired?' I asked solicitously..

'No,' said Joncer blandly. 'Sometimes my arm keeps me awake but they are very good here really and I get plenty of aspirin.'

'You must not take too much of that, you know,' said Marjory. 'I was forbidden it completely after my operation.'

'Here it comes,' I thought. 'Here come all the gory details.' But Janet put paid to that. 'Yes, Mummy, I know. But you had Geoff to look after you then.' Marjory retreated temporarily.

'But you, darling?' said Joncer to Janet. 'How are you coping with everything at Pipers' End?'

'Oh, very well,' said Janet. 'Mummy has been a darling. She got the builder to fix the drawing-room chimney and she's bought us a lovely carpet. I don't know what I would have done without her.'

Joncer smiled at Marjory. 'I don't know how to thank you enough, Mrs Mil——'

'Oh,' she interrupted, 'John. You *must* call me Marjory.'

'Yes,' said Janet, 'I do believe, John, that you're frightened of Mummy.'

Joncer grinned sheepishly. Or pretended sheepishness, I should say.

'Well,' he said, without a wince this time, 'I did feel a bit scared of you. I mean—well, I'm only a jockey and——'

Marjorie rose to it like a queen bestowing a knighthood. 'Arise, Sir Joncer. I hereby bequeath——' that sort of thing.

'Oh, John,' she said, 'you mustn't feel like that. You're one of the family now.' She gave him her royal smile, and they all bathed in its glory. Even I got a bit of it.

They all talked happily then, about the house, Marjory, the Professor and these family matters. And Joncer sat back as if he'd done a hard day's work—which I suppose he had. He'd have been happier if I hadn't been there, I think, and after ten minutes or so I felt the same. After all it wasn't my family. So I left him the latest copies of *The Racing Calendar*, a small bottle of whisky, and an apple tart my wife had made, and I bid them all farewell.

After a couple more visits Marjory became one of his staunchest allies—and in the next few weeks Joncer was indeed in need of allies.

He told me about Marjory: 'She never seemed to like me, you know. Well, it may have been more that she didn't like the situation Janet had got herself into, and I expect that most mothers-in-law are that way at first.' Joncer opened his eyes a bit wider as if suddenly all the music-hall jokes, cartoons, pub gossip he'd heard regarding wives' mothers, was thrown into a new light. 'Why,' he said, 'maybe some of them are like that all the time.'

I nodded. All that he said was true, I would have said.

'But,' he went on, 'that time you all came here and just after you yourself had left—I saw she was a bit lonely, cut off from it all. So I chatted a bit especially to her—even Janet got a bit jealous—seems daft to be jealous of your mum but she was—and soon Marjory was as pleasant as could be. I cracked a few jokes and made her laugh a bit and she went away as pally as you like.'

I don't think that Marjory's change of attitude was quite so sudden as Joncer implied but it was real and, as time showed, it was loyal. She even came to see Joncer ride the first day he resumed after the accident. This was indeed an event, because previously she'd been disdainful not just of the Guses of the racing world but even those of her own class—the tweedy inhabitants of the Members' Enclosure. Racing that day was at Birmingham and Marjory, born and bred in Chelsea, had the sophisticated Londoner's contempt for what must be England's ugliest city. However, she came with us to Bromford Bridge and saw Joncer lose on three horses. Even I have to admit that it was one of Joncer's 'off' days. But then we all have them whatever we do for a living.

There was no question of Joncer not being fit enough —he was and I know that.

In the first race he misjudged the pace. He was on an animal which was a safe but not brilliant jumper. So in my opinion he should have kept well up with the leaders. Instead he tried to come from behind and it so happens that at Birmingham there are four jumps, closely set together, after the turn for the Finishing Post. Although this horse was fast on the Flat he lost ground at every jump. There was too much ground to make up. Joncer was fourth over the last jump, and rode a strong finish as only an ex-Flat Race jockey can. But he came second, beaten by half a length at the Post.

Well, we all said, 'Hard Luck,' and Joncer shrugged his shoulders knowing that we knew that it wasn't luck at all but misjudgement. And after all, that can happen to the great.

In the next they made him favourite. And I saw that

he had a favourite's chance. Singer thought so too and stepped in heavily, as only Singer would. I bet £10 myself. This time Joncer came third. It just seemed to me that the others went better and so I was philo-sophical—you've got to be at times when you're a racing man. If anything could be said by way of criti-cism it might be this. At the first hurdle after the turn the leader ran a bit wide and I should have thought there was room for Joncer to have pushed his horse up quickly on the inside. Mind you, I wouldn't want to do it myself. The horse might close on you and in no time you're having an argument with the Rails. That's if you're not quick. If you are quick enough you gain the favoured position, and this is often worth the race itself.

Joncer didn't go through. Maybe he didn't see it. Or if he did he may have thought—'not this time', and nine jockeys out of ten would have thought the same. I think myself that even if he had gone through he'd only have come second. The winner was a good one—its subsequent form proved that anyway—and Jon-cer's simply wasn't good enough.

Singer didn't think so. 'He's riding like a clown,' he said furiously as the results went up.

'Who is?' I said, although I knew whom he meant.

'Mellows,' he said. And by the way he looked at me he knew I knew. He got a bit rhetorical. 'Didn't you see at the Turn there? He could have come through. What's the matter with him? Don't I see him all right when he gets 'em home? Maybe somebody's paying him more to lose.'

'Don't be daft,' I said quietly.

'Daft! He's costing me money——'

'He's won you plenty before.'

'And I've given him plenty.'

It was becoming one of those pointless arguments.

'And you'll be giving him plenty more shortly—when he wins on *Pentameter* for you.'

He just looked at me quickly and then walked away. There was something about Singer then that I didn't like at all.

In the last race Joncer was riding a four-year-old that had recently come into the Stable. It had shown some very good form on the Flat, but this race was the first time it had run over hurdles. It was a poser for the backers—sometimes these well-bred recruits turn out to be hopeless at the jumping game. But if they do turn out to be good they generally are very good indeed. So if you fancy one you have to back it first time out because that's when you'll get a good price. If it shows promise then in the subsequent races it will always be near enough favourite.

This one was at 10 to 1. I had a bit on and I expect Singer had a lot. Anyway the horse ran well, but inexperience cost us the race and it finished second. No good blaming Joncer—the horse just wasn't quite ready.

I suppose we were all fed up when he rode into the Enclosure reserved for the second horse. There were no cries of 'Hard Luck' this time and Verepont and he merely nodded to each other. We had all expected to have a winning day—as it turned out we'd had a losing one. Terrible—but it happens all the time. There'd be no racing if it didn't.

Joncer was in a bad temper. Perhaps he'd expected to return to the saddle in a blaze of glory. As it happened he'd had a usual jockey's day—winners are indeed rare whatever way you look at it. Because of this Joncer rarely worried, but this day was an exception for some reason or other. Mainly on account of Marjory, I suppose. Probably he wanted to prove his worth to her—to send her back home with a pocketful of winnings. I don't know what she backed but despite Joncer's failings she seemed to have enjoyed herself. As the four of us—Joncer, Janet, Marjory and I—were driving home she said, 'I never realized before how pretty the horses are. That one that beat you, John, in the last race—she had such a pretty little face. That's why I backed her.'

Joncer grunted. We all thought Marjory wasn't being very tactful.

'And although I was cheering you of course, I was delighted that the one that beat you should be my pretty filly.' The winner was a small, squat, tough-looking gelding—but I didn't like to point this out to her. Joncer grunted again. Marjory chatted away quite happily and Janet and I sat back, she keeping a weather eye open for Joncer's mood. The worst anti-climax in the world is the hour or so after a losing day at the races. Marjory, of course, didn't realize this, but I'm afraid Joncer and I know it only too well. It's then that you are most vulnerable to all sorts of feelings. For instance I felt a bit guilty about not taking my missus out more, although she's only too pleased to get me out of the house in the daytime. And then money—I can afford to lose £20 once in a while, but when I do I regret it. The things I could have bought—a new rain-water butt and a coat of paint for the garage, a set of tyres—that's the sort of thing that runs through my mind. It doesn't make you talkative. I suppose the only consolation is that someone like Singer must feel this even more. I grinned as I thought of the savage depression that must have invaded his grey, unhappy soul. Serve the bugger right, I thought.

But that is only being a wee bit vicious.

And who isn't this way at times?

You aren't? Well done then!

In the next three weeks we lost a lot of money. We'd won a lot when Joncer was on form and now that he wasn't, we started to give it back. There's an old punter's saying which not many of them follow—'Never chase lost money'. It means this: if you've gone racing to back two horses, say, and they lose, you should stop. Don't start looking for winners—if the horses you yourself fancy don't oblige, why should those with only chance recommendations? Better to be methodical— wait until the losers run again and then retrieve your losses. And if they get beaten then you've still got to be philosophical. There is always tomorrow.

Well, of course, I tried to be clever—I tried to pick them out—and I lost a lot more.

I can't explain it except by saying it was Joncer's turn to have bad luck and naturally we caught it too. He just couldn't do anything right.

He had about forty rides since he resumed after his accident, and he was only placed six times. It wasn't long before the rumours were circulating—'Joncer's paid to lose' and others. The most persistent rumour was—'Joncer's lost his nerve'.

I almost believed this one myself.

Once or twice I thought he was taking things very carefully. At Warwick he could have got through on the inside but he didn't risk it. He waited and came with a clear late run. He still got beaten. Admittedly, if he had seized the chance and then the others closed on him it could have been nasty. But that's why you have jockeys —to weigh up these chances and to decide in a split second. The jockey who takes the chance and succeeds gets the glory and deserves the glory—that's what the owner pays him for, and it's what the public pay to come and see. Few jockeys get praised for caution, any more than your motor-racing fan praises demonstrations of the Highway Code at Silverstone.

Deep down I knew, of course, that it was a patch of bad, that Joncer was stuck in. Even so, one night at his place I said, 'Even if there's no such thing as luck, good or bad, I must say, Joncer, you're going through something very much like it.'

'I thought you'd have known,' said Joncer. We were sitting in his kitchen drinking beer. He poured me out another glass and he went on, 'I took a chance just getting up on that *Fountain Pen* and I nearly break my bloody neck. You were right—I shouldn't have even considered it—a home-trained, ugly, clapped-out hunter—but the fact was I did.' He drank some beer and then looked straight at me. 'There's only one horse I want to ride. When I was lying in bed I decided that.'

'*Pentameter*,' I said, almost thinking aloud.

'Yes. I was thinking about what the Professor said that night——'

' "The Joy, Delight",' I quoted with mock pomposity. We'd often laugh about that, Joncer and me.

'—in a way, yes, although the Professor talks as if he was in some opera or other. But there's only *Pentameter* I want to ride. I know the horse, he knows me and we can win the Gold Cup next Thursday. That's a horse I enjoy riding. I can do anything with *Pentameter*.'

I nodded. Joncer continued, 'I don't know what price you got but there was some 33 to 1 last week.'

I nodded again. I'd had some of the thirty-threes myself. So had Joncer.

'I'm going to clean up and then I quit riding. I don't know if I told you, but part of the deal I made with Singer when I bought the horse was I was to ride him every time he raced. I've never lost on *Pentameter*—and I never will. Because I'll win on Thursday and that will be it.'

'You'll quit then?' I asked, surprised.

'I'll quit because I'm fed up with it—with Singer, Verepont, the gossip, and the whole daft business of luck, though we won't and don't call it that; though we pretend it doesn't exist, something like luck certainly affects us. And I'm fed-up pretending, being affected.'

'You'll quit just because——'

'—I'll quit because I'll have to. You don't know,

Harry'—that's my name, Harry Sherrif—they all know me—'you don't know what it's like.'

I do, but I let it pass.

'There's Singer. Like a grey, fussy hen torturing himself because he thinks I've lost my nerve and there's thirty thousand pounds at stake.'

He paused and drank deeply. He was becoming confessional and I suddenly realized that though Joncer seemed imperturbable—almost carefree—he really was like anyone else: at times the whole weight of circumstance, doom, destiny, gossip, luck, engenders a loneliness, a necessity to communicate. It was silly of me to think that Joncer was an exception, Naturally the vicious worrying of Singer—himself possibly an exception, one who did not seem to need the ordinary, everyday communication of ordinary, everyday folk—and not only Singer, but the almost unheard and ever-present chatter of the critics, themselves unable to ride a donkey on the sands at Margate—saying, to begin with out of earshot so that Joncer would only feel it, sense it, and then later saying it so that it sounded like a distant echo—saying, 'Mellows—lost his nerve. Did you see him at——' and then the conversation fading into a hypocritical look as Joncer approached them, and they'd grin a bit, slap him on the back, wish him good luck (and possibly mean it). So that the act of riding a race-horse now took on the dimension of something far more. Now it meant demonstrating virility against a dark weight of contrary, not evidence, but opinion. So that the horse was no longer an animal with a possibility of winning a race—it was more a vehicle to be used to re-establish the doubted prowess of its jockey. The horse becoming something to compel destiny to change her forbidding ways.

Putting a foot in the stirrup, rising, and quickly, gracefully, competently swinging the other over, sitting there a while, then bending to test the girths, then straightening the cap, nodding to the owner, trainer and friends, outwardly compelled to show the unperturbed look of assurance, Joncer would have appeared the same during the bad times as he did during the good. Yet, as I say, I now saw that behind the façade of competence—if you can go so far as to say 'façade' because the competence was there anyway—behind the unchanged dignity—the subordinate dignity of the jockey—was this feeling of insecurity, of desperation, lonely and secretive.

The fact that he wanted (needed?) to talk about it was evidence of the desperation. And a jockey who feels this—any man who feels this, this lack of confidence, or even, not feeling the lack so much as feeling that the lack was felt elsewhere, and consequently his performance on the horse was set against a grander back-cloth than merely riding and hoping to win—this man is pledged with a burden that only a grander, more extreme, chance of proof can redeem. Because, what if Joncer had ridden two odds-on favourites home? This would dispel nothing. In fact this would add to the legend, because the Grandstand jockeys and founders of the rumour of his ineptitude would say, 'See—only on a dead cert can he win now.' No. The record, the facts were interpreted and spoken as a complete questioning of talent itself; they say that the earlier brilliance had fled, no longer was there inspiration, that even the form, style of these performances—and no one doubted that Joncer could come second with style—were proof now of an empty, formal talent. No man can see that a jockey can ride brilliantly and come fourth, because that brilliance is unproductive, often unseen and, as such, utterly worthless. I'm a racing man, and I have to say it—I don't see brilliance now unless it benefits me, myself, somehow. It is a jockey's job to be better than the rest. And that's all.

But I saw Joncer's point. Well, more than that really.

I saw the fix he was in. Only a grand redemption—such as winning the Gold Cup in a week's time—would confound the critics (they were legion—even I listened). And I saw beyond this. There was age behind it all. Joncer was planning the last grand gesture—the Getting Out Stakes.

And what is age? Well, youth always has a resilience. Age has to call upon defiance. I was reminded of Harry Smart. And I think Joncer was too.

Even the act of defiance was not going to be easy. Even the mere chance to defy, to confound and therefore scotch the critics—this itself, let alone the ultimate result of the defiance—was not easy to bring about.

'Because this twat, Singer,' began Joncer—he looked blank, perplexed for a moment, as if the void that Singer spanned was suddenly so vast, rootless and ghostly that even the mention of his name was enough to bring communication to an abrupt chasm of silence. But he went on, 'There's this agreement, see? He's got to let me ride, because I fixed it when I bought and sold the horse. He said, "Yes," "Of course," "Why not?" and all that because then he never knew what it would be like to even own a winner. Not even having the ordinary cheap pride of possession—the sort of pride a bloke has when he turns up at his local with a new, cheap car—not even that. And then I won for him—three times. He liked it. He must have liked it—not just winning the money, nor being congratulated, nor everyone drinking his health—he must have liked the idea of owning and, in owning, having the power, the last word. He must have suddenly found that he could be a monster and no one could do a thing.'

'What do you mean, monster?'

'Monster—monster in being Singer, of being Singer —just that. Before—you remember him, hanging around the bars, like a lost child waiting for his dad— before, being a nobody, ignored for the most part, and when everyone was happy, tolerated. And that's as far as it went. Tolerated.'

'And now?'

'Well, now, even the Press listen to him. He under-lines his name every time it's mentioned in the paper—it's true, I tell you—I've seen him do it—and they write him up as if he were the Aga Khan. He tells Verepont what to do——'

'—Everybody tells Cedric what to do—'

'Not the way Singer does. He's trying to wriggle out of his agreement.'

So that's it, I thought, that's what's made Joncer so niggly. I indicated my empty glass and Joncer filled it.

'So he doesn't want you to ride *Pentameter*?'

'He doesn't know. He thinks he doesn't.'

'Who else will he get then?'

'Verepont's boy. That's why it's getting me down. Cedric thinks that pansy son of his can ride. Well, may-be he can—I'd like to see who couldn't ride the arm-chair rides he's had—but I'm buggered if I'm going to let that chatty, bloody kid do me out of a winner.'

This wasn't jealousy—it was a feeling of outrage. It was Joncer, in his forty-fifth year, needing the last opportunity of triumph: it wasn't entrenched, middle-aged opinion fearing youth, fearing youth displacing age. Because, as we both knew, Joncer had only the circumstances of the race itself to worry about, and he was as well equipped to cope with these as any. But he was vulnerable to the opinions of the Grand Stand jockeys, the newly swollen heads of people like Singer and the wavering, weak, spineless *bonhomie* of Cedric Verepont and his rosy-cheeked Oxford son.

'It won't come to that. Singer can't back out of it. But if you're aiming to finish in a blaze of glory, well you know as well as I do how short-lived that glory is—how it lasts only until the next race and then everyone forgets. Even Singer will forget although you'll have won him £30,000 in bets and five thousand stake money——'

'Not everyone forgets. You won't. You know we remember Rae Johnstone winning on *Galcador*—that was twelve years ago—we remember Martin Molony that day at Liverpool—a few of us remember the times when they were brilliant.'

'Yes. A few of us remember and will remember but——'

'—but nothing.' Joncer was certainly tensed up, abrupt, jittery almost. 'A few remember—those who really know. And there's one amongst the few who remembers better than the rest, who looks back at the event with a happy pride, and that sort of sustains him as the years——'

'—I know who you mean, Joncer—I've got you now.'

'Of course you have—that one person is the bloody jockey himself.'

And I said, 'Yes.'

We drank silently for a moment and suddenly we realized there was a hell of a storm blowing outside—March coming in like a lion—and the rain battered against the windows. I sat there thinking as Joncer brought out some more bottles. I was thinking again how even Joncer needed to create a heroic picture of himself, and for himself alone. I'd caught a glimpse of it and it was like a small day-dream of grandeur. It might have been more than a day-dream—might have been the reason for the very act of mounting a racehorse. Admittedly every jockey gets up for £7 and the chance of presents if he rides a winner. That's the basic economics. But that's not enough for any man—no man can live on seven pounds alone—he has to have as well, hidden and often completely unsuspected, his conception of himself as hero.

After a while I said, 'Yes. Yes. Of course,' and I saw that the forty losers had become for Joncer an ever-increasing drain not only on his self-confidence but on the myth that sustained it. Before I'd never thought of Joncer as being that deep; now I realized that all men (except morons and the consciously vain) were the same. Even myself.

He drove me home—he was going to pick up Janet from her mother's—and when we got to my place I said, 'Yes, I see it now.' I must have sounded profound.

'You daft old bugger,' said Joncer with a laugh.

16

THAT week-end the town began to fill up. Even our village pub had two Irishmen staying for the Race Week. Unless you were a racing person you wouldn't have noticed anything different with the town to begin with. In the hotels, however, you would. The heavy-jowled faces behind a brandy-and-soda or behind a hand of cards, the Irish accents, and the sharp-featured trainers, the tweeded, clear-skinned but poiseless English racing ladies with their robust leather shoes and their robust leather voices. The car-parks showed wealth—Jaguars, Bentleys, Bristols, and here and there a Rolls, some dignified black and hearse-like and others gaudy coloured and flamboyant. You soon saw where the bookmakers stayed.

But the town on the Saturday and Sunday seemed about the same. A few strange faces in the pubs and more and more of the conversation centring on the racing—and upon the weather because that affected the racing—snow or frost could finish the whole thing. It would be on the Tuesday morning that the crowds would come—coachloads from London, Manchester, Birmingham, Bristol, and streams of traffic converging on the Evesham Road. Then even the most stolid, unaware spectator would know that the races were on.

On the Sunday I went to meet Joncer at the Stables. It was a regular habit of mine—I'd either meet him there or at Mrs Whitman's for a lunch-time drink. I was talking to Verepont when Joncer rode in.

'How did he go?' asked Verepont.

'He went,' replied Joncer, if non-committally it was because he was dismounting, 'he went well enough.' He was on the ground now bouncing almost with that masculine delicacy, which is only masculine, a prerogative of masculinity at that as well. 'But he'll go better for your boy than he will for me.'

He stood there, the reins in one hand, the other straightening his belt, his very blue eyes rising to meet those of the trainer.

'And he might be a dog,' he added quietly. 'He goes well enough but I can't find all of him. He won't have it.'

Verepont, the suave, the dapper (quaintly avoiding) dirtying his lavender suède shoes as he stood back to look at the horse with a squinting, professional eye) said, 'You surprise me, John, I thought he was honest enough.'

Joncer, handing the reins to one of the grooms, watched the horse being led away. He said, 'That's how it is, Mr Verepont.' He swayed slightly on his feet, easing himself after three hours on horseback, and exemplifying as he said it a certain independence, a certain superiority, even a certain disdain. He added, 'Maybe your son can do better, sir,'—the 'sir' was an afterthought and it carried, although Verepoint didn't, or couldn't, see it, the very reverse of respect.

Verepont said, drawing in his breath in a sort of long-suffering sigh, 'Maybe you're right, John, maybe you're right.'

They moved slowly over to the horse-box to watch the animal being groomed. They waited a few minutes in silence and then Verepont, his hands thrust into his jacket pockets, his shoulders slightly hunched, moved away again.

'About tomorrow'—he stopped in the middle of the yard and stared for a while at a puddle as if it had mesmerized him.

'Yes,' said Joncer, breaking the self-induced trance of the trainer, 'what have you in mind?' He idly swung his foot at a stone. Verepont turned slowly to Mellows (his hands still thrust in his pockets, his shoulders still hunched, gunman style) and then, gazing beyond him, said, 'We'll take *Saltcellar* as well. I think I'll put my boy up on *Lucid*.'

This last sentence he said quickly. And Joncer reacted quickly. 'As you will, Mr Verepont.' He turned abruptly and strode away, 'I'll take my own car and see you on the Course,' and he was through the yard gates as he said this, over his shoulder to Verepont, who was still hunched in the middle of the yard, with all the signs, smells and sounds of the Stable's activity going on around him. He seemed to leave him in a position of insignificant loneliness. Joncer, I could see, was very angry.

We had a drink and he calmed off. The racing the next day was at Worcester and coming as it did before the big meeting it wasn't much more than a curtain raiser. Still a winner is nice wherever you are and it was obvious that *Lucid* would be a winner (it was the four-year-old recruit from Flat Racing that Joncer had come second on at Birmingham; that race had brought him on and he'd been well schooled over the hurdles— there was no doubt about it, *Lucid* was now all set to win). I could see Joncer's point: having done all the hard work he was now going to be denied the reward. That was going to Vivian Verepont, recently from Oxford, a gentleman rider all style and no strength, and as a person as weak and probably as treacherous as his father. So we thought. It was only a small race but Joncer regarded it as the thin edge of the wedge.

'I can't win on *Saltcellar*,' he said, 'I'll get him placed and that's about all. But *Lucid*—well, an armless cripple, blind, dumb and deaf could win on him.'

We drank our pints. 'You see what he's trying to do, Harry?'

'Who's "he"?' I asked.

'Cedric the c——,' he replied.

'No, I don't see,' I said. 'It seems to me he's putting his boy up on an easy ride to give him confidence and maybe earn himself a few quid. I quite see that if he didn't do that the few quid would come your way but——'

'Bugger the few quid. It's more than that. You've seen Vivian ride—he's like a stylish tennis player—makes lovely strokes but misses the ball—he's good to watch, if you don't know much you'd think him bloody marvellous.'

'That's right. Of course, he's only a kid——'

'He'd be made if he won the Gold Cup. Fact is, it would be better for Cedric if his son came second on *Pentameter* than if I rode him and won. The public expect me to win but they don't expect Vivian to do anything. Anyway, tomorrow I'll come third in the Selling Plate and they'll all say, "Poor Old Joncer", and then the boy will ride a stylish finish on *Lucid* and they'll all say, "Ho, what have we here?" '

He paused and lit a cigarette. 'That's when Cedric will say to Singer, "I think, Mr Singer, that my boy ought to ride *Pentameter*." '

'Singer will say no,' I replied, 'because of the agreement.'

'Will he, hell! He's so jittery and changeable he'll forget a thing like that. He'll do just what Verepont suggests.'

'We'll just have to tell Singer a thing or two, that's all. There's no point getting het up about it yet. It might never happen.'

'I'll bet you Lombard Street to a china orange it does,' said Joncer mournfully.

As I left I saw that the Professor had arrived. I grinned hallo and good-bye all at once because I had to go. My Sunday lunch is always on the table at the stroke of one and if I'm late I get shot. So I left them talking together.

Though I have spent nearly all my life training horses, for Flat admittedly, where one rarely comes across them, I have nothing against amateur riders. All racing men remember Lord Mildmay—a stylist, clever, if damned unlucky, jockey. And if a man spends good money on a horse and his trainer, I see no reason why he shouldn't have a little fun riding the animal as well. But with three hundred professionals trying to make a living from the Game I am a bit against the top amateurs bagging the best rides. A lot of owners get an amateur to ride for them just to save paying their fees. Luckily the Stewards step in if they see an amateur getting too many rides and they restrict him to a maximum (generally forty) during the season. Still, there is often resentment among the younger jockeys.

Some of the top amateurs ultimately turn professional and I think that Cedric Verepont had this in mind for his son. Get him in the public eye by winning some big race, ride a season as an amateur, 'collecting' as many owners as possible, and then apply for a licence —that's what he was after. None of the five years' drudgery that Joncer had to go through—none of this for our Vivian. Of course, it raises a point—should any father help his son in this way? Neither Joncer nor I received any from ours, so it may well be we are unduly biased. But whether we are or not it seemed damned unfair that Vivian Verepont's first rung on the ladder to fame should be at the expense of Joncer. I didn't know for certain that even this would happen—I thought that maybe Joncer was being hypersensitive— any man who rides forty consecutive losers is bound to be. So I thought it best to wait and see.

We didn't have to wait long.

Joncer went with the horse-box the following day, so I took my car. I was just leaving the village when I saw the Professor shivering—there was a sharp northern wind blowing—outside his house. He waved me down.

He'd 'come down', he told me, for the Easter vacation.

'Marjory insists that I see this superstition,' he said, when I stopped.

'What superstition?' I said.

'Horse-racing,' he said solemnly.

I laughed. 'I suppose that's what it is. Anyway, you want to come with me?'

He said yes and off we went. It turned out that the Professor had never been before, so I had a bit of explaining to do. He listened and took it all in but I had a feeling that he was after more than a new experience and information about it.

I was right.

'Singer,' he said suddenly, 'what kind of a man is he?'

I thought for a moment. 'Hard to say. Basically he's nasty—I've said he's neurotic but what does that mean?'

'Precisely. I also occasionally catch the common cold.'

'But there's something strange, cold, frigid about him. I'm no psychologist but it wouldn't surprise me if he was a gelding! Anyway, all he's interested in is gambling.'

'He wins?'

'Like all of us, he wins and he loses. Only you want to multiply by a hundred in his case, both his ups and his downs. Joncer says that he's changed a lot lately—becoming the Lord High Bloody Mighty—since *Pentameter* started winning—and Joncer should know. There's no doubt Singer has made a packet out of him, but he's not the sort of man to remember that. I doubt if he remembers anything bar a horse's previous form.'

'You'd say that since he bought *Pentameter* he's won more than he's lost?'

'He'd be a right twat if he hasn't,' I said and meant it. The Professor grunted.

'You've heard what——'

'Yes,' I interrupted. 'Yes, I've heard what Joncer thinks.' I paused and wondered whether to talk about it. What would the Professor know, how could he understand? I thought.

'There's a lot you wouldn't know about Joncer,' I began.

'He's my son-in-law,' he replied.

'Yes, I know that. But what history Joncer knows you could put on a postage stamp and what you know about race-horses—the same?'

He nodded. He said, 'You study history to find out why a thing happened rather than what things happened. You don't get wise necessarily, but you do get a way of looking—an insight. And with that perception, occasionally you can help people—even when they are engaged in horse-racing.'

'You know Joncer as well as I do,' I said. At first I thought he wanted me to gossip about Joncer and the sort of chap I thought he was. I wouldn't do that. I was wrong anyway. He said, 'Of course I know Joncer. Because I know him, and because I know he counts for very little——'

'How do you mean, "very little",' I asked, 'he's the jockey, isn't he?'

'Now, Harry, try to be better. Of course he's the jockey, but you should know that the jockey is the weakest of the three—Singer, Verepont have the last word. They could very easily make Joncer not even the jockey, but an embittered has-been watching from the Grand Stand. I cannot see why Joncer should want so much to ride this horse, but I say that from sheer ignorance; I have never ridden a horse, let alone won a race, I have never seen a horse race even and I have never gambled in my life. So how would I know why he wants—indeed must—ride *Pentameter*?'

'This is why,' I said. 'On the ordinary level of things, if he rides and wins he gets 10 per cent of the stake money at least as a present. So that's £500. But there's a bit more to it than that. Joncer bought this horse and sold it to Singer—*Pentameter* is Joncer's discovery. And he got to know the animal, what with training and riding him, much better than anyone else. Then there is the agreement he made with Singer when he sold the horse—which it seems Singer is trying to wriggle out of. And you can't push Joncer around. But the most important is this—it's going to be Joncer's last ride—after the race he quits riding—and he'd like to finish grandly. Because he half-believes some of the gossip himself— that he's lost his nerve—how else could he explain to himself the forty losers?—and the way he'd look at it is to say one Gold Cup winner would wipe out the forty. For himself as much as the public. Because they will have forgotten the next day and only in the record tables will there be any mention. Maybe in some pub somewhere in ten years' time someone will say, "Snowy Jackson won on *Pentameter*," and someone else will say, "You're wrong. It was Joncer Mellows." Then they'll bet on it, a pint or a pound, and to settle they'll look it up. That's the only permanent glory as far as the crowd is concerned—to them the whole event will be a line of small type in the back of a bookie's rule book.

'To Joncer though—this is how I see it and I may be wrong—it would be a quiet satisfaction, a complacency almost. He'll look back on it during the years to come and he'll say, "that's when I showed them who could ride". He'll probably be an old bore and we'll never hear the end of it, but that's something we'll have to suffer. He's a simple man, is Joncer, and this is one of his simple necessities.'

'I see,' said the Professor. We drove in silence for a while.

'Look,' I said, 'I may be wrong. If I were Joncer I'd say, "if you don't want me to ride, that's it, I won't. Good afternoon," and I'd be off. I wouldn't worry myself sick; I wouldn't be that vain.'

'Vain?' he said, surprised. 'Well, perhaps you're

right. Perhaps it is a sort of vanity that gives each man his place and his dignity.' He changed the subject suddenly. 'Singer is the man to get at,' he said as if that settled everything.

'You're welcome,' I said as we drove into the car park.

I haven't paid to enter a race-course for forty-five years and I didn't see why I should start now.

'Follow me,' I said to the Professor, 'and don't say a word.' He looked surprised but nodded.

'Hallo, Harry,' said the man on the gate, 'still at it then?'

'Yes,' I said, 'we've brought a couple today. This,' I indicated the Professor, 'is the new assistant vet. Give him a badge, will you? He doesn't know his way around yet.'

We collected our badges and in we went. Professor Miller looked a trifle perplexed.

17

'Yes,' I said, 'that's Singer.' We moved over to his end of the bar. 'And that's Verepont,' I said as I caught sight of him too. But then I remembered the Professor knew him. They were talking cheerfully—*Lucid* had just won at even money and Joncer had come fourth in his race. Destiny seemed in an inexorable mood.

'Hallo,' said the Professor briskly to Verepont.

'Oh, hallo,' said Verepont with his public smile. 'I didn't know you were a racing man.' Singer didn't bother to look up from his newspaper.

'I'm not,' said the Professor, 'but I have a son-in-law who is.' He said this meaningfully.

'To be sure,' said Verepont.

'Mr Singer's jockey, I believe?' He looked towards Singer inquiringly and with a slight dash of defiance I would have said.

'Who's this then?' asked Singer. Verepont quickly apologized. 'I'm sorry. Professor Miller—Mr Singer. Professor Miller is John Mellows's father-in-law.'

'Mellows has ridden for me,' said Singer. He wasn't really being rude—just his usual surly self. For when he wasn't being frantic at the betting he was surly, distant, uninterested.

'Yes, I know. The agreement you and he have over *Pentameter* has been a happy one.'

'What agreement?' Verepont looked uncomfortable as the Professor said this.

'You know damn' well what agreement,' I said. 'The agreement whereby he'd turn *Pentameter* into a race-horse for you and ride him like no one else can—the one you're trying to worm your way out of.' There seemed no point beating about the bush.

'I'll see him all right about that,' said Singer.

'Mr Singer is well known for his generosity,' said Verepont.

'And I'm sure Mr Singer is well known for keeping his word as well,' said the Professor easily.

'He's done all right out of me,' said Singer slowly.

'On the contrary you've done very well out of him. And I'm here to see that you don't do anything foolish and ruin your chance of doing even better. It is of course beneath John's dignity to remind you of your obligations. But it isn't beneath mine. And it isn't simply because it could cost me money.'

Even I was surprised. I couldn't see how there could possibly be any financial edge on it for the Professor. He went on, 'Some time ago I asked one of my more dynamic students—and you listen to this carefully, Mr Singer, for when the innocent walks in, the experienced may well watch and be reminded—I asked this student how I would go about backing a horse. I was told. I gave him £3 and I now have a voucher from a bookmaker which says that if *Pentameter* wins the Gold Cup he will pay me £103.'

'A big bet,' said Singer sarcastically.

'No. Regard it simply as a bet irrespective of its size. For a bet is still a bet—any object is still an object, however much you multiply its dimension.'

Verepont seemed half-angry, half-fascinated. Singer remained churlish. What the Professor said wasn't quite true. A bet of £100 to £3 is merely an indication of one's faith. But one of £30,000 to £300 such as Singer had struck—was one which indicated confidence of such a degree that this confidence and the weight of the money at stake, affected the market. *Pentameter* now stood at 100 to 6. It was a small point and I didn't say anything. The Professor went on to answer me anyway.

'I struck that bet in the same spirit as you did, Mr Singer, even if yours was in multiples of hundreds. In the flush of confidence that we all had when Joncer last rode *Pentameter* home—plus two other winners, I believe—I thought yes. I will wager £3 that my son-in-law will ride *Pentameter* home to victory on 5th March—Thursday, as it now turns out. Now'—he looked very keenly at Singer who nervously gulped his drink; the Professor's voice had taken on the colour of sombre incredulity—'now it appears that you are going to be stupid enough to change the very ingredients of that confidence—to change the very nature of the bet, certainly for me, and I would say unquestionably for yourself as well.'

'You back a horse because you like the price, because you think he has a chance and because you want to win money. What's all this crap about "ingredients of confidence" and all that? You sound like some bloody preacher.'

'You're wrong, Singer. It must be a long time since you've been in a church—I can assure you no preacher is so eloquent. But forget that. I know you're superstitious. Any man who wagers money is superstitious for in his act of wagering he says he can predict something of the future and the very confidence of that is a superstition. You just think back to when you struck the bet. You imagined, hoped, probably expected to see your horse, ridden by Joncer Mellows, win—that was the picture in your mind's eye and the motivation for the bet. Now you want to alter that picture. I won't be so inept as to say you're changing horses in midstream—but you'll get my meaning, no doubt. You had enough confidence in a set of circumstances at one time to act in a certain way. I tell you that if you try to alter those circumstances—I use the word since you cannot understand the ingredients—you forfeit any right to luck. You are pestering with destiny itself.'

'You're crazy,' said Singer.

He finished his drink and left the bar abruptly. Verepont, with an expression of worry, bafflement and annoyance followed him. The Professor and I picked up our drinks.

I don't know what effect the Professor's speech had on Singer. It was well delivered, but possibly too rhetorical to reach the depths of his tiny mind. Many other things happened anyway. But one thing about it—it cleared the air and forced Singer to decide. I thought that the Professor had described the absurd beliefs of a racing man (mine certainly) with precision. Almost with grandeur. We waited for Joncer to change, had another drink and then drove home. We were all rather silent and by a telepathic agreement we decided not to tell Joncer what had transpired.

Monday night is my wife's Women's Institute night, so I am allowed out till ten. In fact, I generally have a meal at Joncer's and then all three of us go out for a drink. This particular night the Professor and Marjory were coming over later, so I was thinking of pushing off. Joncer was in a bad mood—I told him, 'You're walking about like a bear with a sore arse,' and that didn't improve matters. Anyway I was just leaving when the telephone rang. Joncer had gone to fetch some coal up and Janet had wet hands, so she asked me to answer it. I did.

'Singer,' said Singer.

'Hallo, Mr Singer,' I said, 'I'll fetch Mel——'

'Tell him he can have the ride like we arranged,' and then he rang off. No good night or anything.

'Arrogant bastard,' I thought at first, but by the time the receiver was back in the cradle I was feeling very pleased. I told Janet the good news and I left no doubt —jauntily and possibly singing a tune, and full of praises for the persuasive oratory of the Professor—at whose door I laid this sudden, if surly, change of heart.

The next morning, however, we learned something else.

Singer had driven Verepont's son away from the race-course. They may have talked the matter of the ride over amongst themselves and maybe Singer decided to stick by Joncer. In other words, the Professor had been persuasive. I don't think he was. I don't think anyone could persuade Singer to do anything. That part of people that gets persuaded didn't exist in Singer. Anyway, it's only my opinion. The fact is that Singer tried to overtake a low-loader lorry on that hill by Kinnersley, just avoided a head-on crash and turned the car over. He, of course, escaped unhurt. But Vivian Verepont didn't.

18

EVEN if he'd been injured when he telephoned, I doubt if Singer would have mentioned it. He was such an obsessive gambler—indeed an obsessive man—that a broken leg, bruises and so on, shock even, wouldn't alter the nature of the obsession.

For a few hours, though, we thought he had changed; that such things as obligation, loyalty, common sense even, were there if you could find them. The Professor preened himself. 'There is a vulnerability towards doing the right thing. I say "vulnerability" because if a man has cut himself off from everyday values—as a crook does—then he is vulnerable to good because he's motivated by evil. Only the fact that he is rich anyway, stops Singer from being a crook. But he has all the motives—incredible selfishness—more than that really —it is an inability to leave the buttressed, porticoed, castellated citadel of himself—a huge villain in a prison lies. And from this stems avarice and its blood brother, cunning. And overriding them all the isolation of implied supremacy, the half-crazed fanaticism of the dictator. That was Singer.' By now I'd got used to this way of talking.

'Still is Singer,' I said, and afterwards I was pleased I'd said it. We didn't then know about the car smash.

'No,' said the Professor. 'No. He was vulnerable. We managed to get through the barriers and touch him somewhere. Into the frosty acres of his loneliness we brought a little thaw.' He put down his glass—we were in Mrs Whitman's waiting for Joncer. Earlier I'd been talking to the Irish lodgers but they left after one drink because the races started at one o'clock and they had all the restlessness of the small-time gambler—until the White Flag went up for the first race everything seemed

like a frantic version of purgatory. Just as they left the
Professor had come in.

'I don't know,' I said. 'I just can't see anyone making
Singer's mind up for him. Perhaps he's superstitious and
you reminded him of something. But I'd bet all Lombard Street to a box of cigars that Singer still doesn't
care—cannot care—about what is the right thing, what
his obligations are and so on. He just isn't that human.'

'You're too harsh on him. What made him change if
it wasn't——?' But Joncer came in then.

He was still in his working tack and breathless as
well. 'So you don't know?' he said quickly, intently.
'Verepont's boy is in hospital, still unconscious from the
car smash and——'

'What car smash?' we both said together.

'Singer turned him over at ten to eight last night.
Legs broken and I don't know what else.'

'Ten to eight!' I said. 'Why, he telephoned your place
only minutes after.'

'Yes. It must have been the first thing he did when he
crawled out of the wreckage. Maybe before he got hold
of the ambulance.'

'So that's why he decided to let you ride——'

'Yes. That's why.' Joncer looked both angry and sad.

'So much for vulnerability,' I said to the Professor.

'What——?' began Joncer. So we told him then how
we'd spoken to Singer at Worcester. And then we told
him what we'd just been saying.

Joncer said, 'You can't talk to Singer, you can't
reach him. Nothing——' The Professor interrupted and
by the way Joncer looked at him I got the feeling that
he was annoyed with us for interfering.

'It's possible Singer had decided to give you the ride
before the smash, John. We don't know what was going
on in that refrigerator he calls a mind. But if he wasn't
vulnerable as a person, the destiny that guides him certainly is. How else explain——'

Joncer interrupted him. 'Destiny nothing.' We could see he was angry now, or exasperated perhaps with us, perhaps with circumstances which the Professor liked to call destiny; I don't know what I call them myself. 'Singer has a car smash. Verepont's boy gets hurt and how the hell Singer managed to escape unhurt I don't know, but he did, and he immediately thinks—perhaps he's even thinking this while the wheels are still turning on the overturned car—*what happens to my bets now? How are we going to clean up so many thousand?* That's what went on in Singer's mind. So he falls back on his second best—me.'

'Look, John. You don't like the word destiny, nor do you like luck—not as a word. But luck's on your side now even at the expense of Vivian Verepont and luck is always at the expense of someone, something. And, even accepting your interpretation of the events, you're only considered second-best by Singer himself, I'd like to think that we were instrumental in making Singer change his mind. In fact, I'm pretty sure we were. But that's vanity on my part. I'd hate to think I'd spoken to that moron for half an hour and left him completely unmoved, that I'd come off second-best. But all this is nothing. The fact is you've got the ride. What are you going to do about it?'

'Win the race and then spit in Singer's eye,' said Joncer. He grinned. 'And then I quit for ever.'

'That's my boy,' said the Professor and we all had another drink.

Well, if you want a mystery you've got one now. When did Singer decide to give Joncer the ride? Your guess is as good as mine. And mine says the minute he regained consciousness after the smash. He wasn't exactly knocked out—not like Vivian was. I mean the minute after the noise subsided and the eye had something still and immediate to contemplate and the workings of his mind resumed their normal (normal for Singer, that is) pace. As soon as Singer saw that Vivian Verepont was no more use to him—that's when he decided that Joncer would be. Anyway, that's how I see it.

Joncer and I arrived at the races at half-past twelve. He wasn't riding this first day; *Pentameter* was to run on the third, so it was a social visit as much as anything. As Ascot is to Flat Racing so Cheltenham is to the Jumping Game: everybody who's anybody and everybody who's nobody was there. We enjoyed ourselves. We had a few drinks with Terence O'Rourke, the former owner of *Pentameter*, who'd come over from Ireland the night before. And after the last race we went down to the Stables to see the horse he'd brought with him and which he was going to ride in the Amateur Riders' Race the next day. I guessed even then that Terence was hoping to sell it. And either we were drunker than we thought, or a sudden madness came over us, but we bought the animal, as a partnership fifty-fifty each. The price was 600 guineas. It could be cheap.

'Can I ride him tomorrow?' asked Terence after we'd concluded the deal. 'I'd like to show you English boys the way round. We'll split the prize money three ways.'

'Well, Terence,' says Joncer, 'since you've come all this way we'll not be hard-hearted. And as far as I'm concerned you can keep your prize. In fact, I'll lay you an even fifty that you'll finish in the last half of the field.'

'I'll have a piece of that too,' I said. I'd never seen Terence ride (in fact this was the first time I'd met him) but I remembered Joncer's account of that day at Tramere when they bought *Pentameter* from him. Admittedly, he'd won, but there's the world of difference between winning there and winning at Cheltenham.

'I'll take you both then—an even fifty each, and just to show I'm not mean—I repeat prize money goes three ways.'

We all shook hands on it. There was prize money only for the first three places and with twenty-six starters we didn't expect much from his offer. Still we tried to keep him fairly sober that night so as not to ruin the very slender chance he had.

That was Tuesday.

On the Wednesday, Terence sets off on what was now our horse, in his usual cowboy style. They go miles away into the country and when they reappear he's still among the middle bunch—which in this race is the best place to be. Anyway they all plod past us (it's a four-mile race) and away round for the last time. And Terence still keeps his position. A few horses had fallen and the field was strung out. But unquestionably he was nearer the leaders than the tail.

'Joncer,' I said, 'this is going to cost us money.'

'Yes,' he said, 'we ought to have got him drunk.'

Terence finished ninth. So we pay him £600 for the horse and £100 for the bet. And thus after a lifetime with horses I now for the first time owned half of one. His name is *Mozart Delinquent*. Only a drink-crazed Irishman would manage to think up a name like that.

And now Thursday.

19

I quote from Thursday's sporting paper:

— AN INTERNATIONAL AFFAIR —
WE SETTLE FOR 'KAVANAGH'S CHARM'

Apart from the residents, three nationalities are represented today at Prestbury Park. Kavanagh's Charm *and* Sparrow's Cottage *from Ireland,* Cherokee *from the U.S.A., and* Amour Galante *from France. The French have never won this race but there is no mistaking the confidence behind* Amour Galante. Cherokee *won the Maryland Chase before he was sent over here ;* Sparrow's Cottage *won by twenty lengths at Baldoyle, so* Kavanagh's Charm *must finish twenty lengths in front of him after his convincing win from* Bellbook *at Leopardstown!—if the form book works out.*

The rest make little appeal. Treble Clef *has never been quite top class and at eleven years of age I feel he's past his best.* Foxy *could go close if in the mood and has a good pilot in* Harry Bullock. *But there must be no tantrums today and* Foxy *is well known for his chancy temperament. The locals have backed* Pentameter *(and for large amounts) but his previous wins, although in good style, have only been in the novice class and it's not often a novice wins this race. I just remember the last time* Hammock *won—and that fact speaks for itself—and I doubt if* Transmission *will get an inch beyond two miles.*

*In an open race I rely on the form choice—*Kavanagh's Charm *to win from* Amour Galante *and suggest* Pentameter *as an each-way wager for small amounts. I fully expect the raucous cheers of our friends from the Emerald Isle to fill the air at approximately three twenty-five today. And it is significant that the Champion has chosen* Kavanagh's Charm *as his mount. I hope and expect he's right.*

'We just rate a mention,' I said to the Professor as we

walked the course that afternoon. It was a bright, cold, windy March day and for some reason the Professor had elected to wear a hat. It was the first time I'd seen him in one. It was one of those dapper trilbys that try to end in a point and which only save a man from ridicule by the fact that you'll see many of them at a race meeting.

'What?' said the Professor. He just managed to save his hat from a particularly sudden gust.

'Why are you wearing that damn' silly thing?' I asked.

'I was under the impression that it was obligatory not to have been a *divorcé* and to be correctly dressed to gain admission to a race meeting.' He said this a bit stiffly.

I laughed. 'That's Ascot,' I said. 'Not here. You could be America's Most Divorced Husband and wear pyjamas and get in here.'

As it was still early and the crowd only a gentle trickle we noticed the roadman with his oblong cart and superior expression watching us.

'See if he'll give you five bob for it,' I said. I felt a bit buoyant that morning. We approached him.

'You see this hat?' began the Professor.

'Ah,' said the roadman with, I felt, a slight feeling of condescension.

'I want to sell it,' continued the Professor. He took it off and exhibited it as if it were some golden casket in a Bond Street sale.

'I reckon to get my hats for free,' said the roadman, 'this weather.'

The wind roared down on us. For a moment I thought deadlock had been reached.

'Oh?' said the Professor.

'I watches where the wind takes them and I starts looking for them somewhere else, helping the owner like. That way I sometimes gets a tip as well.'

'Then what?'

'Well, when the owner gives up looking and clears off I pick up the hat and flogs it to Billy Jenkins down the Lower End.'

'Ah,' said the Professor. The roadman, imperturbable and with a slightly grotesque dignity, nodded. 'Yes. That's what I do.'

The Professor held out his hat. 'Yours for five shillings.'

'Not a penny above two.'

'What! I paid——'

'Not interested. I generally reckon to get 'em for free.'

'Three shillings because I'm——'

'Two. And that's final—but I'll throw in a horse I know about that's home and dried in the big race.'

'What's that then?'

'*Pentameter*,' said the roadman. 'My cousin's daughter married the jockey so she should know, shouldn't she?'

'Unquestionably,' said the Professor. For a moment he was taken aback. Then he added with evident amusement, 'We must be related—almost blood brothers one might say.'

'I dare say we are. Now what about the hat?'

'Yours,' said the Professor, 'for half a crown cash.'

'All right,' said the roadman, producing an old leather purse.

The Professor accepted the coin and passed over the hat. We moved slowly away. The Professor called over his shoulder, 'And please give my regards to Cousin Mary.'

The roadman put down his barrow. 'You mean Cousin Polly,' he said solemnly. 'But don't forget to back *Pentameter*. He's home and dried.'

We nodded solemnly, the Professor bowed, and we both waved farewell.

By the time we got to the race-course the crowd was

thicker. And shortly after, when the London train arrived it began to take on the proportions of a Gold Cup crowd. There were Cockney, Birmingham, Yorkshire, Irish accents, farmers red-faced, boozy and loud, bookmakers even more red and loud, county people, brassy-tongued and all the apparently nondescript, all with a kind of preoccupation—avarice coloured by hope—greed, expectancy, excitement—all these cast upon the diverse ingredients of the crowd and yet giving that crowd an overall feeling of boldness, a feeling vulgar, vociferous and determined. Everything was slightly quickened; people went from place to place with a certain nervous half-run, half-walk; drinks were fought for, gulped and forgotten. Everywhere movement, talk, action.

I lost the Professor in one of the bars. I wasn't sorry because I always feel lost in a race-course bar at its peak—maybe because I'm short and I get overlooked; trodden on, pushed aside by the hearty monsters who always seem to surround me when I'm trying to order a drink I don't really want and certainly do not need.

Anyway I went to inspect the turf. There was no need really, as I knew *Pentameter* would act on any sort of going—except bone hard and you never meet that in March at Cheltenham. For the record though it was good going, inclining a little towards soft—which meant there'd be a few wet patches out in the country. I met Joncer where the Hurdle and Steeplechase courses separate. He'd just walked the whole course.

'Well, Joncer.'

'Well, Harry.'

'What's it going to ride like?'

'All right, Harry. One or two bad patches, but I'll miss them. We should go close.'

He was nervous but then he always was before a race. And so was I even if my 'nerves' were due mainly to the £100 I'd staked. But it was more than that. Perhaps it was the whole idea of the horse, the money, the race, the crowd. Even I, for instance, felt as if I owned a part of *Pentameter*—because I knew Joncer who'd bought the animal and who trained him and because I'd seen the horse nearly every day and certainly listened to the latest reports of his progress with an interest that had more in it than hope of landing a flashy betting coup. In a kind of way the horse had become mine as much as Singer's. Because a horse is just a horse: but a good one is a way of life.

I nodded. 'See you in the Paddock then,' I said, and I moved on. I knew he wanted to be alone. And so did I; we'd have plenty to talk about in a few hours' time.

I had bets on the two races which preceded the big race. And I lost both. I forget what I thought about it, but I probably said, 'that's used up the bad luck'. You say daft things like that when you're racing. It's impossible not to be superstitious. Anyway they started to bet on the big one.

Perhaps I'd better explain about the betting. On a big race the bookies run an ante-post book. This means that you can back a horse some weeks before it runs and get a large price about the animal. However, if the horse doesn't run on the actual day—because the owner's changed his mind, or the horse get injured, or he runs so badly in a race before the big one that the connections decide he hasn't a chance—then you lose your money. But if he does run you'll probably have three to four times the odds of the price he starts at. We had had 33 to 1—Singer in thousands, me in hundreds (and I suspect Joncer the same) and the Professor in pounds. *Pentameter* ultimately started at 8 to 1. When we bet him there were some twenty others down to run. Actually, only nine of these faced the Starter and so already a packet of money had been lost.

I'll quote you the betting report from the *Sporting Life*

the day after—it sounds like the Stock Exchange reports, and in fact the betting itself resembles a Stock Exchange deal.

Ante-post business on Monday night was mainly over Kavanagh's Charm, Foxy *and* Amour Galante, *but no clear favourite appeared until some really good money got abroad for* Kavanagh's Charm *at all rates from 10 to 1 leaving 11 to 2 best at the finish.* Foxy *and* Amour Galante *were solid at 17 to 2 and 8 to 1 respectively although layers wanted special odds a place.* Cherokee *was asked for at 1,000 to 60, but this was refused: 100 to 8 was the best seen.* Pentameter *(previously from 33 to 1 to 100 to 6) was taken to small amounts, and 100 to 9 was laid at the finish of the night's session.*

On the day Kavanagh's Charm *continued to gather strength, going through all the 5 to 1 in a twinkling (evens a place), 9 to 2 (1,800 to 400 was laid many times) and ending up rock-like at 7 to 2.* Foxy *attracted at 8 to 1, leaving six and a half best at the close. The Blower liked* Amour Galante *at 7 to 1 on all rates down to 9 to 2, this in face of a deluge of money (Irish mainly) for* Sparrow's Cottage *at 20 to 1 to eights.* Pentameter *entered the volumes at 10 to 1, 9 to 1 and 8 to 1, again for small amounts.* Hammock *was comparatively friendless but* Treble Clef *was taken at 20 to 1.* Cherokee *drifted and* Transmission *(33 to 1 to 25s) rounded off a hectic session.*

S.P. 7 to 2 Kavanagh's Charm, *9 to 2* Amour Galante, *11 to 2* Foxy, *8 to 1* Sparrow's Cottage, Pentameter, *100 to 6* Treble Clef, Cherokee, *25 to 1* Transmission, *33 to 1* Hammock. *Special place betting 2 to 1 on* Kavanagh's Charm, *4 to 6* Amour Galante, *evens* Foxy: *the rest in proportion.*

That's how the betting went. I quote because I was around the Paddock most of the time and didn't see it myself. I was happy enough with my 33 to 1 and seemingly so was Singer because he didn't budge from the Paddock either. In fact it was a very subdued version of himself that stood, somewhat aloof in the group around Verepont. I'd had a word with Cedric and learned that his boy would be all right. And I was thankful for that. I looked for the Professor but couldn't find him in the huge crowd. And I wasn't sorry about that either. I wanted to watch this race by myself, because like I say, it was a little bit more than just another race to me. All the usual reality was there, of course, the crowd, noise and hope of gain, but somehow I felt a more personal participation this time. I felt as if I was out there taking the jumps, riding the horse, which was already something more than a horse—was already a demonstration of our faith, our hope. And perhaps not only I felt this; maybe people like the anonymous road-man felt it too—if not why did he invent the story about the jockey's wife? Admittedly he must have thought this would lend status to his tip (and humour too, although he'd never know that) but why bother anyway? Because a sort of personal participation was there with him too. It has to be. Racing is just so much noise and vulgarity without it.

They all looked good in the Paddock. *Pentameter* was nonchalant. *Kavanagh's Charm* was a small horse but all of him was good. You could see that. *Foxy* looked on his toes and as if he meant business and the Frenchman would not have been out of place in a Derby Parade. Perhaps *Sparrow's Cottage* was a trifle common but that is often deceiving. I tried to be impartial but I had to admit ours looked the best.

The jockeys came into the Paddock ten minutes before the Start, Joncer and the Champion leading. That was when I left because I wanted a place in the Trainers' Stand and I wanted a good one. The crowd was so thick that I only got there in time to see them parade in front of the Stands. They turned and cantered down, *Pentameter* moving sluggishly, *Kavanagh's Charm* with a lovely action and the rest like good horses.

Those who'd backed *Pentameter* must have had a few misgivings when they saw him go down. But no lazy horse looks well until he's driven. They disappeared for a while because the Start is behind the Stands. Business with the bookies was brisk—I noticed it then while we waited for the Flag.

And then it went quiet. They were under orders. They started.

It's always very quiet at the immediate Start until they reach the first jump. The only worry we had was whether ours would treat the Cheltenham jumps with respect, because they are as formidable as at Aintree—not so high admittedly, but stout and placed where a risky jumper would meet them all wrong. And at the first I thought we'd had it. *Pentameter* just didn't seem to rise but blundered through like a carthorse. I nearly had heart failure; I certainly feared the worst.

Joncer managed to stay on, how I don't know. It would be like rushing full speed on a motor-bike say, through some thickly interleaved, overhanging branches. He stayed on but he was last. They came to the second —an open ditch which they take on the uphill rise to the corner. I watched. I thought: yes we were mad; we should have raced him here before—to get him used to the jumps; he's treating them like hurdles made of feather. He rose at it better this time but dragged his back feet through the birch and nearly turned head-over-heels. Joncer went right up on his neck—the Almighty or the Powers of Darkness kept him on.

We were a long way behind now, forty lengths separating the first—*Transmission*—and us. Joncer settled down—he didn't push him at all but let him go at his own speed. There was a furlong at least before the next jump and I suppose he thought, 'the only thing I can do is to hope he learns in time'. *Pentamenter* raced towards it with his peculiar, almost syncopated, gallop—a huge, slow stride—and luckily he met it well, rose and landed like a good horse should. And I thought, *well*, he's learning; maybe *we'll win it next year*. I'd given up hope then for this race.

They had fifteen jumps to take. The next was the water. Again Joncer sat very still although *Transmission*, way out in front, was taking the jump after whilst we cleared this one. But it was no good me saying there's plenty of time yet to make up the ground—I thought we'd had it.

In that first circuit Joncer let him settle down and acclimatize himself. *Pentameter* looked completely outclassed by the others—like a Labrador chasing greyhounds—but except for pecking a bit on landing after the jump at the top of the hill, he took his jumps better. But he was still very much last and I wouldn't have given a halfpenny for his chance. Nor did the bookies—there was plenty of 20 to 1 being shouted.

Then things began to happen.

As they went over the first jump of the second circuit *Transmission* fell. That only upset a few because he was a tired horse then and I knew he'd never get more than two miles in this company. They went to the top of the first hill and Joncer pushed *Pentameter* past *Hammock*. With one fallen we were now seventh. I'd have given three farthings for our chance then. Going downhill towards the water I could see Joncer was warming him up but he didn't seem to be going any quicker. He took the jump well and we were sixth. All right, a penny for our chance. *Kavanagh's Charm* was a long way ahead of us behind *Cherokee* who'd taken up the running. Third was *Amour Galante*, fourth *Foxy*—and at that point I'd have made *Foxy* the danger. Along the back stretch we were alongside *Treble Clef* in fifth position with just over a mile to go. *Kavanagh's Charm* took the next like a bird and drew up to *Cherokee*. Then the crowd stirred. People half-turned to their neighbours as if to speak, as if to say, '*Yes, you see I told you,*' but they didn't say it, didn't speak because already the leaders were at the top of the hill with three-quarters of a mile to go, and the soft sighs of tension, expectancy, vindication almost, were all they had time for—and that's not right either because what noise they made was involuntary, external, feathery and vast.

Foxy went third and we went fourth with three jumps to go and the long run down the hill. We were a bad fourth. The whip was shown on *Foxy* but Joncer still rode with his hands. If the gap closed it closed or seemed to close only a fraction.

Kavanagh's Charm landed first and everybody said, 'Yes, it's the favourite,' and they said it out loud this time as if they'd expected this—that this was just, was pre-ordained, was in fact a vindication of judgement, of the power of money and the elimination of luck. But I didn't say it. I said, shouted amongst all the other tensions, shouted to the faces filled with a wild surmise, and as I said it others said it too, perhaps with the first tiny inkling of destiny, the first surge of intuition, the—— I said, 'WATCH JONCER. WHAT PRICE JONCER?' and I said it with a strange mixture of hope and triumph.

'JONCER WINS NOTHING,' others said, but at the second last we were third and six lengths separated them. And I shouted it again, 'WHAT PRICE JONCER?' as *Kavanagh's Charm* came to the last and rose. And others said it too and a huge roar of disbelief, glory, greed, hope rose as *Kavanagh's Charm* cleared the last jump and Joncer followed him over a length behind.

Moments of eternity if you like, certainly of suspense. *Kavanagh's Charm* was on the Stands side, Joncer on the far and it looked hopeless—*Kavanagh's Charm* was going like a bomb. A hundred yards to go and everyone shouting. Joncer never looked better—strong and contained, no whip, still with his hands riding a perfect flat race finish, balanced and powerful. We drew level and then we knew. *Kavanagh's Charm* began to swerve

towards the centre. He was a tired, beaten horse. Joncer
passed him thirty yards from the Post. We won with a
ton in hand—two lengths to the good and full of running. Yes, we'd won.

'We've won,' I said. But who heard? Who heard
anybody?

It was over.

There was a crowd round Joncer now as he entered
the Winners' Enclosure. He had nodded to the host of
owners, trainers and gamblers who'd congratulated
him, but I could see he was tired and that he didn't
really care any more. It was over for him too. Because
triumph is an empty thing—it never really happens, it
cannot be lived with. Already the majority of the crowd
were weighing up the prospects of the next race. If
there was a moment of triumph it was when he flashed
past the Post, but it was a quiet, personal moment, in-
communicable, lonely and ultimately worthless. As
worthless as the congratulations or the cheers. It was
over. He'd done it. That was enough.

It was over for Singer, white-faced, eager, ungainly.
Joncer was dismounting now and Singer said, 'Yes. I
knew you'd do it.'

'Liar,' said Joncer as he unhitched the saddle. 'You
liar.' He said it softly but he meant it. Who else heard I
don't know. Verepont probably, maybe the reporters,
and I did, but who cared anyway? Singer didn't. If he
heard, if it registered, he ignored it. And I don't think
it sank in at all as he stood there nervous, jittery, distant, receiving the hearty congratulations of the Irish
earl who owned *Kavanagh's Charm*, with a superior dis-
interest—as if the earl was acting out some absurd,
irrelevant and archaic formality.

'You didn't think any such thing, Singer,' I said.

'What?' he said. This time he definitely hadn't
heard.

'Go to hell,' I said, and he heard that all right.

'What?' he said again. But I moved away. Singer just didn't matter any more.

Joncer weighed in, the Blue Flag went up and the result now was official. You can look it up in the records. *Pentameter* was led away. He showed no signs of exertion, not even sweating, and they told me that when he got to his box he drank his bucket of milk and lay down as soon as they'd done him. He was asleep when they came to collect him after the last race. So it was over for him too—until next year anyway.

I was £3,300 richer. And that's a nice thing to be. So was Joncer. We owned a horse—not another *Pentameter* to be sure—but we reckoned to win a race or two. And that evening Joncer and I went down the Stables to have a look at him.

'How's it feel being retired?' I asked him.

'Harry,' he said, 'I never felt so good. No more kow-towing to the stupid bastards that own horses. No more Singer. No more worrying about weight, about luck, form, nerve—Harry I'm free.'

'You're not,' I said, 'you've just quit one lot of snags for another. Still a change is as good as a rest.'

'Don't be such a misery,' he said. 'Come and see your horse.'

So we looked at the animal silently, and for my part not without a little pride.

20

THAT'S where it ought to end: in triumph. And if Joncer had been like Harry Smart it would have. Because Harry knew that triumph, such as it is, never really lasts long enough for anything to end in it. So he just quit. While they were still cheering even, he put on his bow tie, picked up his bag and left. Just like that. That's why Harry was one of the great, one of the few masters who do not need moments of triumph, neither as a spur nor as a solace; who can, and do, treat the crowd and trainers and owners with utter contempt. One of the great—there are about three every century like Harry.

Well, Joncer wasn't great. He was just very, very good. And the difference lay in the fact that Joncer deep down needed this applause and acclaim and the popularity, whereas Harry knew it to be worthless and would go his own way, isolated, contemptuous, envied. The difference between the great and the very good lies in that. The 'Artist of the Saddle' with an emphasis on Artist: the artist who does something, not so much because he wants to but more because he has to, and on top of that because he can do it supremely well: and not for fame and praise and popularity, but simply for money. Lots of it. And sometimes not even for that. It's much more than self confidence, this; it's self compulsion. That's why I was never a jockey—I had enough confidence, I suppose, but I knew it wasn't enough. Joncer had a sort of compulsion, of course. But I realized, once he'd quit, that he had used his talents cheaply compared with Harry.

I wasn't sorry. In his class he was, as I say, very, very good. And that was something; to be one of the best among the ordinary. And because of this he was a nicer chap than Harry—more restful, genial, human, even.

Possibly that's worth more in the long run. But Joncer didn't take to retirement kindly. He missed the cheers, congratulations, excitement, triumph even. He moped.

There was an old barn at the bottom of Joncer's garden and we spent most of April converting it into stabling for three horses. We weren't being unduly grand in this because 'Mozy'—as we nicknamed *Mozart Delinquent*—was no world beater. He wasn't another *Pentameter*. So we knew we'd probably have to buy at least one more if we were going to make money as owners. Mind you, there was every chance *Mozy* might improve. He was only a five-year-old, he was sound, and we naturally hoped he'd turn into a useful animal. There seemed no reason why he shouldn't win us a few small races even with a name like that! But in case he didn't we'd made room for two more.

We thought of changing the name, but I wasn't all that keen. For one thing it's a lot of bother re-registering the animal at Wetherby's and so on, and I'm superstitious enough to believe that a change of name could bring bad luck. Janet was dead against it too. 'I couldn't,' she said one day, 'have thought of a better name. It's him to a "t". And anyway, it fits his breeding.' Well—what do you think? He was by *Woodwind* out of *Borstal Girl*. Maybe Terence wasn't so drink-crazed as we thought. I wouldn't know.

We had decided to try with *Mozy* at the Devon meetings held in August and September. Consequently, we turned him out to grass during April and May and intended to bring him in for serious training in June. So in May Joncer had nothing to do. He wasn't much of a gardener although he'd bought all the gadgets under the sun. He had a flame-thrower, an ultra-modern lawn-mower, electric hedge-shears, a fork with a spring attachment that was supposed to dig the garden for you as long as you held it upright, and a Rotovator. But all he was concerned with doing was to keep the garden tidy. And he hated that. Janet liked to walk about with a trowel and to pick flowers, but I wouldn't have called her, then, an enthusiast. In fact, one day after I'd made a few suggestions, she said, 'Harry, I'd just as soon concrete the whole area and paint it green.' And I said, 'Well, it's an idea.' I did most of it for them anyway. I let Joncer cut the lawns back and front but I pruned the roses—they had some promising Crimson Glory and Ena Harkness. Old-fashioned roses all of them, and a healthy-looking wistaria over the porch, that was growing nicely through the wrought-iron canopy above it. At the bottom by the stables we'd made a bit of a paddock and we used an old summer house as a tack-room. Janet wanted that changed.

Joncer was sitting in a deck-chair one spring morning, reading the *Sporting Life* with a glass of beer beside him, just like any retired colonel. I'd come over with my wife—she was chatting inside—when Janet came out. She looked a bit drab, although cheerful enough. But when she said, 'I think, John, that we'll have to convert that summer house,' and when I saw her muddy complexion—like a delta at low tide—I put two and two together. Joncer wasn't so quick. 'Convert it to what?' he said, as he put down the paper, perhaps a bit angrily. 'We use it as a tack-room.'

'Well,' said Janet, turning on her heel, 'if that's all the interest you take——' and she went back into the house.

'For Christ's sake,' said Joncer to me, 'what's all that about?'

'Life,' I said. Well, it is, isn't it?

'Life!' he said. 'It's a bloody awful one, I can tell you. I don't know what's come over Janet lately. She wakes up bad-tempered and looks like nothing on earth——'

'She ever sick?' I asked. This was damn' funny. I grinned a bit.

'Yes,' said Joncer. 'She came back from the doctor

just before you——' He must have seen me grinning then. His voice trailed off. 'What's so funny——' he began and then it dawned on him. He was out of the chair and into the house like a flash. I heard all three of them talking and then they appeared.

'Harry,' said Joncer, 'we're going to have——'

'No!' I said. 'You don't say!' I turned to Janet and congratulated her and my wife said, 'Joncer! For heaven's sake stop looking so surprised.'

'Yes,' I said. 'And go and get the whisky. We'll celebrate this properly.

'Not half!' said Joncer and he made towards the house. I shouted after him, 'And after that we'll start on the summer house—it'll make a good nursery.' He returned carrying Gus's tray loaded with bottles and we all had a drink.

Well, well, well, Joncer an expectant father, me a part-owner of a moderate race-horse, and the sun was shining. We'd come a long way. Marjory was delighted with the news especially when Joncer said that he'd make her odds on for the title of 'England's Most Glamorous Grandmother'. She loved that. And about a month later, just after we'd taken *Mozy* in, Janet began to look radiant. I dare say there's a chemical reason for women looking poorly in the early stages of pregnancy and no doubt there is the same to explain how they pick up later and blossom. Certainly Janet went from the extremes of each.

Joncer and I took turns with *Mozy*. Alternate mornings I'd walk him ten miles or so and at the end of June we were going to start some half-speed and fast work on the nearby gallops. I'd leave that to Joncer. Thirty miles an hour when you're my age is all right as long as you've got a windscreen in front of you.

About this time we began to see something of Vivian Verepont. He'd come out of hospital mid-April and gone back to Oxford on crutches to take his final exams. He was walking with a stick by the end of June and that's when I began to see him when I took *Mozy* out.

I stopped one day. 'How goes it?' I asked, resting myself in the saddle and looking down at him. He needed only a walking stick now, so I could see he'd made a lot of progress.

'Well, Mr Sherrif,' he said as he sat on the wall with his right leg stuck out straight, 'by some mystery I've managed to get a "second".'

'Second what? Bad leg?' Well, I didn't know about Oxford.

'No. In my exams—I've passed!'

'You sound as if you were a rank outsider then.'

'I was. There was twenty to one at the Bullingdon against me getting even a fourth. And if I hadn't had this accident it would have been a bad bet. You see, I had nothing else to do but work. But a second! I'm delighted.' I could see he was too.

He was a good-looking boy—perhaps an inch or two taller than Joncer and those inches made him appear slight. Graceful but slight. He had a rather dark complexion—French-looking I would have said, with dark, straight hair, a dead-straight, rather fragile nose and enormous brown eyes. I compare him with Joncer because they were both jockeys. The first impression you had of Joncer was sturdiness and strength, of Vivian it was more grace and style. As jockeys give me the Joncers every time.

'Well done,' I said. 'But what about your leg?'

'Oh. It's coming on nicely, thank you. I hope to be riding in a few weeks. I miss it you know.' I nodded. After all riding was only a hobby with him.

'That's good,' I said.

'What's this one?' he asked, nodding with his head towards *Mozy*.

'*Mozart Delinquent*,' I said. He laughed. 'You certainly go in for arty names,' he said. 'I suppose we do,' I said. I suddenly liked young Vivian. Perhaps we had made him into too much of a villain previously—imagined him as a young upstart in league with the master villain, Singer—when in all probability he'd merely been an innocent participant. He was keen, he was young, and possibly he might be good. We couldn't blame him for making the most out of a certain situation.

'Come round and see him stripped,' I said to Vivian. 'You won't be overdoing your leg?'

'No. I'll hobble round. I'd like to see him. You go on ahead.' So I set off. When I was unsaddling, Joncer came out of the house. He looked as if he'd just got up.

'Morning, Squire,' I said. 'Morning,' said Joncer. He walked round *Mozy* having a good look. I watched him. 'What you looking for?' I asked. 'A fifth leg?'

'No,' said Joncer, shortly.

'Now, Joncer,' I said, leaning on the animal, 'you know *Mozy* is not another *Pentameter*. Terence O'Rourke sold us just a horse this time.' I started to groom the animal.

'You don't mind if I have a look at my half, do you?' said Joncer.

'Don't be a c——, Joncer,' I said. Why should I suffer from his bad temper? I thought. And just to stir it up a bit I added, 'I've invited Vivian Verepont round to have a look at him.' But Joncer ignored that.

'I've got a toothache,' he said.

'Joncer,' I said, looking up from the grooming, 'there's only one cure—have the bloody thing out.'

'You're a lot of comfort,' he said.

'I'm not the World's Bleeding Heart,' I said. 'Have the bloody thing out.' I continued with the grooming. He kicked at a stone and set off abruptly for the house. I could see Verepont and Janet coming towards us, but Joncer must have been very curt as he passed them.

'What on earth is the matter with Joncer?' asked Janet when they reached me. 'He's behaving like a gangster.'

'Janet,' I said, 'he's got the dog on him, because he has toothache.'

'Well,' she said, 'he must have the bloody thing out.' I nodded. Great minds, etc. I was fed up by now with Joncer and his tooth, so I said to Vivian, 'There's *Mozy*,' and stood back from the animal so that he could have a good look. But I said to Janet, 'You send him to the dentist, my girl. He'll thank you for it later.'

'He must certainly go,' she said in her school-mistress manner; she added in a gentler tone, 'But I think, Harry, there's more to it than that. I think he's thoroughly bored.' She turned towards *Mozy*. 'When will he be ready for racing?'

'Not till August,' I said, 'and anyway there's no steeplechasing before.'

'O Lord!' she said. And I nodded.

Vivian Verepont was very polite and pretended not to be interested in all this. More by way of making the conversation general I said to him, 'You must take *Mozy* out one morning when you're fit.'

'Thank you,' replied Verepont, 'I'd like that.'

'We'll be needing a jockey too. If he goes well for you maybe we can arrange a ride.' I was being rash in saying this because Joncer and I had to agree over a jockey, but I felt that he'd see it would be fair and generous-minded to let young Vivian have the ride—it would be some compensation for *Pentameter*. And I felt grand. For the first time in my life I was being an owner!

He said eagerly, 'Now you're talking, Mr Sherrif——'

'Call me Harry,' I said. It always makes me feel so old when I'm called 'Mister'. Even if I am half an owner.

'Thanks. I'd love to try him. I don't expect I'll win but I'll do my damnedest.' He grinned.

'Well, *Mozy* is not another *Golden Miller*,' I began. 'You can see that.'

'He'll win!'

'He'd better!' said Janet suddenly as she gave *Mozy* a pat, 'all those carrots he eats!'

'We'll have a good try,' I said and we moved towards the house.

'Stop for a drink,' said Janet to us both. It was almost a command. 'You can help me cheer the old bugger up!' she added as we went in. Poor old Joncer, I thought.

21

JANET was affectionate, friendly, lively and young. She made friends easily. You were on Christian name terms with her almost at once and you stayed that way. She was interested in you. You felt that from the start but you soon knew when you were becoming boring, self-important or self-pitying. Joncer was never these, but I suppose once or twice I must have been. She told me in no uncertain terms. She gave the impression of being 'fast' but I knew that there was only one man in the world for her and he was Joncer. And he was damned lucky. You might think her a flirt but she was not. She was far too direct—she had none of the flirt's ambiguous equipment. If I had to sum her up in a word I say she was *modern*, whatever that may mean to you.

I think that she liked Joncer's directness as much as anything in him. Joncer couldn't or didn't dissemble. If he was bad tempered he showed it—there was no bottled-up emotion, no sulks, nor ironic attitudinizing. If he'd got a toothache he was bad tempered, if she got on his nerves he told her (and vice versa—believe me!) and yet this was something far more than cold-blooded frankness; there was more intelligence in it than that. Their marriage respected the privacy of each individual in their own special way.

Vivian Verepont began to visit them most mornings. Like all intelligent people they both enjoyed company. He was obviously at a loose end now that he'd left Oxford and because of his bad leg. He hadn't exactly decided what he was going to do with his life. They were talking about this one day when I returned with *Mozy*. They were sitting in the garden—in the patio to be exact, Joncer sunk deep in a deck-chair, Janet in a severe-looking Windsor chair, and young Verepont on a sort of bench that Joncer had made out of two blocks and a plank: maybe he thought it looked rustic, but I tried it once and if you want my opinion I reckon it would give one of those garden gnomes a sore arse! Still Joncer seemed proud of it, although I never saw him sit on it. I suppose he regarded it—as the house agents say—as a feature.

They greeted me and I took a drink and sat on the wall, in the shade. I noticed young Verepont had not brought a walking-stick. He was obviously well on the way to recovery.

'And what did you read at Oxford?' Janet was asking him.

'Modern Greats,' he replied.

'What's that?' asked Joncer.

'It's philosophy, political thought and economics.' He smiled rather nervously and added, 'They are all quite useless.'

'Then why study them?' asked Joncer, not exactly brusquely but certainly with his 'no-nonsense' air.

'I don't know why,' said Vivian. 'Father thought I ought to go to Oxford and my headmaster thought I'd do best at P.P.E. All I was concerned with at the time was to get away from home. So I took the line of least resistance. I enjoyed my time there, That's something, you know.'

'Were you at the House?' asked Janet.

'Well, by a fluke and by influence I was,' he replied. 'I was even on television once during a Union Debate!'

'My,' said Janet, smiling. 'And the Bullingdon?'

'I confess! Yes. The lot.'

'But what now?' asked Joncer like one of the Stewards interviewing a jockey.

'Now?' He paused and then with a mixture of shyness and determination he added, 'Well, now I'd like to ride horses.'

CHAPTER TWENTY-ONE

'And so you shall,' said Janet, 'you must ride ours.'
Vivian gave her a grateful glance. But Joncer sat up and
said, 'If you're any good you can.' He reached for his
drink. He wasn't exactly rude—it was more that there
was no need to say that. It was obvious we wouldn't put
him up if he was hopeless.

So there was silence for a second or so. I said, 'How
are things at the Stable?'

'Promising,' he replied. '*Lucid* has come on nicely and
of course *Pentameter* is as good as ever. Father brought
back two from France and we hope to land the Champion Hurdle and the Gold Cup next year——'

'Who'll ride?' interrupted Joncer.

'I hope I will,' said Vivian quietly. 'Father has
always wanted me to be the Stable Jockey and ultimately to take over the whole business when he re-
tires.'

'Politics, philosophy and economics will be a lot of
use to you there!' said Joncer. He put down his glass
and looked, perhaps grimly, at him. Janet started rescue
operations. 'They can't do any harm,' she said quietly.
And Vivian said with a grin, 'We'll have to wait and
see.'

I nodded.

I'd kept quiet. I know nothing about Oxford and I
didn't know much about young Vivian then either. But
I knew why Joncer was being grumpy. And for all I
knew he might have been grumpy for good reason.
We'd both had to make our own way in the Racing
Game. There had been no Stable Jockey positions for us
to walk into when we were twenty-one. We'd had
seven years of hard and unpleasant apprenticeship behind us then. We'd made money, I admit, but we
made it the hard way.

Does this make us any better? Does it give us a right
to criticize? Well, the answer is, of course, 'No.' There
was no reason to suppose that Vivian wouldn't make

the grade, even if Racing was bread-and-butter to us but was a hobby to him. He could still be very good. But even when you accept this it is still difficult to be logical. I think I managed because I was older and these things weren't so keen, didn't seem to matter any more. But not so with Joncer. In the first place he would have said that the hard way was the only way. He would be wrong but then he was younger and nearer to the Game than I was. So possibly there'd be one attitude that was right for him, and him alone, and one for me, and this one the attitude of the rest of the world. Because, 'the line of least resistance' is no worse than the tougher way. That goes for anything. It all depends on how things are mapped out for you; as Professor Miller would say—it's all something to do with destiny.

Anyway, Vivian would have his difficulties too. Different difficulties to be sure but present none the less. Joncer had had to be good to keep alive—that's all there was to it for him. A simple, if profound, problem. It was his world, he belonged in it, and to remain in it he had to be better than the others. But Vivian would have to earn first even the right to call himself a jockey as opposed to a laughing stock. He was an amateur: he would have to be better than the professionals without their training, without their excuses. A professional can blame the horse; but the amateur who is supposed to be riding anyway for his own sport can only blame himself. Because if he blamed the horse people could say, 'Well, why did you ride him then—you don't have to.'

I understood only too well why Joncer was being uncharitable. And I think Janet did too. But I could not approve it. I knew that this was one of his limitations. And after thirty years in a cut-throat, highly competitive world the strength and the weaknesses of his character had become clearly defined, unchangeable, deep rooted. You could hardly expect anything else. So when I say I didn't approve, I didn't disapprove either. All I did wish for was a quiet life. But Joncer, being younger, didn't value this as much as I did.

I nodded and I kept quiet. Well, quiet for me, that is.

'You'll be all right,' I said. 'Learn to stay on—that's the main thing. Never forget elementary horsemanship. That's why Joncer was so good——'

'Thank you, Harry,' said Joncer with a smirk.

'—and don't be choosy what you ride. Not until you're really good, that is. The more animals you get up on the more you'll learn. No two are alike.'

Joncer interrupted, 'You know who you suddenly remind me of, Harry?'

I didn't; not at that moment that is. 'Harry Smart?' I said on the off chance.

'No,' he said. 'No. You remind me of Stowy Rook.'

'That b——,' I began and then I laughed. I expect that's how Stowy instructed the kids at Penfield's. And then we reminisced for a while and Janet and Vivian listened enthralled. That morning ended pleasantly.

A week later Vivian took *Mozy* out. And when he returned Joncer and I watched him while he groomed the animal. We'd more or less agreed we'd let him have the ride at Buckfastleigh but we made him work for it. Grooming was something he'd not done a lot of, but he seemed willing enough to learn. So we watched him silently, perhaps we were a bit formidable. But then, we were the owners now. It was a pleasant feeling.

'Joncer,' I said, loud enough, 'I think this kid is shaping well.'

'He might be all right,' said Joncer. 'He could ride at six stone if he had a haircut though.'

'His cap wouldn't fit.'

'Oh, we'll have a new one made.'

'Better to dye his hair our colours.' (They were scarlet and gold, quartered!)

'That's an idea. We'll make that our present if he wins.

'Yes. A free hair-do.'

Vivian Verepont, red faced and sweating, because grooming on a hot July day is warm work, believe me, looked up from his work and said succinctly, 'Get stuffed!' He was learning.

'Now that's a fine way to talk to your owners.'

'Stuffed, indeed. I wonder where he picked up that expression.'

'They're a rough lot, these stable-boys!'

'I think we'd better send him down.'

'Yes. We can't have that kind of language in our college.'

'Though we mustn't be too harsh. We'll fine him this time?'

'That's it. He can do tomorrow's work.'

'Do you hear that, boy?' I said. 'You'll be here to-morrow at seven. Muck out first, then take *Mozy* ten miles, groom him when you return, clean all the tack and bed him down. You should be finished by four. Have your lunch then and return to feed him at six. We'll be back at six ourselves.'

Vivian looked up again. 'I'll do it,' he said, 'but you can still get stuffed!' He was learning very well indeed.

'Quite incorrigible,' said Joncer. And we walked pompously into the house.

Janet was reading the *Sporting Life*. 'Bath today,' she said. She meant that the races were at Bath that day, of course—at Lansdown to be exact, just outside the town. She just looked pregnant now—in fine fettle but unquestionably round. The habits of pregnant women have changed since my day. She said, 'I want to go. And you two layabouts can take me. And I want lunch in the town first—a good lunch, mind you. This will be about the last time I'll be able to have a day out. So——'

It was a good suggestion. We had three hours to get there, the sun was shining, the car ready and the 'boy'

—poor Vivian—on hand to see to *Mozy*. So I said, 'Delighted, my lady.' Joncer said, 'Ought you to?' but Janet was determined. 'Of course I ought. I'll show you boys how to win some money.'

So we went. We ate smoked trout—I didn't like it much—roast chicken done in wine somehow, cheese, peaches, coffee and brandy all washed down with two bottles of Burgundy. We left the restaurant in the right mood—carefree, satisfied and slightly wicked. And then we went Racing.

I like Lansdown. There's free parking for one thing, it's easy to approach and leave (no traffic jams and irritations after the last race) and even on the hottest day a pleasant breeze comes off the Downs. Joncer liked it too. He always had connections with the Lambourn Stables and they regard Bath as their home meeting. So, although we were only going as ordinary punters, there'd be a few familiar faces there.

Well, the first familiar face we saw was Singer's. He was just ahead of us as we barged our way through the Owners' and Trainers' Entrance. I flashed an out-of-date badge at the man on the gate, said, as I indicated Joncer and Janet, 'Stable-girl and jockey,' and before he had time to wonder about pregnant stable-girls I was patting Singer on the back. We were in. I still hadn't paid after forty-six years in the Game.

'How's the car, Mr Singer?' I said. Singer was well known at the entrances too so the man on the gate thought twice about interrupting us. Anyway, we all moved rapidly towards the bar.

Singer greeted us blankly. He just remembered us, it seemed. 'Got a Porsche now,' he said. 'It's all right.'

'Well done,' said Joncer. He'd got a Jaguar himself which he drove like a dream. 'Time for a drink?' he asked.

'Yes,' said Singer, 'I'm not betting the first.' We all had a drink. Now this was a Flat Race Meeting, and we hadn't attended one like this for over a year. We were out of touch. Naturally we could prowl around the Stables and find out what was fancied and what wasn't, but as good a source as any was Singer. The tables were turned with a vengeance. I ordered the drinks and Joncer said quietly and with mock astonishment, 'Why, Mr Singer, *Magician* is a good thing in the first.' Considering that he'd only just glanced down the runners this was cheeky. But I nodded and whispered to him, 'That's the bet for us anyway.' Janet looked coyly at Singer. 'I'm sure Mr Singer has his own ideas. Don't you listen to these two, Mr Singer—just because the trainer tells them he's going to win doesn't mean it's a foregone conclusion, does it?' As is well known this is as near a foregone conclusion as can be. Singer said, 'What? He told you. I hadn't . . .' His voice trailed off as he searched rapidly in his form book for *Magician*'s credentials. Singer hadn't changed. 'Oh, have I let a cat out of a bag?' cried Janet. She winked at me. 'Yes,' said Joncer sternly, 'we don't mind Mr Singer knowing, of course, but we don't want the whole world to know.' The bar was fairly crowded.

'Oh, I'm sorry,' she said.

'It's a good thing?' asked Singer eagerly.

'We want ten to one,' I said, 'don't touch it until you see tens.'

'Right,' said Singer. Nervously he swallowed his drink.

'Well, it's only fair that Mr Singer tells us what he is going to back,' said Janet primly.

'What?' said Singer.

'One good turn deserves another.'

'*Hell's Bells*,' said Singer almost under his breath. He picked up his papers and left. Janet and I watched him go, stunned into silence.

'Well,' said Janet, 'what an absolute pig of a man!' Joncer, however, was roaring with laughter. 'You asked for it,' he said, 'and you got it. That's the name of the horse.'

It's a strange sport. We laughed when Janet bet a pound on *Magician*. We laughed when we saw the price tumble from 100 to 8 to 4 to 1. 'That's Singer,' I said, and I thought how odd he must be to bet hundreds of pounds on something as flimsy as our story. And we thought ourselves very clever indeed. We hadn't bet anything.

Then we watched the race. It was a five-furlong Selling Plate. *Magician* broke first. At the two-furlong mark it was *Magician* by a length. At half-way it was *Magician* by half a length. At the four-furlong post it was *Magician* by a length again. And at the finish, it was, as you may have guessed, *Magician*. By two lengths. We looked at each other.

'Mellows and Sherrif,' I said, 'psychic consultants!'

'Well, I'm blowed!' said Joncer.

'Excuse me, boys,' said Janet, sweetly, 'I must go and collect my money.'

We looked at each other again and burst out laughing. It was the only thing to do.

After that we decided to wait for *Hell's Bells*. Janet said she'd be quite happy sitting in the sun, 'counting her money', so Joncer and I wandered over to the Weighing Room. I could just hear the rich tones of Gus coming across from the Cheap Ring—'So I said, "Thank you, your Grace, and I——",' he seemed to be saying.

And then we went in. One person I didn't expect to see was Billy Locker, my son-in-law. He generally rode up North and the fact that he'd come South was a tip in itself. We talked for a while about family matters and then I asked him his chances. 'The only one I fear, Dad,' he said, 'is *Hell's Bells*. Apart from that we're home and dried.' Billy wasn't a cocky type, so I took a lot of interest in this. We made a date to meet after racing and I rejoined Joncer. He was in the thick of it.

'Hallo, Grandad,' said Wally Jones to Joncer. Wally is fifty-two this year and still rides at eight stone.

'Hallo, Tich,' said Joncer, 'not drawing your pension yet?'

'Pension!' said Wally with contempt, 'the only pension you get in this game is when they club together to buy you a tombstone.' That's true enough too. Joncer laughed.

'Looking for a job, Joncer?' someone shouted.

'Job! He's running for Steward.'

'Chaplain to the Jockey Club!'

'J. J. Joncer, Archbishop of Newmarket—I can just see that.'

'Now you be careful, fellows,' said Joncer with a grin. 'Remember I'm an Owner now.' A chorus greeted this.

'Attention. His Grace the——'

'Disgrace, you mean.'

'The Count of——'

The bell rang then and they all got up to leave for the Paddock.

'Good luck,' said Joncer to one and all. And he suddenly seemed lonely.

'Come on,' I said, 'you're well out of that.'

'Yes,' he replied, 'but I wish I wasn't.'

We rejoined Janet.

I wasn't the only one who thought that Billy hadn't made the trip from Malton for nothing. He was riding *Advice* and *Advice* was 5 to 2 favourite. *Hell's Bells* was 6 to 1. So, like Singer I did some calculations—a hundred pounds to forty *Advice* and two hundred and fifty to forty *Hell's Bells*. (I always ask for the extra point— instead of 24 to 4 I ask for 25 to 4: they'll generally give it you if you're backing in tens. Likewise a horse at 8 to 1: ask for £250 to £30—you should get it.) Anyway if *Advice* won I'd be £60 to the good and if *Hell's Bells* came up I'd be £210. I thought myself pretty clever.

I think the Almighty was in a playful mood that day. The race was a two-mile Handicap and for 1 mile 7½ furlongs I thought I couldn't lose. With two hundred yards to go *Advice* and *Hell's Bells* were neck and neck. But the unexpected happened. Out of the blue came a nag called *Good Money*, ridden by a sixteen-year-old boy and *Good Money* was coming like a train. I couldn't bear to look. But everyone was yelling their heads off. Well, it was a photo finish. While we were waiting for it to be developed the bookies quoted prices on the verdict. I saw *Advice* at 3 to 1 on, *Good Money* 3 to 1 against. That's it then, I thought. *Advice* wins it. But some bright spark shouts down to the books, 'What price a dead heat?' and Goldbergs laid him five score. It was catching. Everyone tried to get on and there was only 6 to 4 available as the Voice said, 'Dead heat between No. 12 and No. 27. No. 7 was third.' Well, as soon as the words 'dead heat' crossed my mind I knew that such was the colour of my luck that day, that a dead heat it would be. Thus *Good Money* and *Advice* dead heat, *Hell's Bells* short head third. Now you lose half your stake in a dead heat. So instead of receiving £140 I only got back £70 : i.e. £50 to £20. I'd laid out £80 altogether. So I was £10 down. And I deserved to be.

I didn't dare ask Joncer how he'd fared. He backed the same horses as I did but I don't know for how much. Janet, systematic as in most things, had backed *Hell's Bells* on the Tote for a place. Consequently she won about £7. She was delighted.

'Drinks on me, boys,' she said when she'd been paid.

'A tomato juice for me,' I said. Dead heats always make you feel like that.

22

WE enjoyed ourselves at Bath, but it stirred up nostalgic memories for Joncer. Although he realized when we visited the Weighing Room that the jokes were only jokes and were meant well, he also saw he was no longer of that fellowship: he was an outsider. Personally that would never bother me a bit, but then, I never was a jockey. Of course it's not really a fellowship: it's too competitive and cut-throat for that. But one thing bind's all jockeys together; they ride horses and they, for the most part, enjoy riding horses. And probably they all (except the Harry Smarts) enjoy the shouts and cheers of triumph. As Joncer had.

But he'd quit. It had been his own choice. And as the month of July advanced it seemed to me he regretted it more and more. To own half of a moderate steeplechaser was poor consolation.

I suppose he'd quit because he was tired of coping with clots like Singer; there was no need any more. He had enough money, he had a wife and a nice house. He had a horse. And then there was always the risk of injury, like the time he rode *Fountain Pen*—three months in hospital—that was something to bear in mind. But the main reason was that every jockey has to quit sometime. Perhaps it's as well to let age dictate the quitting. When you know without question that you are past it. And that would be when rides are hard to get, when everyone is whispering, 'So-and-so has had it!' When no one wants you any more.

Joncer didn't do it that way. He did it like Harry Smart had—implying an utter contempt for the gossip, and creating a kind of legend, a mystery. Harry meant it, the gesture was more than a gesture; it was a decision. But with Joncer I felt it was merely a gesture: a grand, rather vain one. He just wasn't big enough to rest on his laurels. He still wanted to show 'em.

You can't blame him. He still had capabilities: we knew he was still good. Maybe he'd still be good in five years' time. But he'd said he had quit—made his gesture implying that he could control circumstances and not let circumstances control him—said or implied that he wasn't going to be one of those who fade away—his gesture meant he'd had all he wanted of Racing and out of Racing. It was a grand gesture. Too grand.

We got through the rest of July, and on the last Sunday in the month Vivian Verepont came round on a three-year-old from his Stable and we took *Mozy* and this one up to the Gallops for some winding-up work. Since Vivian was going to ride *Mozy* at Buckfastleigh, Joncer got up on the three-year-old and they went six furlongs fast. *Mozy* couldn't stay with him but he wasn't disgraced.

They pulled up near me. 'Not bad,' I said.

'*Mozy* is faster than that,' said Joncer bluntly. He turned to Vivian, 'Why didn't you let him go?'

'I did,' said Vivian, also bluntly. Joncer jumped off. 'Look,' he said angrily, 'I had a ton in hand and you couldn't stay with me.'

'You want me to flog him to death?' said Vivian. He jumped off too. 'Where do you want him to run best— here or at Buckfastleigh?' It looked food for a bust-up.

'Be your age, Joncer,' I said. 'This three-year-old has eight stone three in the Cambridgeshire. *Mozy* can't live with him. We didn't expect him to.'

'I could have got him closer,' said Joncer.

'Oh, Joncer! Do me a favour! Please!' I said. 'You expect a five-year-old moderately bred steeplechaser to live with a *Hyperion* colt? Even Harry Smart couldn't do that.'

'Look,' said Verepont. 'If you aren't satisfied with my riding get someone else.'

'We're satisfied,' I said. 'Forget it.' Joncer was silent.

When we got back and Vivian had left I had it out with Joncer. We were by the stables, so we could cuss a bit if we wanted.

'Now look, Big Head,' I said, 'you've quit now. Mr V. Verepont is our jockey. You're just an owner. Remember?'

'I don't think he's good enough,' said Joncer.

'He's twenty-two. He's got a lot to learn but he's good enough.'

'Twenty-two! You're an old man at that age. Piggott had won the Derby by then.'

'Joncer!' I said. 'What's biting you?' He had a whip in his hand. He suddenly threw it against the stable-door. 'Nothing's biting me. Except this.' He stood squarely before me and said, 'That kid hasn't got it in him. He isn't tough enough. And I'll tell you why—you ought to know anyway—he's had it too easy. He hasn't——'

'Suffered?' I interrupted. I said it ironically.

'Harry, you know what I mean. He's soft. Of course he can ride good animals. At any gymkhana you'll find kids good enough for that. But he hasn't been through the mill, like you and me. There's always Cedric the——'

'Now you listen to me. Vivian Verepont is keen. And not only that. He's indebted to us because we know he's keen and because we've got faith in him.'

'I haven't got faith in him. Why should I? He's got money—it's just a hobby with him. He probably rides so as he can show off in front of a lot of debs.'

'So did you. Only you showed off for one deb; but you were basically the same.'

'It was my job.'

'All right then. Get some professional to ride *Mozy*. Get one of the Devon boys. They'll say, "Thank you very much, Mr Mellows. That will be £7." Because they won't win. They won't risk their necks on an unknown and obviously moderate animal. They can't afford to. They'll take it very easy and come gracefully third. You know that, Joncer. But young Verepont? He's keen. He'll try. He might fall off—you know as well as I do anything can happen—but he thinks we believe in him, he knows the horse, and he won't cost us a penny. Penfield believed in you a long time ago, Joncer.'

'Penfield? If Verepont had been through what I had to, I'd give him the ride. I'd know he knew his stuff.'

'Joncer. Who else you going to get?'

'I'll ride *Mozy*.' He lit a cigarette. He knew what I was going to say. He thought he did anyway.

'You big-headed twat!' I began. 'The "do-it-himself" man. I'll tell you something. You're finished, Joncer. You're no good any more. You've stopped riding horses. You remember? You quit last March. So you won't be riding a horse any more if you get up on *Mozy*. You'll be trying to thrust down someone's throat—whose I don't know—that you're brilliant. The main thing won't be *Mozy* or the race: it will be you. Showing off. Being a c——.'

'I own enough of this horse to ride him.'

'Oh, I won't stand in your way. You can buy me out for £400 now.'

'Right,' said Joncer, white with anger, 'you can have the money whenever you like.'

'C——,' I said again. He stormed into the house and I stood watching him. Then I climbed into my car and drove away. I wasn't very good tempered for the rest of that day.

A week went by. And I didn't do anything to stop it. Not that I was sulking or anything like that. Nor was Joncer. You don't sulk in the Racing Game; there isn't time.

It was more that I'd said my piece and Joncer had

said his and neither of us would give way. I hadn't intended to let things go as far as they did but once you start a slanging match you never know where it will end. I still say that ethically Joncer was in the wrong. We'd promised Vivian a ride and on the strength of that promise he does a lot of the dreary donkey work for us. So, when at the last moment Joncer broke the promise, he had done wrong. It wasn't so much that, that upset me. It was the fact that it was such an uncharacteristic thing for Joncer to do.

During the week that followed I rationalized it. I couldn't really blame Joncer; but I certainly couldn't admire him. In the first place he didn't think Vivian would ever be any good and he was quite entitled to think it too. But he should have said so at the beginning. It was vindictive the way it all came out at the end. Maybe he held a grudge against the Vereponts for the passive way they'd allowed Singer to be such a monster, but Singer was the owner and you can't roar down an owner's neck.

Anyway, that was it. Joncer didn't think Vivian would be any good because he hadn't been through the mill. And on top of that he thought to himself, 'They messed me about, now I'll mess them about.' And that attitude, of course, is plain stupid whatever your job. But there are times when it requires the mind and powers of a saint to avoid it. I didn't get around to thinking this way until a couple of days had passed. But when they had, I'd cooled off a bit. And I thought that Janet would have something to say about it too. She liked young Vivian, and she wasn't the sort of girl to sit back and let an injustice be done.

So I thought.

I was in Mrs Whitman's about a week later. I was reading the *Sporting Life* and I saw that *Mozy* was entered at Buckfastleigh in my name. It was nice to see my name in print, even though technically I'd resigned my rights to title. I hadn't asked for the money for my share—that was a suggestion done in anger and I'd come around to thinking that I'd turn the other cheek this time. And when I saw my name in the paper as the owner I felt magnanimous. Then Janet came in. I'd expected her to be an ally but I soon learned that not only was I wrong but that I was mad to think she'd oppose anything Joncer did. She was nothing if not loyal.

'Hallo, soldier,' she said gaily. She was wearing a smock-type thing and looked radiant. Since she was pregnant she'd improved no end—become rounder, softer I suppose. Before she'd tended a little towards the skinny and that's not my taste, although I dare say I'm unfashionable.

'Morning, ma'am,' I said as I put down my name in print. 'What will you have?'

'Stout,' she said stoutly. 'A dirty great pint of stout.' I bought a dirty great pint of stout and she drank half of it before I'd picked up my change. That made me thirsty so I had another myself.

'I expect you're looking forward to Saturday,' she said. Saturday was the day for *Mozy's* début.

'In a way,' I said cagily. She came straight to the point.

'Harry,' she said, tapping my arm, 'John told me what happened. And I think he's right. Vivian Verepont has a lot to learn. Let him learn on his father's horses.'

'All right,' I said, 'but you can't expect me to feel happy when we promise him a ride three months ago and then take him off at the last moment.'

'It seems to me,' she said, 'that that sort of thing happens all the time in racing. When Vivian Verepont shows that he's good enough, then we will give him a ride. Not before.'

205

'My dear girl, you don't suppose he'll ever ride for us. after what's happened!'

'Harry,' she said solemnly, 'I think he will.'

'Well, he's softer than I thought he was. Have you been talking to him?'

'I have,' she said with a smile. 'I used all the charm I've got left after being amongst roughs like you and John, and I'm happy to say it worked.'

'I'm sure it did.'

'Harry, don't be cheeky.'

'The poor kid didn't have a chance. I'm not being cheeky.'

'On the contrary, he is a very clear-headed young man and he saw our point of view. When I say I used my charm, I mean that there was no need for unpleasantness. Not every owner need behave like Mr Singer.'

'Janet, the whole thing has been very much like a Singer trick. That's what got my back up.'

'Well, you can put it down again. Vivian Verepont understands completely and will be delighted to ride for us whenever we want him. You're the only one who's being stubborn.'

'All right then,' I said, after a pause. 'I'll look forward to seeing Joncer Mellows make a triumphant return to the saddle on Saturday.'

'That's my boy,' said Janet. 'And no more sulking.'

I wasn't sulking but I didn't say anything to Janet. To her the whole matter was tidied up—she probably thought that we were all very childish—and now that she was six months pregnant she had a more important thing to think about. We had one more drink and then we left. I was in a hurry because of my lunch so that when I saw Vivian Verepont in the street I had time for only a few words.

I said, 'Will you be going on Saturday?'

He said, 'Well, I may as well. There may be a chance

206

of a spare ride.' I nodded. 'I'm leaving early Saturday morning. Would you like a lift?'

'Yes, I would indeed.'

'Okay then, I'll pick you up at seven.'

'Fine, Harry,' he said. 'And thank you.'

I waved and drove away. I was pleased he didn't bear a grudge against me (and if Janet was to be believed that he didn't bear one against Joncer). And although I wasn't a hundred per cent happy about the way we'd treated him I wasn't prepared to pioneer any more on his behalf. No doubt it would all come out in the wash as they say. It was, however, to be a very strange wash.

23

A BRIGHT day to begin with—a slight mist over Bath but by the time we were approaching Exeter it began to cloud over.

On the way Vivian and I talked about many things after we'd cleared up the trouble over *Mozy*. He said about that, 'I know I'm powerless at the moment and I don't blame Mellows for behaving like he did. You can't expect him to trust his first horse to a comparatively unknown jockey, No, I don't mind waiting until people know I'm good. Of course, I would have loved to tell him what he could do with *Mozy*—and any other horse he owns come to that—but no jockey gets very far if he starts cussing the owners.'

'That's true,' I said.

'And anyway,' he went on, 'they were quite nice about it when it came to a showdown.'

'Janet was, you mean.' I said.

He blushed slightly. 'Yes,' he said, 'I do mean her.' And I laughed.

From then on—we were in mid-Somerset now—we forgot the whole matter. I said, 'I'll see if I can get you a ride. There are bound to be a few folk I know down there.'

He thanked me and just outside Radstock we stopped for a drink. They'd just opened.

It began to rain when we hit the A30 road and I could see that it was going to turn into one of those soft wet and warm Devon days. And knowing Buckfastleigh race-course there would be plenty of mud as well. Vivian had never been there so I told him what I remembered.

'It's a field,' I said. 'Fairly flat with a sharp turn and run-in of a hundred yards to the Finish. You'll find it like a Point-to-Point really—it's railed by the Finish but out in the country the course is marked by posts— red ones for the Hurdle and white for the 'Chase. I think I'm right about the colours. You'd better walk the course before hand. Even if you don't get a ride today it will be useful next time.' I glanced at my watch. *Mozy* was running in the first race at two o'clock. It was half past twelve now and we had thirty miles to go. 'We'll be there easily on time,' I said.

I might have been over-confident. We were in the thick of the holiday traffic and the rain cut down visibility. So much so that I nearly missed seeing the damaged Bentley on the side of the road and an enormous figure—almost completely covered by a camelhair coat, and binoculars—who stood alongside the damaged car and impatiently thumbed the passing traffic. He looked familiar. I stopped.

He ran up to us like a bull chased by bees. He shouted through the window, 'Been in a smash. Got to get to Buckfastleigh in time for the first race. Can you give——'

I lowered the window while he was saying this. 'Get in, Jack,' I said, 'you talk too much.' I thought I'd recognized him. It was Jack Cassell. Vivian opened the rear door for him and with a grunt and a sigh the purple face appeared.

'Well, I'm——'

'Yes, Jack. You'd better call me "sir". I'm an owner as well now.' He lowered himself into the seat and the whisky fumes wafted across to us. Jack hadn't changed. He said, 'Harry—when I saw Mr H. Sherrif's *Mozart Deliberate*——'

'*Delinquent*,' I said.

'*Delinquent* then—some bloody silly name, anyway—I wondered if it would be you. But I thought to myself— "No, Harry may be soft but he'd never be soft enough to own a horse" and now, there's yourself like a bloody duke !'

'Ah, well,' I said, 'we all weaken towards the end. How come you're hitch-hiking at your age, Jack?'

'Skidded,' he said. 'One of these midget cars came at me from nowhere. I braked—right where some cows had been—so I end up in the ditch. And the midget never stopped.'

'Damaged?'

'A dent or two. But I couldn't get her out. And I've got *Rag Bag* running in the first. No jockey booked and I've got to declare the animal yet. So I decided to thumb my way. It isn't the first time.'

I don't want you to think that car smashes are an everyday thing with racing people. With Singer, maybe, but the rest of us are no worse than any other drivers. However, this one of Jack Cassell's was to be as timely for Vivian as Singer's had been for Joncer. I said, 'Your jockey problem is settled, Jack. Meet Vivian Verepont—Gloucestershire's most promising amateur. He'll ride *Rag Bag* for you.'

Jack and Vivian nodded to each other. 'You're Cedric's son, then?' asked Jack.

'Yes,' said Vivian.

'Well, if you want a ride you can have *Rag Bag*. He's no *Pentameter*, mind you, and although he's never won a race he's never fallen either. And with the going heavy like it will be today he has a chance.'

I grinned. 'Come off it, Jack. You know as well as I do that *Rag Bag* is terrified of the Winning Post. He must have had a difficult childhood or something.'

'I tell you, *Rag Bag* is not a wonder horse. But I know he'll win one of these days and I know someone who'll have twenty to one many times when he does. It might well be today.' Jack sat back with the air of a philosopher. Vivian said, 'Thanks for the offer, Mr Cassell. I'll see what I can do to bring the twenty to one home.'

'That's my boy,' said Jack. He gave us each a cigar. The traffic was thick along the by-pass and I began to wonder if we'd get to the races in time. You have to declare a horse half an hour before he runs so that meant we'd have to get there by half past one. *Mozy* would be all right because Joncer had taken him down the night before but *Rag Bag* was entered in two races and Jack had intended to decide at the last moment— when he'd weighed up the opposition—which race he'd go for. The horse was there but the stable-boy in charge of him had been instructed to wait before declaring *Rag Bag* a runner. Jack had made his mind up now; in the first race there would only be five runners, so he might come third if two fell down! That, therefore, was the race for him, even though we were trying too.

We'd never have made it, if Jack hadn't shown me a short cut. We turned down a lane that was an inch wider than the car and which twisted and turned like spaghetti in a bowl. Jack kept telling me to put my foot down, but you know what those Devon lanes are like— high hedges either side and visibility, therefore, as far as the next bend—I couldn't. So he cussed. And I cussed. Anyway we started to climb and after a while the road became a track and then a farmyard, and then a gate and beyond that mud.

'Well, genius,' I said, 'what happens now?' I'd given up hope by now of ever getting there.

'Someone opens the gate,' said Jack. 'That's what happens now.' Well, it was obvious that Jack wasn't going to move, so Vivian got out and we drove through. There were enormous ruts in the track and mud every-where and Jack wanted me to do fifty miles per hour. I wouldn't. We went on for a mile it seemed—through woods, gates and wild country and suddenly we came to a road. The rain now was a soft continuous drizzle.

'We'll walk from here,' says Jack. 'Park in the bushes over here.'

I switched off the engine. I was properly fed up. 'Why the hell—' I began. And then I heard the crowd.

Jack grinned like a successful conjurer. 'What did I tell you,' he said, easing himself out of the car, 'round the next bend you'll find a race-course.'

'Catterick Bridge, I suppose,' I said, but the wind was taken out of my sails. I looked at my watch. It was just one o'clock. We'd made it.

We wandered down the lane, Jack like a cardinal, Vivian and I like the incense wallahs, and then we came to a stile. Beyond it over a field lay the back of the Grand Stand.

'If you're ever broke,' said Jack with a grunt as he clambered over the stile, 'this is the way in.'

'Thank you,' I said with dignity.

The going was soft. Not too slippery—there'd been a fair amount of rain that summer in Devon—and as far as I could judge it would be perfect for *Mozy*. Vivian was walking the course while I looked for Joncer. It dawned on me then that he'd never ridden at Buckfastleigh either. I found him in the Weighing Room.

At first you'd have thought you were at a market instead of a race meeting—the place seemed full of farmers. It's the same at all the Devon meetings—farmers round that way are sporty. Joncer was talking to a group of them. He saw me.

'Here's my partner,' he said grandly. 'The brains of the syndicate.'

'Gentlemen, one and all,' I said with a bow to the ruddy faces.

'Mind you,' Joncer went on, 'Harry here thinks I'm past riding now, so I'm just going to show him.' He'd had a drink or two—I could see that.

'Me!' I said. 'I don't think anything. I'm only the owner. Half the owner I should say.' They laughed.

'Which half do you own?' asked one of them.

'The tail when we win and the head when we lose,' said Joncer. 'That's right, Harry, isn't it?'

I held out my hands. 'You see how it is, gentlemen,' and they laughed again. I took Joncer on one side.

'How's *Mozy*?' I asked.

'Fine,' said Joncer. He put his hand in his pocket and brought out a wad of notes. 'There's a hundred there,' he said. 'We're bound to be favourite, but see if you can get two to one.'

'All right,' I said. I took the money. 'You ever ridden here?'

'No,' said Joncer, 'but it looks easy enough.'

I looked at my watch. 'You've just time to walk it first if you want,' I said.

'Harry,' said Joncer, 'stop worrying. I'm not a kid, you know.'

'Okay, okay,' I said, 'I'll see you in the Winners' Enclosure.'

'You can bet on that,' said Joncer. I grinned and walked out into the drizzle.

It's a holiday crowd you find at Buckfastleigh. Those staying at places like Teignmouth, Brixham, Paignton, Torquay, and on a wet day you'll find more of them racing than on a fine one. I suppose they reckon it better to stand in the rain hoping for a bit of excitement than to doze in their boarding-houses. I wandered amongst them. I saw the 'Wages of Sin' man.

I don't know his name but he's been around the tracks now for donkey's years. He used to be a tipster—the confidential, whisper-in-your-ear type as opposed to a brassy know-it-all like Gus. Then one day I saw him at Epsom with his sandwich boards handing out leaflets and yelling for all he was worth that we were all damned. We'd just won the City and Suburban, so I didn't mind if we were. I knew him well by sight, so I nodded and asked him how he was. He lowered his voice and said, 'Two quid a day and expenses—I'm better off doing this than "working" a horse.' I remember saying that he must be and he asked me if we were trying in the last race. I said, 'Yes, but only put a bit on —it's a tricky race.' He winked and away he went shouting, 'JESARS IS COMING.' It amused me no end.

That must have been all of ten years ago, and now, like the legendary bad penny, here he was again.

'How goes it?' I asked. We were standing by the Tote, slightly sheltered from the rain, but even so, he was very damp. He looked at me for a moment with his large, soft, pale blue eyes, then he shook away a drop of rain from the end of his nose, eased the sandwich boards and said, 'Doncaster. The year *Ridgewood* won?'

'Epsom,' I said, 'but the year's right. We won the "City".'

'That's it,' he said as if he'd been right all along. 'I never forget a face.'

'What are you doing down this way?' I asked him.

'Headquarters is Plymouth,' he said, 'and they've given me the National Hunt tracks to work this season. Better class of person.'

'Ah,' I said wisely. 'And they see you all right?'

'I work on commission now. Ten bob a convert.' He pulled out some leaflets. 'Here,' he said, 'I'll show you. You see this form?' I nodded. Underneath a map which tried to make out that the Thames was really the Jordan, was a space for your name and address. 'Well, you fill that in and send it—it's only a request for literature— and I'll get ten bob.'

'No catch?' I asked.

'No catch,' he said solemnly and he thrust the form in my hand.

'Like a drink?' I said.

'Not when I'm working,' he said, perhaps regretfully, and added, 'And there might be some of the highups here today, seeing as it's their home meeting.'

'Ah,' I said again as I put the form in my pocket. 'Do you know anything for today?' I was curious to see if he still followed the horses. He looked over his shoulder, lowered his voice and said, '*Semantics*. In the last. Can't lose.' He moved out into the crowd. He hadn't changed, either. Nor had his war cry. 'JE-SARS IS COMING,' he shouted. I grinned to myself: it's one way of making a living, I thought.

When I got back to the Paddock the horses were there and the bookies were just beginning to do business. *Mozy* looked lively enough and, of the five runners, the most useful. *Rag Bag* looked like an arm-chair and the one we'd have most to fear from was a strong-looking chestnut by *Precipitation* called *Insoluble*. He was owned by a local farmer and ridden by the son, and the bookies thought the same as I did because they'd gone 6 to 4 *Mozy*, and only 5 to 2 *Insoluble*.

There wasn't much form to go on, as this was a Novice 'Chase and none of the runners had ever won. As much as anything the crowd were backing the jockeys and with Joncer the best known we had to be favourite.

The jockeys came into the Paddock, all five of them wearing mackintoshes. Jack Cassell was patting everyone on the back. I went up to the boy we'd got to lead *Mozy* round, slipped him a quid, and took *Mozy* round a couple more times. The market seemed to be warming up but no one would lay more than 6 to 4. I couldn't hear any more anyway.

The bell rang for the jockeys to mount and I led *Mozy* over to Joncer. I took off the paddock sheet and Joncer tested the saddle.

'Okay, Harry,' he said. I helped him aboard and picked up his mac and the sheet.

'There's no two to one,' I said.

'Get what you can then,' he said quietly.

'You reckon it's worth it?' I asked.

'A six to four winner is better than a twenty to one loser, isn't it?' said Joncer.

'All right,' I said, 'I'll get it.'

A lot of things probably decided me against backing *Mozy* for myself: the change of jockey, the rain, even the 'Wages of Sin' man—possibly all these contributed towards a slight feeling of misgiving. But the main reason was the price. Here was a horse, first time out, with no form to go on, and only one and a half to one in the betting. It wasn't worth betting. If we won I'd get half the stake money anyway—and that would be £80; to risk a lot of money to win only a little more, seemed to me to be mad.

I saw Jack Cassell going down the line taking a £100 to £5 off each over *Rag Bag*. 'There's nothing like having the courage of your convictions,' I thought. The bookies must have thought the same, because they all knew Jack and Jack's horse and the price didn't budge from twenties even after his onslaught.

Mozy was rock-like at 6 to 4 so I took £150 to £100 for Joncer with the Exeter bookie and that was me done. I followed Jack into the Stand.

'Well, Mr H. Sherrif?' he said.

'Exactly, Mr J. Cassell,' I said. And I lit another of his cigars.

The five horses were down at the Start. And just for the record, it was then that I noticed that my right shoe was leaking. Still, I forgot that for the next five minutes. The Starter got them away nicely. Those few seconds, when they race towards the first jump are one of the best parts for a spectator. All the hectic wagering is over and the horses are moving, all of them seemingly at that juncture with equal chances. You almost relax.

Joncer got there first and *Mozy* took the jump well. *Insoluble* landed second, a thing called *Paper Back* third, and *Rag Bag* was last behind a 6 to 1 shot called *Trade Mark*. And they kept that order for the next three jumps. As there were no Rails in the country I got a good view of *Mozy's* action. It was good; he covered a lot of ground and it was nice and easy. He might have got a bit too close to the third jump but with Joncer up that didn't matter. None of the horses—with the exception of *Rag Bag*—were experienced jumpers; they all had to feel their way.

They turned at the top end and came down towards the Stands.

Jack said, 'He sits a horse well, that Verepont.' And I nodded. And then I expect he wished he hadn't said it for Vivian took *Rag Bag* very wide indeed on the turn and lost about ten lengths. *Mozy* was eighty yards in front of him now with *Insoluble* close on his heels. *Rag Bag* plodded on with Vivian sitting very still, taking each jump sedately and carefully as if this were a gymkhana or something.

'He sits too damn well, if you ask me,' I murmured, but Jack didn't hear me.

They came past the Stands the first time. Except for *Insoluble* and *Mozy* it was a procession. The others turned for the country as *Rag Bag* came in front. I heard a few ironic cheers as Vivian went by the Cheap Enclosure. I couldn't make him out. It seemed almost as if he wasn't trying. I could see that even *Rag Bag* would go faster than the dignified gallop he was taking him. And he put him at the jumps as if this were a riding school—careful and correct, dressage stuff, really.

Joncer was two jumps in front of *Rag Bag* and *Insoluble* was still close on his heels. As I saw it, it was going to be difficult to shake him off. They turned at the top again. After what must have been a full minute *Rag Bag* took the corner. And again Vivian pulled him out on the wide outside. I still couldn't understand it. The other jockeys were trying to keep as close to Joncer as they could but Vivian seemed to be riding a race of his own. Jack Cassell was very quiet.

They turned again at the top and came towards us.

One thing I saw now was that *Mozy* got two miles easily—his jumping was patchy but he'd stay for ever. *Insoluble* was alongside him but Joncer had the Rails position. There were two jumps to go. *Trade Mark* had moved up behind them but I saw Joncer sitting still so I wasn't worried. They took the second last together with *Trade Mark* a length behind and as they turned into the straight Joncer showed slightly in front. And he hadn't moved on *Mozy*; *Insoluble* was under the whip but *Mozy* was being nursed in front. They took the last and *Insoluble* blundered. He seemed to put his nose through it first. Anyway on the run-in *Mozy* was ten lengths clear of *Trade Mark* with *Insoluble* a bad third. That's how they announced it anyway. *Paper Back* was fourth and *Rag Bag* last.

We left the Stand and we were down in the Paddock just as *Rag Bag* passed the Post. I waited by the Winners' Enclosure and a few types I knew congratulated me. As it happened Vivian was first through the gate that leads to it. I nodded to him and he nodded back and quite calmly rode *Rag Bag* into the position reserved for the Winner. There was a crowd round there already. I looked at him—queerly, I suppose.

'I'm objecting,' he said. He dismounted. Jack had barged his way through.

'What to?' Jack asked.

'Yes,' I said, 'objecting to what—the weather?'

He slipped the saddle off before replying. 'I'm objecting to the first four.'

Jack and I looked at each other and I was about to say he must be mad. But the news spread as only news can at a race meeting. The crowd round the Enclosure looked at each other with a sort of laughable surmise. A few rushed over to the bookies.

'Objection,' I heard shouted. 'What price *Rag Bag*?' And Joncer came in then.

Over in the Cheap Enclosure there was a lot of activity and I could see the 'Wages of Sin' doing a roaring trade as he came towards us. Vivian had gone into the Weighing Room and Joncer looked at *Rag Bag*, placid, nonchalant and supremely unconcerned, with a mixture of laughter and surprise.

'What's going on?' he asked. I took hold of *Mozy* as Joncer dismounted.

'Verepont's objecting,' I said. Joncer stopped loosening the strap and looked at me. 'What to?' he asked. There was no laughter in his voice now; just some enormous surprise.

'He's objecting to you and three others,' I said. 'What went on out in the country?'

Joncer yanked the saddle off. 'The stupid——' he began. 'Come on, let me pass. We'll soon see about this.'

'What went on?' I asked. I barged through the crowd with him.

'Nothing,' said Joncer. 'I never saw him, the cheeky twat.' Joncer was angry. I don't know how I felt. In nearly fifty years of racing I'd never seen anything like this. A few came up to us. 'What's going on?' they asked. And all I could say was, 'Objection.' The loudspeaker said it just as we got to the door of the Weighing Room.

'Number Seven objects to the first four horses,' and we met Jack Cassell coming out.

'Joncer,' he said, 'the Stewards want you and the other three jockeys. I do believe I've got a winner.' He wasn't exactly grinning: he seemed merrily dazed.

'Don't talk bloody stupid,' said Joncer. He barged his way in. I stood outside not knowing whether to laugh or cry.

You can bet over the result of an objection. Normally the second objects to the first and normally you've seen the grounds for the objection yourself. It generally happens on the run-in when the jockeys get over-excited and bump each other or the horses, because they are tired, tend to roll or swerve—go off the straight course anyway—and if one has interfered with the other—these are the grounds. But when a horse has been last all the way round and finishes about a minute after the others and then the jockey objects, you begin to feel that the world, as you know it, is coming to an end. A scare on the Stock Exchange is nothing to this.

Even the bookies thought so. Some were laying ten to one against *Rag Bag*, others fives, some went even money on *Mozy* and from the activity going on you'd think it was the day that fivers were given away.

I caught up with Jack. 'What gives?' I asked. He was about to answer me when the loud-speaker announced, 'Number Seven objects to the other horses on the grounds that they took the wrong course.'

'That's what gives,' said Jack.

The news settled the Market. I leapt in for a bit of the 10 to 1. You've got to be quick but I wasn't quick enough. All you could get was even money *Mozy* and even money *Rag Bag*.

Most of the crowd now were just dazed and were standing like expectant fathers outside the maternity ward. Jack, to cover himself, had an even £50 over *Mozy* and I was just about to do the same when the 'Wages' came through the crowd.

'It is prophesied,' he intoned, 'it is in the Holy Writ.'

'What is, you daft bugger?' yelled the Exeter bookie, and the others took up the cry.

He mounted the first step of the Grand Stand, turned towards the crowd and held out his hands for silence. This was his big moment.

'It is written,' he began, 'ye unbelievers. It is written, "AND THE LAST SHALL BE FIRST".' A profound silence, and something stirred in my mind. Vivian had gone very wide at the top corner. He'd walked the course beforehand. Joncer hadn't. Yes, I thought. Yes.

I don't know if the crowd had seen and remembered what I had. I doubt it. And they certainly aren't religious. But deep down they're a superstitious lot and 'Old Wages' gave them enough of a direction. They all stepped in (me included) over *Rag Bag* and gave the bookies a clouting, just before the loud-speaker announced, 'Objection sustained. Number seven is placed first and the rest of the field disqualified.'

Well, we looked at each other. I'd just about seen everything. It wasn't just unique: it was unbelievable. But the money the bookies were forking out wasn't. That was very tangible. I collected mine and waited for Jack who had many hundreds waiting for him. He came up to me. 'Now, tell me that Racing doesn't pay,' he yelled—he had to yell, the whole crowd had gone mad.

'I won't tell anyone, anything, any more,' I said. 'I've seen the lot now.'

'Wages' came up to us. 'That's worth a drink, isn't it, guvnor,' he said, more or less to me, but with an eye on the wad of notes Jack was arranging in his hand.

'It certainly is,' said Jack. He gave him a fiver. But that wasn't enough for 'Wages'. 'Thank you, sir,' he said, 'and I'm sure you won't mind filling this form in and sending it back to us.' Jack took it. 'Wages' put on his plummy voice. 'Salvation comes to us,' he said, 'in many diverse ways.' This was as much to the crowd as to us.

'All right,' said Jack, 'but this gang need it more than me, you know'—he indicated the bookies—'you'd better see to them.'

It didn't do for the bookies to upset a good customer like Jack so they all accepted meekly as 'Wages' went solemnly down the line. He changed his cry though, this time. 'As it is written,' he was saying as he went out of earshot. Jack and I turned for the Weighing Room. He looked at the leaflet as we walked over.

'You know, Harry,' he said, 'there may be something in all this after all.'

At first I thought he was joking.

24

WHETHER or not Jack became a convert I don't know. If I were to bet on it, however, I'd want 33 to 1 against.

When we got back to the Weighing Room the inquiry had just finished. The Stewards were going to fine Joncer £25 and he'd get a caution from the Jockey Club when the report went through. And he deserved it. And he knew it. Vivian and he were talking.

'I'm sorry, Mr Mellows,' he said politely, 'but I had to do it.'

Joncer grinned. 'My boy,' he said, 'you cost me £25, stake money and my reputation. I only wish I could have done it to you.'

'You'll be able to get your own back,' said Vivian, perhaps a bit nervously.

'I won't,' said Joncer. 'This is where I really quit. You can ride *Mozy* from now on.' He was taking his boots off. Sitting opposite was a young apprentice waiting to weigh-out for the next race. Joncer yanked the boots off and said to the apprentice, 'You're nearest. They're yours for the carrying away.' He lobbed them over—twenty quid's worth of leather. The apprentice caught them. 'Thanks very much, Mr Mellows,' he said.

'If they don't fit,' said Joncer, 'chuck 'em in the dust-bin—like I should have done last March.'

'They fitted you then,' I said.

'No, Harry, they didn't. I was getting just a little bit too big for them even in March.'

'Well,' I said, 'we won't argue.'

'I expect we will,' said Joncer, 'but not over that any more.'

And up till now we haven't.

PRINTED IN GREAT BRITAIN
BY EBENEZER BAYLIS AND SON, LTD.
THE TRINITY PRESS, WORCESTER, AND LONDON